TROUBLE
COMES
IN THREES

Books by Michael Jenet

FICTION
Trouble Comes In Threes

SELF IMPROVEMENT
ASK: The Questions to Empower Your Life
A Better Life

CONTRIBUTING AUTHOR
Imagine: 29 Days To A Better You
Peanut's Legacy

TROUBLE
COMES
IN THREES

MICHAEL JENET

Wordbinders Publishing
Journey Institute Press, Colorado

Wordbinders Publishing
An imprint of Journey Institute Press,
a division of 50 in 52 Journey, Inc.
www.journeyinstitutepress.org

Library of Congress Control Number: 2023936122
Names: Jenet, Michael
Title: Trouble Comes In Threes
Description: Colorado: Wordbinders Publishing, 2023
Identifiers: ISBN 979-8-9875066-5-3 (hardcover)
Subjects: BISAC: FICTION / Mystery & Detective / Women Sleuths |
FICTION / Thrillers / Crime |
FICTION / Crime

First Edition

Printed in the United States of America

0 1 2 3 4 5 6 7 8 9 10

This book is typeset in Garamond / Minerva

To Dafna, for everything, always; and for believing in me and my writing.

THE LUMBERJACK MURDERS

DEATH BENEATH THE SURFACE

LIGHTS, CAMERA, MURDER

NOTE FROM JOURNEY
INSTITUTE PRESS

In February, 2020, we launched our publishing company, the Journey Institute Press. A few weeks later, the global pandemic surrounding COVID-19 changed everything. All the plans we had made disappeared overnight.

In those first days of the pandemic, we, like so many others, sat at home staring out our windows pondering what life would be like. We feared the unknown of this invisible global killer and we worried about the future.

It was in that moment we decided to do something. We wanted to help take people's minds off of the worry they were facing. An alternative to the news that dominated every screen and every minute of every day.

The answer came to us in the form of 'daily writing prompts'. The idea was to provide people a respite from the uncertainty of life and the never-ending grimness of news about the pandemic. We wanted our community of writers, aspiring authors, and anyone else who wanted to join to take a break from the realities of life and get lost, even if only briefly, in the world of creative writing.

So, we began posting a daily writing prompt alongside a photo on a public Facebook group. The first post was simply a photo of rain outside the literal window we were sitting at staring out of. Next came a photo we found on a copyright free website and a corresponding writing prompt alongside it. The assignment was simple; use the prompt or the photo or both, and write. It didn't matter what you wrote, how long the writing was, or what genre you chose to write in. Just write.

People began joining the group. One or two even commented on the prompts. Few people, however, actually posted what they were writing. So, after a few days, our publisher, Michael Jenet, began posting answers to the daily writing prompts as short form stories.

Every day, he would post a few hundred words in response to that day's writing prompt. People began to engage. Some commented on the story, or poem, or whatever it was that Michael posted. Others joined in and posted short prompt responses of their own. The community began to grow.

One day in July, the prompt was a photo of a mountain stream. Michael dutifully posted his response. It was a short story about a detective inspector in the north of England whose young constable has found something macabre in the stream.

The post got a few likes and one or two comments, and that was that.

On to the next day's post.

Or so he thought.

People in the group began asking, 'What happened in that detective story?' 'What happens next?'

After a few days, another prompt inspired him to write a follow-up piece, hoping to quell the group's curiosity. The effect was exactly the opposite. Cries of 'we want more' began flooding in and thus the Jillian Scotte Mysteries were born.

Months upon months of writing prompts, usually not in successive days but over several weeks, would elicit a slow but steady series of 'episodes' in the stories. Not unlike the old Sir Author Conan Doyle stories published in The Strand Magazine in England, these episodic chapters appeared on the writing prompt group interspersed with other prompt writings over several months.

Eventually, as time and the pandemic wore on and live began crawling back to some sense of normalcy, the work of being a publisher took hold and his time for answering daily writing prompts came to an end. In fact, at one point during the summer of 2021, we actually informed the group that since the pandemic was almost over, we were going to stop the daily prompts altogether.

The backlash we received from even thinking of stopping the daily prompts changed our minds and we continue to provide daily writing prompts to this day.

A year passed from Jenet's last episode featuring DI Scotte, and then another, and some members of the group began suggesting that the stories ought to be published in a book. The sentiment continued from the group, along with strong encouragement from his wife. And that, ladies and gentlemen, is how this volume of the first three stories in the series were compiled, edited, and published as *Trouble Comes In Threes*.

We hope you enjoy these mysteries and the characters that inhabit them as much as we did in publishing them.

Let the hunt begin!

Journey Institute Press - 2023

THE LUMBERJACK MURDERS

CHAPTER 1

There was something in his eyes that left detective inspector Jillian Scotte uneasy. His face was flushed, and his breathing was coming in short bursts. She initially put it down to nerves or inexperience, but as she paused and looked closer, she realized it was something else.

It was fear!

This was not how she imagined her day when she left her house an hour ago.

The mountain stream bubbled and swirled as it made its way through the fells of the Lake District toward Ravenstonedale in Cumbria, Northwest England. A still-unspoiled township at the foot of Howgill Fells, this quiet, picturesque farming village was often frequented by tourists. Nothing exciting happened there.

Jillian Scotte, with an *e*, as she often felt compelled to say, had chosen the Eden Police Department, serving Cumbria, for this very reason. A newly decorated detective inspector from the Thames Valley Police Force, she had played a major role in a widely publicized serial murder inquiry. She thought of it as just doing her job. Others said she alone had broken the case wide open.

Just two months later, Jillian had walked into her boss's office and asked for the transfer.

"What, Cumbria?" he asked, astonished. "But that's in the middle of nowhere!"

"I know," she replied, standing before him, having refused to sit. She knew if she sat, it would give him more time to talk her out of it.

"Jillian, come on," he said rather forcefully. "This is ridiculous." He stared at her for over a minute, waiting for something that would never come. "Look, if you want a transfer, that's fine, I can help you there, but

13

you are far too talented a DI to go God knows where out in the middle of bloody . . . I mean, it's damn near Scotland!"

Jillian, all five foot five of her, had stood her ground. Now, six weeks later, she had just finished her first full week, having replaced the departing inspector who had been in Ravenstonedale for almost five years. Having never required training in criminal investigations and lacking a Criminal Investigations Department to be attached to, he had remained a uniformed inspector for years.

The brass in London had shaken their heads as Jillian's request passed up the line to the detective chief inspector and even the superintendent. "But DI Scotte," the super had said, "you're bound to make chief inspector soon, and I daresay one day you'll be sporting for my job." Shaking his head, he added, "Going to Cumbria will put paid to that."

Nevertheless, Jillian had packed up her life, such as it was, and headed north.

Ravenstonedale served as a central location for several other villages and towns around it, so they had built a police station there five years ago. Jillian would be the first DI there. The station was small, with a staff of five, Jillian included. One detective sergeant, one police constable, one police constable in training, and a retired sergeant who manned the desk and phones as a volunteer.

It wasn't much, but it would suit her just fine.

Jillian drove slowly down the narrow lane in the department's only unmarked vehicle, an ageing Range Rover in desperate need of a new clutch. Trying to hold her thermos of coffee in her right hand while holding the steering wheel, she ground the shift into fourth gear with a lot of colorful encouragement.

Her light brown hair was blowing all around her as she drove with the windows down, despite the early spring chill. She navigated a turn without spilling her coffee. Having been here just over a week, she still marveled at how beautiful the countryside was.

Smiling to herself, she took a sip of her still-hot mocha. Her motto being *"What is the point of drinking something bitter unless you can add chocolate to it?"*

The smile faded as she crested a small hill and saw the flashing lights of PC Worhington's car. He'd called in to the station, but she had heard the call on her car radio and answered before (retired) Sergeant Pallwell could respond.

Worhington's voice had seemed odd. He said a body, of sorts, had been found. Not wanting anything more to go over the police radio lest someone was listening—God forbid some tourist heard about it and came out with their camera—she had turned around and headed out straightaway.

Pulling into the small dirt path off the road, she stopped behind the yellow-and-blue police car.

Police Constable Jack Worhington was nice enough, if a bit on the inexperienced side.

"Hello Jack," she said as he approached her. "Tell me what we've got."

She could see he was uncomfortable, so she gently turned him around by the elbow and kept him moving. "Well," he said, clearing his throat, "Merrick Thompson, he's the one that owns this land." He paused and swallowed.

"Yes, go on," she said, walking beside him.

"Well, he found . . . uhm . . . he was walkin' 'is dogs this mornin' and they was diggin' and when he came up on 'em, he saw . . . well . . ." It was clear he was not comfortable. "It's a head, mum," he said quickly, wanting to get it out.

Jillian looked at him. His face was flushed, and his breathing was coming in short bursts. He had likely never seen a dead body before. Putting her hand on his shoulder, she stopped him. She initially put it down to nerves or perhaps inexperience, but as she paused and looked closer at him, she realized it was something else.

It was fear!

"All right, Jack, take a deep breath. That's it. Now, tell me everything you've done since you found the body. How much did the dogs disturb the scene? Have you roped it off yet?"

Something in the way PC Worhington looked at her told her there was something else. Something she was missing. Frowning, she opened her mouth to ask him, but he beat her to it. "That's just it, mum . . ." he said, again swallowing heavily before the next words out of his mouth changed everything.

"There's no body. It's just a head."

CHAPTER 2

The ditch wasn't far from the road, Jillian thought, looking back over her shoulder as she sat on her haunches.

She'd told PC Worhington to call in to Eden and tell them they needed a scene of crimes team right away. "Oh, and the coroner as well." And then she told him to set up crime scene tape and create a perimeter.

Jack Worhington had only been too happy to get away. If he never went near that head again, it would be too soon. He knew he'd be having nightmares about it for days.

Jillian returned her attention to the head. The landowner's dogs hadn't done too much damage, mostly licking, even so, it would contaminate any evidence they might get. The victim was female, early to mid-thirties, Jillian thought as she pushed a strand of her own hair out of her face.

Standing up, she surveyed the scene. It was impossible to tell, given the trampling of the dogs, but it looked an awful lot like the head had rolled. Squatting down again, she pulled out her cell phone and took a few pictures.

Jillian knew the crime scene photographer would document everything, but just in case someone got it wrong and stepped in the grass, she wanted to look back at it as it was now.

The sirens could be heard from quite a distance in this remote part of England. Two more police cruisers pulled up. The entire department, such as it was, was now on scene.

She watched Detective Sergeant Mark Halloway, tall with sandy blond hair and dark eyes, get out of the first car. From the second car, PC (in training) Kara Devanor emerged. She was a young black woman with dark curly hair and wide brown eyes.

Jillian watched as DS Halloway pointed toward where Worhington was putting up crime scene tape, and PC Devanor headed off in that direction.

17

Jillian kept an eye on Halloway, who was looking for her footprints and trying to step into the same ones, cautiously making his way across the grass to where she was still squatting down.

As he approached and saw what was beside her, he took in a sharp breath. "Bloody hell."

She saw him look away and then at her. "Quite," she said. Then, dropping the formal tone she often used, she said gently, "Mark, do you recognize her?"

Halloway seemed surprised by the question, his brow furrowing. Then he looked at the head again. Shaking his head, he said, "No, she's not from around here."

Jillian pursed her lips. That's what she'd been afraid of. Standing up, she nodded toward Halloway's car, and they carefully made their way back the way they had come.

Everyone gathered round and looked at her. "Right," she said. "Here's what we're going to do. Mark, you stay here and wait for SOCO and the coroner. When they arrive, I want everything in the crime scene area photographed, documented, and pored over with a fine-tooth comb."

"Yes guv," he replied.

"I also want you to call in to Eden and talk to the DCI. Fill him in on what we've found in case he doesn't already know. I have a feeling that once this gets out, it's going to spread like wildfire, and who knows who the landowners talked to already."

At that, she looked over across the road to where the man was resting against an old post with his two dogs sitting beside him. Turning to PC Devanor, she said, "Kara, take a statement from him. Write down every word he says and ask him the same question two or three different ways to see if you can jog his memory about something he may have forgotten."

The young constable reached into her jacket for her notepad. "Yes, mum," she said, and walked off.

"PC Worhington, you and I are going to search up and down this road, both sides. Then we're going to make our way into the grass and work back and forth until we reach the ditch." Looking in both directions, she said, "We'll probably have to go a half mile in either direction."

Worhington looked at his new boss. "What are we looking for, mum?" he asked.

She studied the young constable and his naïve face, wondering how long it had been since she had been so unspoiled by crime and the evil that permeated society's darkest corners. She took a deep breath and said, "We're looking for the rest of the body, Jack."

As she and her PC walked in their separate directions, she called back to her DS, "Oh, Mark, tell Eden we're also going to need to dredge that ditch."

CHAPTER 3

"Fields of Gold," the popular Sting song, was playing on the radio as Detective Inspector Jillian Scotte drove to work. It reminded her of growing up and going for family drives through East Midlands , where rows of wheat grew in late summer.

A stark contrast to the rolling green hills of Ravenstonedale in Cumbria and North West England.

The clouds were dark and grey, and the rain was already falling steadily, her car's windshield wipers straining to keep up. Sting's golden, sun-swept fields seemed a long way off.

Walking through the door into the police station, she said good morning to retired police sergeant Frank Pallwell. Frank had been lukewarm when she'd first arrived, but she was determined to win him over. To her surprise, this morning he didn't just nod or mutter something, but said "guv" and motioned for her to approach the welcome desk where he worked.

"Yes Frank, what's up?"

"Coroner," Frank replied, turning his large round face toward her . "From Eden. In your office."

"Really?" Jillian said, somewhat surprised. "Right. Thanks, Frank."

Frank grunted and went back to his paperwork, which Jillian understood meant *You're welcome.*

As she walked through the back into the working area of the station, she saw DS Mark Halloway look up at her, then over at her office with his eyebrows raised. It seemed everyone wanted to know why the coroner was making a visit this morning. Jillian just said hello to everyone and went into her office.

Dr. Daniella Morales was a striking woman with long jet-black hair, high cheekbones, and black eyes. She was dressed in jeans and a burgundy silk blouse. Her handbag sat on the floor next to the chair she was waiting in. Her raincoat hung over the back.

No wonder Mark had raised his eyebrows, Jillian thought. Hearing her enter, Dr. Morales stood up and extended her hand. "Hello, Detective Inspector, I'm Dr. Morales. I'm the coroner for the region here in Cumbria."

Jillian smiled and shook her hand. "Please, call me Jillian."

The doctor smiled back, pleased. "I'm Daniella."

Jillian motioned to the seat and took her own place behind her desk, thinking she had detected a trace of accent in the woman's voice, but she wasn't sure where from. She said, "What brings you here so early, Daniella?"

Dr. Morales waved a hand as to say it was nothing. "I was on my way in to work, and I thought I'd say hello and drop off the postmortem on the head." She reached into her handbag to pull out a yellow envelope and, leaning forward, placed it on Jillian's desk.

It had been a frustrating two days since they'd found the head. Searching the ditch had proven more difficult than Jillian had expected. When DS Halloway had put in their request, Eden had come back saying they couldn't send a dredge or dive team because either would create as much mess as it would solve. The ditch, while wide, was too shallow for diving to do much more than stir up the bottom of the slow-moving water. Dredging would be worse and would likely damage anything they found.

The solution, so said the chain of command, was to get sonar to go over the area. There were new sonar-equipped drones that would do just the trick, but they were at the Met in London and would take a day to come up, assuming they were available.

Luckily, they were. Yesterday, a SOCO technician who still looked like he belonged in school had appeared and run his drone one mile in either direction but found nothing.

The only break had been the fast-track of the DNA from a hair sample. They now knew the victim's name was Sarah Longwood.

Grabbing the envelope, Jillian pulled out the report and glanced at it.

"There's not much I can tell you, other than that ditch did not kill her," Daniella said.

Jillian looked up. "Can you tell how long ago?"

Daniella nodded. "It's all in there. It's a little difficult to be exact, but I'd say she was killed about two weeks ago. There's an indication the head was frozen after decapitation. I'd put it somewhere between ten and fourteen days."

Jillian shivered, noting that she had only arrived in Ravenstonedale eleven days ago. Daniella then added, "That's not the only interesting bit."

Jillian looked up, meeting Dr. Morales's eyes, waiting for her to continue.

"The head was severed with a chain saw."

That made Jillian sit back in her chair. Placing the report back on her desk, she said, "That's not usual is it, for decapitation, I mean?"

"I'd say not," Daniella said, "but that's your area of expertise, not mine." And then she smiled a knowing smile. Obviously, the good doctor had done some research about Jillian's past at the Thames Valley Police Force.

"Well," she said, standing up, "I'd better be off. Just wanted to give you that and say hello officially."

Jillian stood up and came around from behind her desk. "Thank you. It's great to put a face with the voice on the phone."

"You as well," Daniella said.

As she was walking out of her office, Jillian said, "Oh, you said you were on your way in. Do you not live in Eden?"

Daniella looked back over her shoulder. "No, I live in the next village over. Much more peaceful."

Just then, PC Kara Devanor called out from her desk, "Guv, there's a call for you from Norwich. A DCI Sanderson."

Today was full of surprises, it seemed. Frowning slightly, Jillian walked back into her office and closed the door. Detective Chief Inspector Maryanne Sanderson was more of a celebrity among the English Police than Jillian ever wanted to be. She was considered among female officers as a trailblazer for women in British policing. She also had a reputation for being tough as nails.

Jillian picked up her phone and punched the blinking "on hold" line. "DI Scotte, how can I help?"

"Hello Jillian," said the voice on the other end of the phone. "This is DCI Maryanne Sanderson from Norwich."

"Yes, mum," Jillian replied respectfully. She noted Sanderson had called her by her first name, even though, to her memory, they had only met once at a London conference. "What can I do for you?"

"Other way around, I think," DCI Sanderson said in her sharp voice. "I'm your right hand."

"Sorry," Jillian said, confused.

"Right arm, more precisely," the DCI said.

"I still don't . . ." Jillian began, then it clicked. "Wait. Are you saying you've found an arm belonging to Sarah Longwood?"

DCI Sanderson chuckled down the line. "They told me you were quick."

"Did you find anything else?" Jillian asked, holding her breath.

"No," came the reply. "Just her right arm."

CHAPTER 4

The ladder that everyone climbed in their career didn't just belong to the corporate world. The ladder, rickety, rusting, and unstable, was just as prominent in the United Kingdom's police service, Jillian thought as she hung up the phone after talking with Detective Chief Inspector Sanderson of the Norwich police.

Sanderson's team had found a human arm the afternoon before. Word had already reached Norwich and the rest of the local constabularies of Great Britain about the discovery of a severed head. DCI Sanderson, who had more pull than most, got a DNA test run on the spot, and the name had matched when Jillian's own result had come in.

Jillian and the DCI had discussed what little they knew. The arm had, by all appearances, been thrown from a moving vehicle near a bus stop in the early hours of yesterday morning. It appeared to have been cut from the torso.

When Jillian suggested a chain saw, DCI Sanderson had gone quiet. Jillian could hear her chewing on something, a pen maybe, when she said, "Yes, that could be it. I should get the coroner's report sometime today. When I do, I'll send it your way."

After going over a few other minor details, the two women inspectors said their goodbyes.

Jillian walked out of her office, across the small room of desks, and into the conference room. Earlier, she had told PC Devanor to remove all the furniture, and they had set it up as their murder incident room.

Approaching the maps they had put on the wall, Jillian studied one of the country. Taking a blue Magic Marker, she circled the general area of Cumbria and then Norwich. That was quite a distance. It made no sense.

She called her team, minus PC Worhington, who was out making rounds, into the incident room and gave them the update on the arm. "Mark," she said, addressing her sergeant, "Where are we on the victim?"

DS Halloway stood by the door, his dark eyes showing bags underneath and his blond hair a little disheveled. Jillian wondered if he'd even been home the night before. She tried to recall what he'd been wearing the previous day, but she'd been too distracted by the case. "We managed to track her down to a flat in London that she shared with a roommate." He consulted his notebook. "A Vicky Wells, but we have yet to reach her by phone."

Halloway continued, "The victim has parents just outside Oxfordshire. Local nick has been to see them. They haven't seen their daughter for close to a month."

"Is that all?" Jillian asked.

"Yes guv. They weren't too bothered, to be honest," he said, referring to the Thames Valley Police in Oxfordshire.

Jillian had little time to ponder that thought, however, as at that moment, Chief Superintendent Roger Smalton from the Eden Police Department walked in and began looking around for her.

Unable to prevent the exaggerated sigh that escaped her, Jillian walked out of the incident room and approached him. "Hello sir," she said.

"Scotte," he said in his deep, gruff voice. "Do you have a moment?"

Jillian motioned toward her office and joined him there, closing the door behind her. She found herself nervous at the sight of his uniform and tried to calm down. She knew if she had been male, this would have been a phone call, but because she was a woman, he felt the need to come in person. He told her he wanted to let everyone in the station know that he was in charge of the region and would oversee the case personally.

It was all Jillian could do not to vomit. "You will, of course, run the investigation, but I expect you to report to me daily." He requested an update. She gave him what little information they had and then decided she might as well ask for what she needed.

"Sir, we could use more resources to help manage everything here." She watched as he considered it. Then he nodded, saying he would send two constables to help. She decided to push a little more. "Thank you, sir. Actually, I think I'm going to need to go down to London and Oxfordshire."

"Why?" he asked.

"I want to check into the victim's life, her roommate, friends, et cetera, and then see her parents."

"Surely the local police are doing that?" he retorted.

"Yes sir," she said, "but this isn't their case. They're hardly going to give it their all, are they?"

She knew he couldn't argue with that, and ultimately he relented, but with a caveat: "Just don't go stepping on toes, Scotte." And with that, he looked her in the eyes before walking out of her office.

Message delivered. He knew about her reason for leaving Thames Valley. He was making it clear that he thought it her fault, by telling her not to step on toes when it ought to have been the other way around.

"Kara, grab your coat," Jillian called out, grabbing her own off the rack by her office door. When she told Kara where they were going, she saw both surprise and a flicker of a smile on the young constable's face.

Jillian was tired of the men sitting on top of the ladders, always pushing her down. She wanted a friendly face with her when she went back into enemy territory. She was not looking forward to this visit down memory lane.

CHAPTER 5

The rails clacked against the wheels of the train as the green countryside of Northern England slipped by. PC-in-training Kara Devanor, having run home earlier to grab an overnight bag, was now busy on her phone securing two hotel rooms in Oxfordshire.

Jillian Scotte was glad that Kara was busy. The five-hour train ride would give Jillian plenty of time, and she needed it to prepare herself.

She had to be ready in case he was there. Chief Inspector Paul Davies, early fifties, tall, tan, and full of himself. It had happened at a forensics conference in Manchester. He'd flirted with her mercilessly, and nothing she could do or say seemed to deter him. On the afternoon of the next-to-last day of the weeklong conference, he'd cornered her alone, away from the rest of the group.

She remembered the smell of his awful cologne and what she was sure was vodka on his breath at one in the afternoon—probably from his lunch with the senior officers in attendance.

First, he tried flattering her about her looks, her shape, and when that didn't work, he tried her intelligence. He laid it on thick and added promises of promotion and advancement he was in no position to give. When she still tried to get by him, he dropped the pretense.

His manner turned smug and condescending, and he blamed her for flaunting herself, for wanting what "he could give" her.

She let him grope her breast; her back against the wall of the alcove he had cornered her in. She let him kiss her neck, creating the pretense that he was gaining purchase. He moved closer to her, giving her the opportunity to shift her hips slightly. Once he was in the position she wanted, she waited for him to finish kissing her neck and look at her.

She could see the lust-crazed look in his eye as she met his gaze. Shifting her weight slightly, she brought her right hip and leg back as far as they would go and smiled at him. He smiled back, thinking he had her.

The snap of her knee shooting into his groin was quick and direct. She watched his smile turn to pained surprise. He recoiled, and he attempted to grab himself, but she had her hands on his hips, and her arms prevented him. Pulling back, she kneed him a second time, even harder now, as she had more leverage. He fell to the ground, half curled up, unable to breathe, his face turning red.

Straightening her blouse, she took a step over him and glanced down the hall. It was empty. Drawing her leg back, she aimed a full-on football kick directly at the back of his hands, which were covering himself. Every ounce of her body went into the kick. She heard a bone in his hand crack, and he cried out through clenched teeth as her toe landed once again on his groin.

He didn't attend the rest of the conference, nor the train ride back with the rest of the group from London. Everyone just assumed he'd used his privileged rank to get another way home.

Jillian had filed a report, but she had no proof. He said his broken hand was from an accident at home. Then he claimed she had been the one coming on to him, but that when he refused her, she filed a false report. Her word against his. He won. She lost.

Had it not been for her work on the serial killer case that had taken over West London soon after, he might have been able to make her life miserable. As it was, she took great pains to avoid him as much as possible, but she knew she couldn't stay. If she remained anywhere in the London area, she would be within his purview as a chief inspector who would make superintendent by the end of the year.

She took the only way out and put in for her transfer.

"Guv," PC Devanor said forcefully, and Jillian realized she'd been off in a daze. "You all right?"

"Yes, sorry," Jillian said, shaking her head. "What's up?"

"I've got us sorted for tonight, and your contact at Thames Valley has come through and arranged to bring the parents in for us to interview."

"Great," Jillian said, returning to the task at hand. She and Kara spent the next four hours on their laptops, searching digital records for anything that might give them a clue to who the killer was. They cross-referenced decapitation with serial killers and again with chain saw killings. There was little in the way of results.

The well-publicized killing of a man on the Isle of Wight in 2019 was, of course, among the results, but that had been an attack with a chain saw followed by strangulation, not the carving up of a body. There were a number of attacks involving chain saws, but nothing like what they were dealing with.

The famous Jigsaw Man back in 2009 had been dismembered , and the killer had previously worked for a crime family. He had used a meat cleaver, meat knives, a hacksaw, or a chain saw to cut up bodies. However, he was still in prison and not eligible for parole until 2046.

A search of recently released offenders who might be considered suspects left them with one name, and he was nearly seventy years old. That seemed an improbable lead, but Jillian told Kara they would need to look into it, just in case.

They arrived at the Kidlington Police Station on Oxford Road at just past four in the afternoon. Jillian was stiff and a bit on edge until they were taken back to the incident room, where some of her old team approached her and gave her hugs.

Everyone chided her about being up in Cumbria and gave Kara their sympathy for having DI Scotte as a governor, but it was all good natured. Everyone got caught up on life and, of course, the case Jillian was working on.

They moved to an interview room along with Detective Inspector Norland, the man who had replaced Jillian, to talk to the parents of the deceased. If DI Norland was upset about having his predecessor in his "patch," he didn't show it. In fact, he was nothing but professional, letting the pair from Cumbria know he would help however he could and that they could lead the interview.

Jillian took a seat next to DI Norland. PC Devanor sat in a chair against the wall, taking notes.

The mother was understandably shaken. The father, however, seemed disinterested, stiff, unemotional.

They began with the basic questions: When did you last see your daughter? When did you last speak to her? Can you think of anyone who would want to harm her?

The mother had a hard time answering, as she was prone to breaking out in bouts of crying any time her daughter's name was mentioned.

"Mr. Longwood," Jillian asked. "Did your daughter have a boyfriend?"

He shrugged as if he couldn't care less.

Jillian frowned, then said, "A girlfriend, then?"

This struck him. "What are you getting at?" he retorted.

"I'm just trying to get a picture of your daughter's life, Mr. Longwood."

"She lived her life, and we lived ours," he said gruffly. "Who she saw was her own business, the silly tart."

That earned a renewed fit of tears from his wife, at which he rolled his eyes.

They kept at it for a little over an hour, but there was nothing much to glean. The mother calmed down enough to answer some questions that her husband refused to consider. Yes, she thought her daughter had a boyfriend, but she couldn't remember the name. She worked a lot and came home infrequently.

As the trio of cops watched the couple leave, Kara voiced what they were all thinking. "He was a bit odd, wasn't he?"

"You see all sorts in this work, love," Norland said. "Everyone processes grief differently."

As they walked back to the incident room , Jillian said, "Not sure I would call that grief."

The day was ending, and Jillian's old colleagues invited the two ladies to their local for a round of drinks. Since they had yet to reach the victim's roommate to arrange a time to visit, they agreed.

Two hours later, amid laughter and a few admonishments from Jillian to two of her former constables that Kara was out of their league, she looked at her phone and stepped outside to take a call.

After coming back inside, she walked up and grabbed Kara by the arm. "We'd better get to our hotel. DS Halloway just called with news, both good and bad."

That calmed the small group down.

"Good news is that he finally reached the victim's roommate, and she can see us, but it has to be before she goes to work, so we're going there at half-past six tomorrow morning," Jillian said.

One of her old detective sergeants said, "Not sure I'd call getting up before half-past six in the morning good news, boss." The "boss" had been added automatically, and she could see his face redden as soon as he realized what he'd said. She just smiled at him warmly.

"What's the bad news?" Kara asked.

Jillian dropped her smile. "A call just came in from Dartford. They've found a severed leg, chewed up at the cut." She paused. "Too early for DNA, but I'll bet the next round it's ours."

CHAPTER 6

Morning came far too early for Detective Inspector Jillian Scotte. The wake-up call from the front desk assaulted her senses and added to her growing headache, courtesy of the pints she'd had with her former coworkers last night.

The night sky was fading outside her hotel window as Jillian pulled on the clothes from her overnight bag and brushed her teeth, all the while replaying the second conversation she'd had with her sergeant on the phone last night.

"Hello boss," he'd said when she picked up the call at nearly eleven o'clock. "Sorry to call so late."

"S'all right," Jillian responded, having not quite made it into bed yet. "What's up, Mark? Why are you up so late?"

"Just got a call from the desk sergeant at Eden," he said, still sounding half-asleep. All of Ravenstonedale's calls were routed after-hours to the larger station in Eden. "Another leg and another arm have been found."

"What, together?" Jillian said, surprised.

"No," he said, "the leg was down in Guildford, the arm near Worcester."

Jillian relaxed ever so slightly. At least the killer was being consistent. It would have been odd to have them both together. As if reading her mind on her next question, he said, "No DNA yet, but I've put in a call to have the DNA tests rushed."

"Good work, Mark," Jillian said, meaning it. "Listen, tomorrow morning I need you to run a background on a Gareth Longwood, victim's father. Find out all you can. There's something odd about him."

She could hear him typing on a keyboard. "Also, any headway yet on the victim's boyfriend?" She knew he'd only gotten the name of the room-mate a few hours ago, but she and Kara needed to track the boyfriend down if she was going to have any hope of interviewing him herself before they had to catch the train back later in the afternoon.

"Not yet, guv." Mark sighed.

She could sense the frustration in his voice, so she jumped in. "I know you have had little time. Just thought I'd ask."

Mark seemed nonplussed about it. "Eden has sent us a couple of constables each day and we've got them working on CCTV and searches. I'll get one of them on it first thing."

That conversation had been a little over six hours ago, and she doubted anyone was coming in this early, so she'd just have to wait.

She spotted Kara in the lobby, holding two takeaway cups of coffee.

"I could kiss you," Jillian said, reaching for one of the offered cups.

Kara half laughed. "I've also checked us out, so we're clear to go."

Jillian took her first sip of coffee, feeling the caffeine shooting into her bloodstream. She knew part of PC Devanor's enthusiasm was because she wanted to impress her boss—she was, after all, still in training—but it was the little things like this that made an inspector's job easier, and it didn't go unnoticed.

She let Kara drive so she could focus on drinking her coffee and trying to fit all the pieces together in her head before they met the victim's roommate.

Vicky Wells was a hot mess. Her hair, purple, stood out at all angles as if shouting to the world. Her black lipstick seemed out of place with her blue scrubs. Jillian, flashing her warrant card, wondered which hospital would allow such an unusual appearance.

Ms. Wells was like a Tasmanian Devil, opening the door wide and rushing about the apartment looking for "me fags" and "me bloody phone." It was easy to see how they might have gotten lost in the flat. It looked like it hadn't been cleaned up in weeks.

"Sorry," she said, noticing Kara and Jillian looking for a place to sit down. "Sarah was always straightening up." Then adding, as though it were an excuse, "I don't have the time, do I?" as she swept rubbish off the sofa to give them a place to sit.

Jillian thought "straightening up" was putting it mildly and that sending in a hazardous materials team would have been better, but she kept that to herself. Vicky, having found and lit her cigarette, took a seat and leaned forward with her elbows on her knees. The cigarette burned between her fingers, which she held up next to her face.

After going through the preliminaries of when she last saw her roommate, how they came to know each other, how they got along, Jillian got down to it. "Can you think of anyone who might want to harm Sarah?"

"No," Vicky said immediately. "I mean Dom's a right twat, but I can't see 'im harmin' 'er, not really."

Jillian leaned forward a little. "What do you mean, not really?"

"Well . . ." she said, hesitating a bit.

"Vicky," Jillian said, keeping her tone even. "Sarah has been murdered. Anything that you can think of could help us catch this killer."

Jillian watched as Vicky thought about it, and apparently deciding that it was safe to say something, she said, "Well, Dom, that's . . . 'e was 'er boyfriend, you see. 'E knocked 'er about sometimes, you know."

Jillian thought, *No, I don't know*, but kept silent and let Vicky go on.

"But 'e was all right most of the time," she said as she began chewing on her nails, holding the cigarette dangerously close to her eyes. It occurred to Jillian that if her wild hair were being held in place by hair spray, the burning end of the cigarette could ignite it, and the whole wild mess would go up in a flash.

"It sounds like you don't care for him much?" Jillian said. "You called him what . . . a right twat?"

"Yeah . . . well . . . I mean . . ." Vicky said, flicking her hand about, dropping ash everywhere and seeming not to notice. "Most men are twats, aren't they? 'E was better 'n most, but 'e was far from an angel."

"How so?"

Vicky was getting nervous. Her right leg was bouncing at the ankle, making her cigarette jump, so she lifted her elbow off it. "Look, I don't wan' git no one in trouble."

"Just tell us what you know, Vicky," Jillian said, her voice getting a little sterner.

"Well, 'e does a little dealin' on the side, I know that. My mate Babs was tellin' me just the other day how she saw 'im handin' off packets to people who'd put money in 'e's palm as they walked by."

Jillian looked over at Kara, who was busily writing everything down. "Do you know Dom's surname?"

"Yeah," Vicky said, taking another cigarette and lighting it from the embers of her first one. "It's Lesther. Used to give 'im a right hard time they did, they'd call 'im Lesther the Molester in school." Suddenly, she put her hand up to her face. "Ooohh . . . I shoudna tole you that, should I?"

"It's all right, Vicky," Jillian said soothingly. "When was the last time you saw him?"

"Well, 'e came round looking for Sarah about a week ago, and then 'e called me last Monday sayin' 'e wanted to know where she was. I tole 'im I 'adn't seen 'er in weeks meself." Then, as if it was an afterthought, she said, "'E can be a right bastard on the phone."

They stayed as long as possible before Vicky became overanxious about getting to work on time. There was nothing else of relevance they managed to get out of her.

As Jillian and Kara stood outside Vicky's flat, they watched her walk down toward the tube station, catching glances from passersby in awe of her hair and general appearance. "Come on," Jillian said to Kara. "Let's find some breakfast.

Since Vicky had provided them with his phone number and last known address, they wanted to plan their approach before going to see Mr. Dominic Lesther.

CHAPTER 7

The umbrella wasn't big enough for both of them, but Jillian did the best she could, wrapping her arm around Kara and pulling her in close as the two ran from the car up the steps of a rather posh looking building and pushed through into the lobby.

They were both half-wet from the storm that had come out of nowhere while they ate their breakfasts. The block of flats was nondescript, but upscale. The lobby was well-appointed and clean, with two lifts side by side, rather a luxury in this part of Oxfordshire.

DI Norland would once again accompany them, and he was already inside, his raincoat still damp, indicating he hadn't been waiting long. Although this was Jillian's investigation, it was now DI Norland's patch, and to avoid the "stepping on toes" she had been warned against, she and Kara had called him so that he could take the lead.

As they rode up in the lift in awkward silence, Jillian reflected on the two calls she had received over breakfast. The first was from DS Halloway, who had sounded apprehensive. "Guv . . . umm."

"What is it, Mark? Spit it out." Jillian still had not gotten her breakfast yet, and she was both hungry and annoyed. The term these days of "hangry" felt very appropriate.

"Have you seen anything on the news or online yet this morning?" he asked.

Just then, across the table from her, she saw Kara's eyes go wide as she looked at her phone. Looking up, Kara saw the quizzical look on Jillian's face and turned the screen toward her.

It was a post on social media with the headline:

LUMBERJACK KILLER LEAVES BODY PARTS ACROSS ENGLAND.

"Bloody hell!" Jillian yelled, causing many patrons of the restaurant to turn and look at her. She couldn't care less, and she shot the table next to them such a stare that they turned back and resumed their meal. "Mark," she barked into the phone, "how the hell did this get out?"

Halloway assured her he had talked to everyone on their team, and he was certain none of them had leaked to the press. Jillian wasn't convinced and told him in no uncertain terms that if she found out who had leaked the information, she was going to boil them alive.

The server, who had stopped by to deliver their food, raised her eyebrows and stood staring down at both of them. Jillian stared back, her face flushed, and Kara looked down at her food as if it were the most amazing sight she had ever seen.

No sooner had Jillian hung up the phone with her sergeant than it began chirping again. Jillian was so annoyed with the leak to the press that she considered ignoring it, but the number was from Cumbria, so she answered sternly, "DI Scotte."

"Hi Jillian, it's Daniella."

It took her a few seconds to process; then she remembered meeting Dr. Daniella Morales in her office the other day. "Oh, hello."

"Is this a bad time?"

"What? No, sorry, it's been a bit of a rough morning."

Dr. Morales said, "I saw the news. I'm sorry, that must be frustrating for you."

Jillian thought frustrating was putting it mildly, but said, "What can I do for you?"

"I just wanted to let you know that I've been in contact with the coroners in Norwich and Dartford, and we've been comparing notes."

That made Jillian sit up a bit in her seat.

"We all agree that although we can't pinpoint the time, there were some indicators in the leg and one or two things in the arm—we can now say with confidence that the victim was killed either the eleventh or twelfth of this month."

Jillian didn't have time to ask how they had determined that. There was just too much going on, but she made a mental note to follow up later with Dr. Morales and find out. "That's good to know, thank you," she said.

Daniella wasn't finished. "There's more. The hand, specifically the fingers, have been scrubbed clean with bleach."

Jillian's eyes narrowed. Talking out loud to herself, she said, "Perhaps trying to eliminate defensive wound evidence."

"That would be my guess."

"It means our killer knows a thing or two about our methods," Jillian said.

"That," Daniella responded, "or they watch a lot of criminal television shows."

Jillian snorted at that one, knowing it was truer than she liked to admit.

"There is one more thing," Daniella said. "We found traces of dirt in the foot's heel."

"Anything special about the dirt?" Jillian asked.

"Too early to tell," Daniella said, "but if you find a location, they might match dirt from it."

For the first time, Jillian felt as though they had something. It wasn't much, but it was something. There was hope.

"Thank you, Daniella," she said earnestly. "I appreciate this."

"All part of the service," Daniella said, and rang off. But Jillian knew that wasn't true. Daniella didn't have to follow up with the other coroners, and she certainly didn't have to go to the trouble of connecting some of the dots. That, Jillian knew, was her job.

Back in the upscale block of flats, they had to knock for quite some time before the door was answered at number seventeen on the ninth floor. Although it was closer to noontime, Dominic Lesther answered the door in pajama bottoms and nothing else, looking as though he had been woken by their pounding on the door.

"Mr. Dominic Lesther?" Norland asked.

"Yes," he answered with a sneer. "What do you lot want?" He clearly knew the trio standing before him were police before they even identified themselves.

Holding up his warrant card, Norland said, "I'm Detective Inspector Norland with Thames Valley Police. This is DI Scotte and PC Devanor. We'd like to ask you some questions about your girlfriend, Sarah Longwood?" He'd spoken in an even tone up to the end and then posed it as a question.

The mention of Sarah's name did not improve Mr. Lesther's mood. If anything, it worsened it.

He stood scowling for a few moments as if deciding what course to take. Maybe it was because there were three of them, or perhaps because two were women. Whatever the case, Dominic Lesther sighed heavily, dropped his arm from his doorframe, and turned back inside. "All right, come on then, let's get this over wif."

Once everyone had found somewhere to sit in the plushly appointed flat with a fifty-two-inch television screen taking up one entire wall, and Lesther had retrieved a T-shirt, Norland began.

"When was the last time you saw your girlfriend?"

"I dunno," he said lazily. "Ten days ago, maybe longer."

"Can you be a bit more specific, Mr. Lesther?" Jillian asked, prompting a reproachful look from Norland.

"Why?" he responded, before adding, "She's dead, i'n' she." And for good measure he added, "Got noffin' to do wi' me."

"When did you learn she was dead, Mr. Lesther?" Jillian asked. Norland was now leaning forward and tilting his head at her in reproach.

"That bitch of a roommate tole me, didn' she," he said.

Jillian let that comment go and was about to ask another question when Norland cut her off. "Mr. Lesther, you don't seem all that upset at finding out that your girlfriend is dead. Why is that?"

Dominic sneered at him in response. "I got more'n one, don't I. Was gonna end it soon anyway."

"And why was that, Mr. Lesther?" Norland asked.

He shrugged. "Not worf it anymore."

Jillian jumped in this time. "Can you account for your whereabouts on the eleventh and twelfth of this month, Mr. Lesther?"

"You're joking," Dominic said, laughing. "I can't tell you wot I was doin' last Tuesday, love, much less goin' on three weeks."

"Give it some thought, Mr. Lesther," Norland said testily, displeased with the way Jillian was now firmly stepping on his toes.

"Wot?" Lesther said. "You lot gonna arrest me for not rememberin' which slag I was shaggin' or what pot I was pissin' in?"

After twenty more minutes of insolent answers, rude looks, and even more disgusting innuendos, Jillian felt like she needed a shower. Kara shuddered as they got into the lift to go back down.

Once the door closed, Norland turned and stuck his finger in Jillian's face. "Look, this may have been your patch once, and I've seen all the headlines from that case, but this is mine now. You want my help in the future, you can bloody well piss off." He paused, lowering his finger, then leaning in with malice, he added, "Chief Davies was right about you. You'll do anything to get what you want."

The doors opened to the lobby and Norland stormed off, leaving the two women to watch as he rammed open the front door and stomped into the rain.

Kara looked over at her boss. "What was that all about?"

Jillian kept looking straight ahead as they exited the lift. "I've no idea," she said, but something was clearly wrong. Lesther had been off, and regardless of whether she'd stepped on his toes a little, Norland's response was off as well.

The more they worked on this case, the less they learned, and the more questions were added to the list.

CHAPTER 8

The office of the Thames Valley Police Kidlington in Headquarters South on Oxford Road wasn't as big as it ought to be, and that had created problems, mainly to do with space—and especially space needed for what had once been known as the drug squad.

Scotland Yard had reshuffled the police who worked in the drug squad into the newly created Serious Organized Crime Agency, or SOCA for short, in April 2006. In 2010, the part of the unit that worked drugs and typically fell under the Vice Squad was renamed in a politically correct makeover across the force.

Thus, those whose work involved the criminal underbelly of the biggest cities in the Metropolitan Police Force across the UK now fell under the Serious Crime Directorate 9: Human Exploitation and Organized Crime Command, otherwise known as SCD9.

Inside the Kidlington Police Station, Oxford Road, SCD9 had been relegated to a small area of offices at the far back of the building, down the hall from the admin section.

Jillian and Kara were walking through the admin section, which included the 999 incident control center, when Denise Conley walked up .

Conley was a communications officer and worked both with staff and in the control center. She and Jillian, while perhaps not friends, had been good acquaintances during Jillian's time there.

Officer Conley said hello, then dropped her voice. "Thought you'd want to know, but Chief Inspector Davies has been lurking about since he heard you was here. Was in DI Norland's office yesterday making a right fuss."

Kara watched as Jillian's face turned white, and her back stiffened. Taking a breath, Jillian thanked the officer and continued walking down the hall toward SCD9. A detective in jeans and a leather motorcycle jacket who looked like he hadn't shaved in weeks approached. He stood with his hands on his hips and looked at Kara, who was standing slightly behind Jillian.

"Sorry, love," he said, his cockney accent thick. "Tarts have to be processed downstairs before they come up here for interviews."

Kara's eyes opened wide, and she found herself unable to make a sound. She looked at Jillian, who was staring at the man who had just accused her of being a prostitute. There was an awkward moment of silence, and then the man broke out into a smile. Turning to Jillian, he opened his arms and gave her a big hug.

"Good to see you, Jills," he said.

"You can be a right arsehole, you know that?" Jillian said as she let go of his embrace.

"Yeah, well," the detective said, "goes with the territory, dun' it?"

"Kara, meet Detective Sergeant Milston," Jillian said, "DS and resident scum with SCD9. Braggart, rogue, and every once in a while, a good copper." Then she added, "Rob, this is PC Kara Devanor, who's already showing signs of being better than you'll ever hope to be."

DS Robert Milston offered his hand to Kara, who shook it. "Whatever you do, don't aim for being better'n me." Then, pointing to Jillian, he said, "Shoot for being better'n 'er." He smiled, leaned in a little closer before whispering, "Just listen and do what she tells you, there's no one better."

Kara, already blushing from Jillian's comment, stood a little taller.

"Now then," Milston said. "What brings you two lovely ladies down to sex, crime, and drugs?" It was his private moniker for SCD9.

Jillian asked what he knew about Dominic Lesther.

"Dealin' Dom? Yeah, we know about 'im. 'E thinks more of 'imself than anyone. 'E's not high level, but I'll give 'im credit, somehow that piece of sludge keeps working 'is way up the ladder."

"Is he a player, then?" Jillian asked.

"Not quite yet," Milston replied.

"Can we get a copy of his file?"

Milston said he didn't see why not, and of course asked what it was all about. Jillian filled him in. He'd heard about the head and the other body parts, though he hadn't known it was her case.

As he was handing Kara the copied files—SCD9 didn't have the resources to digitize everything, so a lot were still old-fashioned paper—Jillian's mobile phone rang. "Sorry Rob, I've got to take this."

"No worries, love," he said, giving her a peck on the cheek. "I've got to go see a man about some heroin, anyway." Waving to Kara, he went through a door at the back.

"DI Scotte," Jillian said into her phone.

"Hello guv," PC Jack Worhington said. "DS Halloway asked me to give you a call to fill you in on our progress."

"Fire away."

"We've set up coordination with all the stations that found . . . uhm . . . the parts and we're trying to scour CCTV to see if it caught anything, but so far all the locations where the drops were made are remote and there are no cameras."

Jillian had expected as much, but they had to check.

"Also," Worhington said, "we've been in contact with the victim's employer and have done phone interviews with a few people she worked with, but honestly boss, it sounds like she just did her shifts and went home. No one really knew much about her."

Jillian nodded to herself as she, and Kara made their way down to the police station entrance. "Keep at it, Jack. We need a break with this thing. Someone has to know something."

"Well . . . uhmmm . . ." he began.

Jillian could sense there was something he'd been waiting to tell her. "Yes," she said impatiently.

"You asked us to check into Gareth Longwood, the vic's father?"

"Yes," Jillian repeated.

"Turns out he's a long-haul lorry driver. Goes up north as far as Wales and down to Bristol," Worhington said, but Jillian could tell there was more, and the hairs on the back of her neck were standing up. He continued, "Here's the thing, mum, he sometimes drives loads for a logging company."

That made Jillian stop, and it took Kara a step or two to realize her boss wasn't moving before she half turned around.

"Jack," Jillian said after a moment, "I want you and DS Halloway to look into Mr. Longwood's recent driving history, especially around the eleventh and twelfth of this month. I want to know if he was at home or on the road."

Jillian began walking again. "Also, check into his whereabouts last Thursday through the weekend?"

"Yes, mum," he said, then asked, "Why start on Thursday?"

Jillian never wanted to discourage questions from her officers, but she was wondering if PC Worhington might not benefit from a little less talking and more thinking. "We found the head on Friday morning, but it had clearly been there for a bit, so likely the killer was in the area the evening before."

She asked if there was anything else and then disconnected.

As they climbed into their car, Kara wanted to ask so many questions, especially about the phone call she had only heard one side of, but clearly something was up with the victim's father.

Surprising even herself, she didn't ask about the call first. Instead, she said, "Mum, what was that comms officer saying about Chief Davies when we arrived?"

She was looking over at Jillian as she started the car, and although it wasn't much, there was a definite catch in her boss's breath. After a moment, Jillian turned to her and, looking at her straight in the eye, said, "Nothing."

Kara knew when she was being lied to, but she also knew better than to press the issue. Putting the car in gear, she pulled out and headed toward the train station for their long trek back up north.

CHAPTER 9

Flowers sat on top of a small table just inside the door. Tall orange irises with bright green leaves and baby's breath in a contemporary glass vase. It all seemed out of place for the entrance to a coroner's office.

Jillian stopped, taking in the flowers and reflecting on how much had happened already this morning.

The train ride back the night before had been long and uneventful. She and Kara spent some of it taking brief naps after their whirlwind trip to the west side of London and Oxfordshire.

Kara was turning out to be much more than she had seemed at first look. Jillian had always hated the term "PC in training." While she understood it took time for a constable to get the basics, she always found the term demeaning when called out in public. It was the reason she almost always left it off when introducing Kara to others.

Perhaps it was Kara's young age and generation, or that she was new to being a copper, but she was fearless when it came to asking questions and taking in new information. Jillian tried to think whether her younger self would have had the nerve to press a superior officer the way Kara had pressed her on the train and struggled to think that she would have.

Kara had seemed to sense Jillian's internal struggle after they left Kidlington Police Station, and once they had settled in for the long ride up north, she'd jumped back in. "Guv?" she asked. "Are you sure you're all right?"

Jillian had been sitting deep in thought, mostly about the case, and it took her a moment to realize what Kara was referring to. She answered automatically, "I'm fine."

She should have known that her flippant answer wouldn't be the end of the conversation. "What happened?" Kara asked, brazenly.

Jillian took a deep breath and looked directly at her. It was complicated. She wanted to tell someone, to confide and share, so she wasn't alone with everything that had happened. Still, PC Devanor was her subordinate, her charge, her responsibility. It would be inappropriate for her to unburden herself to someone on her team, let alone someone at such an entry-level position.

Kara was a female officer, and what had happened to Jillian could, and likely would, happen to her as well. She was young, pretty, and vulnerable in the sense of having older and senior men who would always look for a way to take advantage.

These thoughts entered her mind in a flash, and before she could process them, Kara said, "We all knew about the case when we heard you were coming up to Cumbria. What I couldn't understand is why someone so accomplished would want to come up to a small place like Ravenstonedale."

Jillian had ultimately decided it wasn't the time to go into everything. Besides, she was too tired. "Leave it for now, Kara," she said decisively.

Kara looked down apologetically and turned the conversation back to the case, reviewing her copious notes.

After arriving home late, Jillian had not slept well and woke up tired, sore, and unsettled. Her mood didn't improve when she checked her phone and saw an email from Chief Superintendent Smalton calling her in to Eden for an update.

As if surprise visits to her office weren't enough. It felt like being called into the headmaster's office at school. He had invited her to sit upon entering his office, and he sat quietly as she updated him on the past few days.

"So," he said, "you've managed to gather a lot more information, but not much in the way of leads."

"Well, sir." She answered his derogatory tone with an even-keeled, measured one of her own. "We're taking a hard look at the father, and the boyfriend is still in the frame. It may not be much, but it's a start."

"Look, DI Scotte," he said condescendingly, "I don't know how things were done in Thames Valley, but the press has got their bit into this thing and they will not let go. We've already been fielding calls from all the majors, and comms have told me that the BBC is sending a camera and reporter up, possibly as early as today."

Jillian flinched. She knew the press were having a field day with their self-described "Lumberjack Killer," but she had hoped they would focus on the body parts closer to London.

Smalton brought her mind back to the present. "I don't want to face the lion's den with nothing to feed their appetite. It won't be long before Scotland Yard calls, and then soon after, the home office will want me to explain why we haven't caught the killer. We need results and we need them fast; do I make myself clear?"

"Yes, sir," she said as Smalton stood to show their meeting was over.

Politics and the press were the ever-present masters the police had to serve. People always thought it was the public to whom the police were responsible, but in reality, the press and the higher echelons of government ruled the day.

She had stopped at the coroner's office, which was just down the road, to see if Dr. Morales had anything new to give her. It was her voice that had snapped Jillian out of her daydream with the flowers. "Oh, hello. I didn't know you were coming by."

Jillian turned to the smiling doctor, returning a weary smile of her own. "Sorry, just dropped in. I was called in for a talking-to up the road. Thought I'd see if you or your cohorts down south had anything new to report?"

"As a matter of fact," Daniella replied, "I just got off a video call with them."

That piqued Jillian's interest.

"We were discussing the similarities between the parts, and some rather disturbing ones at that."

"Go on," Jillian said, her eyes narrowing.

"Well, as you already know, the arms and legs were deposited near the sides of roads. Based on their positioning and various marks found, we can say with some credibility that they were thrown, not placed."

Jillian nodded; they had discovered this from the severed head as well.

"All the fingers and toes, in fact the hands and feet, had all been scrubbed clean with bleach."

Jillian frowned. "But I thought you said you found some soil on one foot?"

"Yes," Daniella said, grinning with appreciation that the detective had been paying attention. "It might be the one and only mistake the killer has made. The dirt was caught in a crease at the narrowest part of the ankle and thus was not part of the foot that was scrubbed. The killer would have had to look closely to see it. My counterpart down south said he missed it the first time and only caught it because he was curious how far up the bleaching had gone."

"What's most disturbing, Jillian, is that our killer seems to know his, or her, I suppose, stuff. The bleaching, the tossing of the pieces so as not to leave trace evidence near the crime scene. Whoever is doing this is being very careful not to leave us anything to go by." Daniella's face had turned very serious.

Jillian asked a few more questions and then left to get back to her team. As she walked in the door, she found DS Halloway and PC Devanor anxiously waiting for her.

Mark let her get her coat off first; then glancing at PC Devanor, he said, "We've been tracking Mr. Longwood's movements. According to the firm's logs, he was definitely not driving on the eleventh of this month. He did, however, make a trip down to Bristol, leaving on the twelfth and returning on the fourteenth."

"Right," Jillian said, tapping her lips with a pen. "What about last week?"

Kara responded this time. "I've just got off the phone with them, mum. The firm only collects driving logs from the drivers twice a month. They had just collected the midmonth ones, which is how they were able to give us the information on those two days. They said they won't collect the end-of-month records and process them until next week."

Jillian cursed under her breath. "You're joking?" she said exasperatedly. "Are these logs manual ones? Because if that's the case and he's our man, he could write whatever he bloody wants to in the damn thing."

Mark spoke up now, trying to calm his boss. "They're both manual and electronic. The lorries have GPS trackers on them, so they know what their drivers are up to. It also allows them to compare to the manual logs to see if the drivers are being honest." He finished with one eyebrow raised, clearly thinking the firm was more than a little suspicious of its employees.

Turning to Kara, Jillian said, "Well, get back onto them and tell them it's bloody important that we get those records straightaway. Mark, if you have to, drive down and make some noise in person."

They both nodded and went back to their desks. Jillian put her head in her hands. They desperately needed a break before this spiraled out of control. She was not immune to the pressure the chief super was putting on her, but more than that, she was worried about what no one wanted to say out loud.

What if the killer does it again?

CHAPTER 10

The shower filled with hot, muscle-soaking steam. Kara let her head tilt back and the hot water just cascade over her. Her muscles were taut, her arms heavy. She was wound up tight with stress.

Nothing could have prepared her for the brutality of the severed head, the intensity of the investigation, and the stress that she brought home with her each night. She would get to her small flat above the baker's and make herself something to eat, which usually involved something frozen and premade, or a quick takeaway.

Then, she would sit down with her notes, going over everything they had learned, doing more research, and looking for anything that could be important to the case.

As a police constable in training, she had no delusions of seeing or finding something that her more experienced team members had missed. In reality, she didn't want to be the member of the team that dropped the ball, or somehow didn't do her bit.

She would work well past midnight before crashing. Sometimes she would simply fall asleep on the broken-down couch that had come with the flat. She didn't want to think about how that might just be an excuse to avoid sleeping in her bed and be reminded that she was single with few to no prospects. Far from being an attraction, once a potential suitor found out she was a copper, they ran away, and fast.

Having stayed in the shower far longer than she should have, she quickly put on her uniform and ran out the door.

She made it to the station with five minutes to spare, and yet when she walked through the door in the back, she found she was the last one to arrive. Even the two constables on loan from Eden had already turned up.

Chiding herself for not realizing everyone was going to come in early, she made a mental note to leave home at least thirty minutes earlier tomorrow.

DS Mark Halloway, who had just emerged from the gents, approached her. "Good morning. We're going to have the morning brief in a few minutes. Make sure you have the data from yesterday handy, in case the boss wants to reference it."

"Yes, Sarge," she said, depositing her bag and coat by her desk, then quickly logging in on her computer and printing the latest dataset pulled the night before. This was not a good start to her day, and she needed to get back on track.

***

Detective Inspector Jillian Scotte finished the team brief and strode back to her office. She could see that the team was trying. Everyone was on board, but they had so little to go on.

She called DS Halloway and PC Devanor into her office.

"Mark, where are we at on Mr. Longwood's employer?"

Mark looked a little pained. "They say the lorry he was driving last week left yesterday morning for a trip up to Scotland and won't be back until tomorrow." He could see that Jillian was about to explode. "They did, however," he said, cutting her off before she could get started, "say that last week Mr. Longwood was scheduled to drive up to Manchester, then on to Liverpool and Cardiff before coming back to base."

He waited a beat before adding, "If the GPS log checks out, he couldn't have made all the trips it would take to drop off the body parts, much less come all the way up here to leave the head."

Jillian was not happy about the news, but knew she couldn't dwell on it. Turning to Kara, she asked if they had anything new on the victim or boyfriend. Just as Kara opened her mouth to speak, Jillian's phone rang. Holding up a finger to Kara, Jillian picked up the phone. "DI Scotte."

Jillian listened a beat, then said, "Hello Rob, what's up?" She listened for a moment more, asked a few questions, then hung up.

Looking at her team, she said, "That was DS Milston from SCD9. Turns out our victim's boyfriend has been misbehaving for quite some time. I asked him to look into Mr. Lesther's past, and he found several connections between Lesther and not only some work SCD9 was doing but also with Vice. Our victim, it seems, was also part of Lesther's ring of girls he was running on the street."

She noticed that both Kara and Mark were taking notes. "He's sending everything over via encrypted digital transfer. We should have it soon. Kara, I want you to go through it and put together a dossier on Dominic Lesther."

Kara nodded and made herself another note.

"Mark, I need you to look into Lesther's activities as best you can. Look at ANPR," she said, referring to the automatic number-plate recognition system the Met uses to track vehicles moving all over Britain. "We need to see if he was making trips up north and around the circle last week. Either we find him, or we prove he wasn't there, but either way, we have to get to resolution on him. He's a loose end that cannot remain untethered."

"Yes guv," Halloway said, and he and Kara turned to leave their boss's office.

They filled the rest of the day with the slog of police work that the television shows never mention. The endless phone calls, the data checking, cross-checking, and rechecking. The tips that came in from crackpots but had to be run down or at the very least cataloged.

Jillian took two calls from Eden, asking for updates. Neither of those calls went well.

Kara came in midway through the afternoon and laid a folder with several typed sheets on Jillian's desk. "Here's the dossier on Lesther, mum."

Jillian lifted the cover off the folder and quickly perused the sheets. The presentation impressed her, and on the initial pass, it looked quite thorough. "That was quick," she said, smiling.

Kara beamed. "I thought it best to get to you as quickly as possible, mum."

Jillian thanked her, and the day wore on. Far past teatime and going well into suppertime, Jillian emerged from her office and called out for everyone's attention. "All right, you lot," she said once everyone quieted down. "You've put in a long day, and I know it's been rough. There's nothing more we're going to get tonight. All the contacts you're trying to reach will have gone home or are out for the night. Let's call it a day and try again tomorrow."

There was a mumble of reluctant agreement. Mark spoke up just as people began to move. "Tomorrow we'll be starting an hour earlier than normal, so make sure you adjust accordingly."

At first, Kara thought this was a dig at her, but judging by the grumbles and mumbling, she realized he just wanted the team in early. She made a large note in all caps on her pad to wake up in plenty of time to be the first one in.

By the time Kara got home, her brain was mush, which matched the frozen meal she put in the oven to warm up—mashed potatoes and some sort of squished peas, mixed with what the box claimed was fried fish. It all looked like piles of the same slop, but she was too tired to care.

Despite her promise to herself to get to bed early so she could wake up even earlier and arrive at the station before everyone else, she couldn't turn off her brain. Pulling out the dossier and the full printouts she'd made from the information at SCD9, she began going through it all again.

Perhaps it was the change of scenery, or simply the quick break she'd taken since leaving the station and eating her supper, but as she spread out the sheets and reviewed them, something began to form in her brain.

She'd spent most of her time creating the dossier around Lesther's criminal record and exploits, but now she was looking at the full picture, which included his history.

Dominic Lesther hadn't grown up in London. He actually went to school and grew up in North Yorkshire, not far from Cumbria. Going further, she discovered that he spent one year at the University of East Anglia on the outskirts of Norwich, where he apparently began his wayward path. He was caught up in a rather large-scale drug ring and sentenced to three years in Her Majesty's Prison at Belmarsh. HMP Belmarsh, it turns out, was nine miles from Dartford.

These coincidences made Kara sit and stare, dumbfounded, for several minutes. Without thinking, she picked up her phone and dialed. Just as she noticed the time and her heart began to pound, the call went through.

"Kara?" Jillian said. "Is everything all right?"

Kara didn't know what to say first. She stumbled, but finally got her voice. "I'm so sorry, mum. I didn't realize how late it is."

Jillian, sounding wide awake, said, "S'all right. What's up?"

Kara gave her the information, methodically, piece by piece, not embellishing, just laying out what she had found. She finished and waited. There was silence on the other end of the phone.

She looked at her phone to see if it was still connected and was about to say something when Jillian replied, "Kara, this is brilliant."

Kara felt her heart bursting, but didn't have time to revel. "Well done. Let's talk first thing in the morning and come up with a plan."

***

Jillian, on her end of the call, was impressed with PC Devanor and made a mental note that she needed to honor her in some way.

The call, of course, caused Jillian's already manic mind to go into overdrive. She, too, wondered what else they might have missed and began going through the dossier. She logged in to her laptop to go back over everything they had.

By two o'clock in the morning, she was spent. Despite going back over everything, she had found nothing new. She opened the dossier that Kara had put together for her and, carrying it to her bed, she lay down and went back over Dominic Lesther's life of crime one more time.

When she saw it, she didn't believe it. It just couldn't be. Going back to her laptop, she started back-checking, cross-checking with other pieces of the case. The more she looked, the more she saw.

One thing was certain. Detective Inspector Jillian Scotte would not be getting any sleep.

CHAPTER 11

Traffic was mercifully light as Jillian drove down the M6, headed south toward London. She enjoyed driving and wasn't afraid to push the limits both of her Ford Fiesta and the law when she drove on motorways.

Her electric-blue supermini wasn't big, nor all that unusual, being the most popular car sold across the UK for several years, and while she'd bought hers used, it had been in top shape, and she did her best to keep it that way.

It was already after midday, and she still had a few hours' drive ahead of her as she reflected on the morning's events.

She'd arrived at the station in Ravenstonedale early, though not as early as the rest of the team. They were digging into their various jobs with fervor, which she appreciated. Her discovery last night changed everything, and yet . . . She was hesitant to jump the gun. She'd spent the better part of the early hours of her morning reviewing the details.

In the end, all she had was a lot of coincidences. She was loath to pull members of her team off their assignments if she was wrong. Ultimately, she decided she needed to go back to London herself to gather the evidence she needed.

Before she could leave, however, she had some work to take care of in her office. She called Kara in and asked her to close the door. As Kara sat down, pen and notebook in hand, Jillian noticed Mark looking quizzically at them from his desk. She didn't have time to worry about his sensibilities. "Really great work last night, Kara," she began.

"Thank you," Kara replied, clearly pleased with herself.

"I know you want to follow this up, but I need you to do something for me instead." Jillian could see Kara's disappointment in her changed disposition, and Jillian held up both of her palms, facing outwards. "Don't worry. If anything, and I mean anything, comes from the follow-up on Lesther, you will get full credit and the collar."

That perked Kara up a bit, but now she frowned. Jillian didn't give her a chance to say anything. "Something else has come up and I need to follow it up. I'm going to London again, but I need you to do some digging for me while I'm headed south."

Kara nodded.

"I need you to look through ANPR for this number plate." She handed Kara a piece of paper where she'd written down a car number plate, make, model, and color. Coming around her desk, Jillian got right in front of Kara and, leaning on the edge of her desk, she bent slightly forward and looked her young constable directly in the eyes. "Listen carefully to me, Kara. This is very important."

Kara sat back in her chair, her boss's eyes boring into her.

"You need to be incredibly careful with this search. I want you to go all the way back to the eleventh and twelfth of this month, and then from last Thursday through Sunday night."

Kara took down some notes.

"If ANPR doesn't find anything on the Thursday through Sunday search, I want you looking at any relevant CCTV for a match to that car within those time frames. We have to know if that car was anywhere in the area during that time frame. It's likely that you'll get hits for the car in the London area for the eleventh and twelfth, but we need to be sure."

Kara nodded again, not sure what the fuss was about.

Jillian's voice dropped low as she said, "Kara, look at me."

Kara looked up, and seeing the look on her boss's face, she froze, pen in mid-stroke on her lap.

"This is the important bit. I do not want you doing a number plate license check on this plate. Just one ANPR search, that's it. Don't repeat it or dig deeper. One search. Got it?"

Kara frowned, but nodded.

"I will let DS Halloway know you're going to be doing something for me. If he pushes you, tell him I told you not to say anything. This has to stay between you and me for now, understood?"

"Yes, mum," Kara said seriously.

When she told him, Mark wasn't happy about the secrecy, but Jillian was stern with her instructions to him. She promised to fill him in tomorrow. After a few more phone calls and required meetings, she got in her car. She hadn't bothered to let Chief Superintendent Smalton know she was going because he would never agree unless she explained why, and she wasn't ready for that yet.

When she finally pulled up at Thames Valley Headquarters, sunlight was already beginning to fade. She was stiff from the long drive, but eager to get in and out of the station. One call she had made on the way was to Denise Conley, her old friend in comms.

Denise had said she was happy to help, but when Jillian told her what she wanted access to and then wouldn't tell her why, she hesitated. It had taken a little cajoling, but Denise had eventually relented. As to Jillian's questions about who worked that afternoon, it seemed a large takedown was happening in SCD9 this evening, and half the station, from top brass to lowest PC, were involved. Comms officers not so much, though Denise would help coordinate things from the station.

So, when Jillian was buzzed back by the desk sergeant, she approached Denise's desk to find her with a headset on, busily coordinating what sounded like an operation in full swing. Denise, looking up, smiled, then pointed to her headset and rolled her eyes in the universal signal among women that whoever was on the phone was some twat male officer who thought too much of himself and liked to hear himself talk.

Jillian made the appropriate sympathetic face and placed a bottle of wine on the desk. It was an admission that she was asking something that Denise was going out of her way to accommodate.

Denise mouthed "thank you" excessively, then pointed to an unused office and handed Jillian a slip of paper with a passcode on it.

Jillian wasted no time in entering the office and closing the door. After making sure the blinds on all the windows into the station were closed, she logged in and began searching.

She was just getting started when her phone buzzed. It was Kara.

"Hello Kara." She placed the phone in the crook of her neck as she kept searching.

"Hello guv," Kara said. "I'm in your office. I hope you don't mind, but thought you'd like to keep the conversation private."

"You thought right," Jillian said, once again thankful for the bright young PC. "Whatch'ya got?"

"Well," Kara began apprehensively. "Not much I'm afraid."

Jillian stopped typing.

"You were right about the eleventh and twelfth. The car was mostly local to the London area, and frankly, it wasn't driven much during that time. It stayed parked most of the time during the day." Kara paused, letting her words hang in the air.

Jillian knew what she was saying, but didn't take the bait. She simply said, "What else?"

Kara took a breath. "That's it. No hits on ANPR, and I watched every close hit on multiple cameras up and down the motorways and across the area. Nothing. That car was not in the area last week or this past weekend."

Jillian took her phone out of the crook of her neck and into her hand, and leaned back in her chair. "You're sure?" she asked.

"Yes, mum," Kara replied confidently.

Jillian sighed in frustration.

There was a long silence before finally Jillian said, "Okay, Kara. Thank you. I'll get back to you if I need anything else." She ended the call before Kara could ask questions.

She finished the searches she had been making, but now it made little sense. The car had to have been in the area. Then something on the screen caught her eye. She dug a little deeper, and another thought came to her. Maybe . . . just maybe.

The problem was that she couldn't get the information she needed from this computer. She needed a different system, and she didn't have access to it or know someone who did.

Out of desperation, she called Detective Chief Inspector Maryanne Sanderson in Norwich and explained what she needed.

"Yes, I know someone who could get it, but why not just put the request in through normal channels?" Sanderson answered.

"I'm in a bit of a hurry. I wouldn't ask if it wasn't important." Jillian said.

DCI Sanderson paused on the other end, and Jillian could almost hear her thinking. "You're on to something, aren't you?" she said. "About this case?"

Jillian weighed her options. Finally, she said, "Yes, but it's only a thin lead, probably nothing, but I'm getting pressure from my super, and I need to chase everything down or he's going to have my arse."

She heard what sounded like a cross between a laugh and a sigh. "All right, is this your mobile?"

Jillian said yes, and Maryanne said she'd get back to her soon.

After thanking Denise, Jillian left the station, not wanting to outstay her welcome. She hadn't eaten since breakfast, so she found a pub down the road packed with early evening revelers and ordered a sandwich with salad and a coffee. She wanted something stronger to drink, but she had a long drive home again tonight and she couldn't risk falling asleep.

She hadn't realized how hungry she was until she took the last bite off her now-empty plate. As she sipped her coffee, her phone buzzed. Hoping to see something from Maryanne, she was surprised to find a text from Detective Sergeant Milston. It read *Just finishing up but need to talk to you.* He mentioned a café not too far away and suggested they meet there in three-quarters of an hour.

She texted back that she'd see him there. Another coffee wouldn't hurt and might keep her more awake for the drive. She kept going over everything in her head, trying to think of what she might be missing.

With her head swimming with facts and theories, she got in her car and headed over. As she pulled up to the café, her phone buzzed again. This time it was Sanderson with the information she had asked for: a name.

Pulling into a parking spot in the half-filled lot behind the café, Jillian quickly dialed Kara as she got out of the car.

Kara picked up on the second ring. "PC Devanor."

"Kara, it's me," Jillian said. "I need you to run another number as soon as, but I don't have the number. I have the name and address."

Kara took down the name.

"Kara, listen, it may not be under the full name, so check Bob, Rob, or any derivative of it."

"Yes, mum."

"Oh, and one more thing," Jillian said.

But she never finished.

She felt a presence behind her, but before she could react, a powerful arm wrapped around her and a hand with a soft cloth pressed against her nose and mouth, at the same time knocking the phone out of her hand.

She smelled the sweet scent of ether . . .

Somewhere in her brain, she remembered a lecture on chloroform and its sweet taste . . .

Her brain concluded that none of that mattered.

One more thought managed its way into her brain as the ether took hold.

She'd walked right into the trap.

Then everything went black.

CHAPTER 12

The candle flickered in the windowsill as Kara sat cross-legged on her bed, laptop open and phone in hand. Although no voice came from the phone, she still held it to her ear, straining to hear something, anything. The candle, its flame swishing back and forth in ever-quickening irregular intervals, moved as if to say *Now what?*

Jillian had been in the middle of a sentence when there was a muffled cry, a loud thud, some indiscernible sounds, and now silence. And yet there was still sound. She could hear a car in the distance, something that sounded perhaps like a scrape or a footfall. It was hard to tell.

There. That was definitely a door closing, or perhaps the boot of a car, difficult to say. An engine starting in the distance. Now more of the quiet sounds that emanate from the night. Sound and yet no sound.

Kara looked at her phone for perhaps the sixth or seventh time. The call was still connected. Why would Jillian not respond to her questions? If she'd meant to hang up, surely there would be other sounds, like the muffled movement heard in the case of a butt-dial.

This wasn't like that at all. The phone was still on, still in the middle of the call with Kara, but there was no sound, no movement, no . . . anything. While she had been sitting on her bed, she'd absentmindedly typed the name and address Jillian had given her into ANPR. Suddenly, a ding notified her that there had been a hit in her search. Check that, several hits.

It was close to eight in the evening, and Kara realized she needed another phone. She didn't dare do anything with her mobile that might cause her to drop the open call. One downside to modern technology was the death of landline phones in homes—at least for members of the younger generation, of which Kara was one.

She went across the hall to Joan Watson's flat. Joan was a bit of a mess, but she was always friendly, especially since she'd found out Kara was a copper. Joan answered the door with her baby boy on her hip, her hair up in rollers, wearing what looked like either a jogging outfit or pajamas, likely both.

Kara explained why she needed to borrow her mobile without going into detail, just that she didn't want to drop the—now muted—call she was on. She said it was an urgent police matter, which, of course, it was.

Joan was more than happy to help, being somewhat of a gossip. Kara realized she was going to have to talk in front of Joan, as she couldn't exactly borrow her phone and walk out with it.

DS Halloway answered the phone skeptically, not recognizing the number. Kara got straight to the point, explaining how her call with their DI had ended. She then explained about the ANPR search and what it had produced. Halloway didn't seem convinced, and she had to go into far more detail than she would have liked. Joan was in her kitchenette pretending to busy herself making tea, but Kara could see she had one ear to the living room where she was standing. None of it could be helped.

She could sense her sergeant's indecision, so she pushed the bit about how the phone call, now going on for over twelve minutes, remained open with no sign or sound of Jillian. It was that, perhaps more than anything else, that got him to agree to meet her at the station straightaway.

***

Jillian Scotte felt groggy and nauseous. The room was pitch black. She could hear rumbling, and as she tried to wake up, she felt a smashing headache coming on. Nothing made sense. *Where am I?* she thought.

Slowly, she began to feel. The headache slowed her progress, but after a time, the fog moved slightly away. She wasn't in a room. She could feel movement, or rather, she could sense and feel it. Suddenly her body bounced, and her mind, like a light bulb going turning on, made the connection. She was in the boot of a car.

The moving sensation and rumbling were on the road beneath her.

God, her head hurt, and the movement wasn't helping her nausea any. That made little sense. She was almost never motion sick. Something wasn't quite right. Her brain, trying desperately to reconnect with her normal, logical self, was trying to make sense of these nonsensical pieces of information.

Why am I in the boot of a car? What car? Where is it going?

Something in her mind told her to breathe. To take slow deep breaths, to calm the rushing of blood to her brain and the anxiety of not knowing. She could smell something musty. Oil or something covered in oil was near her. The air was neither cool nor hot, mostly comfortable in temperature if not in scent.

Jillian took in more slow breaths, willing her mind to focus. She began doing simple things. She knew her name was Jillian Scotte, and that she was a policewoman. Something about that was important, but she didn't know what. She flexed her hands and fingers; they moved. Good sign. She wiggled her toes. Another good sign.

Now, all she needed to do was try to remember why she was in this dark, musty boot and how she'd gotten there in the first place. She thought about crying out. Perhaps the driver of the car didn't know she was in there. Something—instinct or perhaps just a feeling, she wasn't sure— told her not to. So she kept her mouth shut and tried to focus through the pain and the nausea.

***

Kara got to the station just as Mark was pulling up.

"Look PC Devanor," he said, getting out of his car in jeans, a wool jumper, and a lightweight, zip-up dark blue jacket. "I appreciate that you're concerned about the boss, but this other bit. You're going to have to get more before we can go down that line. That is a *very* serious road you're traveling down, and I, for one, don't fancy following you, given your big-gest piece of evidence is a car driving around England's countryside."

As he approached the main entrance and pulled out his keys to unlock the door, Kara said, "Yes Sarge, I understand how serious it is to accuse another copper, but sir, look at the ANPR hits. They match, almost pound for pound, what the killer would have had to drive to make all the drops in that short period."

Moving into the conference room, she spread out the papers she had quickly printed on her way out. Mark Halloway looked down at them, nodding. "I don't disagree, but that still doesn't put your man in the frame, does it?" He looked up at her.

Kara looked defiantly back, biting her lip. She knew he was right.

Noticing her determination, he said, "What about the call?"

Pulling out her phone, she said, "Going on thirty minutes now," and she handed it to him. He looked at the screen, seeing the call still con-nected, and pressed it to his ear. Frowning, he hit the speakerphone but-ton and put the phone on the table.

Voices could be heard, first in the distance, then getting closer. A woman, a different woman, a man. They were laughing. None of them sounded like Jillian Scotte. The voices came a little closer and then faded away again.

Kara looked from the phone to Halloway. "There's no way the boss would be without her phone this long, and it's clearly just laying somewhere.

That sounded like people walking by."

Mark was nodding when a ding erupted from Kara's phone. A message from the ANPR system to her email. Glancing down, Kara ran to her desk and turned on her monitor. Opening her email, she punched up the message from the ANPR system. She had put in a search request for driver-photo hits on all the relevant dates.

Two images were included in the email.

Kara felt her heart race. "Sarge," she said.

She could hear him approach, then he bent down and looked over her shoulder.

She looked sideways at him as he took in the images. "Bloddy hell!" was all he could say. Walking over to his desk, he pulled open a drawer, flipped through a small book, then picked up his phone.

"Chief Superintendent Smalton, this is DS Halloway, Ravenstonedale. Sir, I'm very sorry to bother you at this hour, but we have an urgent situation."

***

Jillian had fallen back asleep. She knew because she could feel herself waking up, and she remembered waking up before. The headache was much better now. The nausea too. Her immediate environment was still dark—very dark.

The road had turned from relatively smooth to a bumpier ride . Was that what had woken her up?

Jillian blinked to try to will her eyes to find light. Her eyes suddenly shot wide open in the dark.

She remembered.

The car was slowing down, turning sharply to the left until it came to a halt.

The engine shut off and she could hear a door open. She felt a slight shift in the car as the driver exited. It was incredibly quiet. She could hear the familiar rattle a car makes after it's been driven. She could also hear insects and other sounds, the type made at night in the middle of . . . well, the country. No city noises here.

She heard footsteps coming around the side, and then to the back of the car.

A key was turning in the boot's lock. This was not a new car. No key fob or automatic opener, Jillian thought.

There was a click, and then the boot lifted quickly and completely open.

CHAPTER 13

Light flooded in and blinded Jillian. For a moment she was so disoriented that she thought it must be daylight and wondered just how long she had been out. Lifting a hand to shield her eyes from the white beam, she realized it was a torch—powerful, but not the sun. She could see darkness around the edges of her vision.

A man's voice brought her fully to her senses.

"Good. You're awake."

The sound made her skin crawl.

"Get out of the car," he said, an edge in his voice that she quickly placed as anger. No, more than that, it was the sound of contained fury.

Jillian got out of the boot and stood up, facing him. Her body was still not fully back, but the cool night air was helping to clear the effects of chloroform from her mind.

She didn't see it coming. In retrospect, she should have expected it. Her instincts, still somewhat dulled, had no chance to respond in time, even though some part of her brain registered the change in shadows along the edge of her vision.

His fist landed deeply in her stomach, expelling every ounce of air from her lungs and knocking her back against the car. Her backside hit the edge of the trunk. The shock of both impacts weakened her knees, and she fell helplessly to the ground. Pain coursed through her as she fought to get air back into her lungs.

She rolled slowly onto her back, hoping as she let her arms fall to the dirt road beneath her that she could expand her lungs. It was her second mistake.

His foot landed on her side. She cried out sharply, her vision flashing white with sparks as the pain shot up her right side. Tears welled up, and despite some distant part of her brain that seemed reluctant to let them show, they fell down the side of her face as she curled up into a fetal position to protect herself.

Though her stomach and ribs ached, tiny breaths seeped into her lungs, and her eyes, though blurry from the tears, were no longer seeing shards of bright light. She flinched as she heard him crouch next to her on one knee.

Fearing another blow, she brought one arm up to her head.

Holding the torch so she could see his face, Paul Davies looked down at her with snarling contempt, his face contorted with such hatred that he was almost unrecognizable, and far from the chief inspector he portrayed to others. "How does it feel, Scotte?" he said, spittle spraying her face as he said her name. "Do you like being on the ground, writhing in pain?"

***

Mark Halloway had caught Chief Superintendent Smalton just as he was leaving a dinner engagement with his wife and some friends. Smalton had not been happy to have his evening interrupted by the information DS Halloway related, especially since it concerned a well-respected chief inspector of the Thames Valley Police.

Mark pushed as hard as he could, and while Smalton eventually accepted that there was enough circumstantial evidence to warrant further investigation, he would not approve extreme measures against a fellow officer without more proof. As for DI Scotte's phone, he seemed to think that it had likely fallen out of her purse and she hadn't yet noticed it.

All this frustrated Halloway to no end, mainly because he didn't think the chief superintendent was taking things seriously enough. Adding to his worries was the fact that he was driving like a madman, trying to keep up with Kara, who had bolted out of the station. He hadn't gotten a word out of her, but as he got into his car, he had seen her talking animatedly on her phone as she drove away.

What should have taken close to fifty minutes took them just over half an hour, and Mark was certain they had broken more traffic laws than he had written tickets for in his entire career. That thought, fleeting though it had been, disappeared when he saw their destination.

After screeching to a halt, he scrambled out of his car and chased after Kara, who was sprinting for the helicopter pad of the Cumberland Infirmary in Carlisle. A dark blue-and-green Great North Air Ambulance Eurocopter AS365 Dauphin sat on the pad, its lights flashing and its four propeller blades spinning rapidly.

An EMS medic in an orange jumpsuit with reflective silver stripes and what looked like a pilot's helmet from Star Wars stood just outside the wash of the rotors. Mark caught up just in time to hear the medic say, "Constable Devanor?" to which Kara nodded. "Follow me and keep your head down."

There were four rear-facing seats behind the cockpit, where two pilots were already occupied. The medic helped Mark and Kara buckle in, then handed Kara a headset that was plugged into the wall beside her. Mark sat at the opposite end as Kara began talking to the medic, showing him a map that she unfolded on her lap. The twin-engine helicopter roared, shuddered, and then leaped up into the dark night, angling forward, and began accelerating toward its top speed of 190 miles per hour.

***

Paul Davies grabbed Jillian by her hair and the back of her coat, dragging her along the ground behind him. The pain in Jillian's side was agonizing, and almost made her forget the pain in her stomach. She tried to reach up to stop him from pulling on her hair, but the movement sent jolts of pain across her ribs.

He took her into a dark building. She couldn't quite get a look at it. It was primitive inside, one big room with tools and a workbench. He let go of her once they were inside. As he pulled the chain on an overhead bulb, she got a better look. It was indeed a workroom of sorts—lots of tools, gardening equipment, and there, off to one side, a long wooden table with black straps trailing off the side.

The table, however, wasn't what made Jillian's heart skip a beat. Sitting on the floor, near one end, was a chain saw, its metal teeth glinting menacingly from the light.

Davies grabbed a wooden chair and set it near Jillian. Reaching down, he grabbed her arm and yanked her to her feet in one fluid motion. The movement stole her breath as her ribs, either cracked or broken, protested with new shards of pain. He slammed her down on the chair, then took her wrist and yanked it behind her. Grabbing her other wrist, he pulled them back and bound them with two zip ties, interlocking them. Taking a third zip tie, he connected her bound wrists to a slat in the chair.

If Jillian thought it was hard to breathe before, it was doubly so now.

Moving in front of the chair, Davies stood and looked down at her.

"Why are you doing this?" she asked, her voice barely audible as she observed the scorn on his face.

"Why?" he said, laughing. "Why?" Then his face turned angry again. "Do you know what happens to a man when you repeatedly kick him in the testicles?" His face contorted in anguish as he continued, "You can cause testicular rupture." He paused, then said, "That's what you did to me, you stupid bitch. I lost one, and the other is now infertile."

Jillian thought of telling him he was too old to be thinking of children, but thought better of it. She also thought of reminding him that he'd had it coming, but given her current predicament, she kept her mouth closed.

Davies was still seething. "And all for what? Because you changed your mind about having a little fun at a conference."

"I never said . . ." she began, but Davies cut her off, his voice rising. "Shut up, you little slut. You were begging for it. Wearing those tight-fitting outfits and smiling that coy little smile of yours, you know you wanted it. You were practically begging for it, and when I answered the call, you turned on me and ruined my life." He finished leaning in close to her with his breath, hitting her straight in the face, making her flinch.

"Well," he said, leaning back and smiling with a look that she did not like. "I'm going to make you pay now."

"Why did you kill Vicky Wells?" Jillian asked, wanting to keep him talking. She was desperately trying to keep her anxiety down. She knew from her training that as long as she kept him talking, she could try to think of a way out, though given that she couldn't move her arms, her shoulders were screaming from being stretched back behind her, and her ribs protested every time she took a breath, she did not know how she could get out of this.

He began walking around, talking to himself as much as to her. "Vicky was a slag. I did the world a favor, but she was just the means to an end." Turning and pointing a finger at Jillian, he said, "The great DI Scotte. I knew when you ran away to fuckin' Cumbria that I was going to ruin you. Give you a case you could never solve. Make you the laughing-stock you should be instead of the stupid poster child for bloody female inspectors!"

Jillian tried to lean back in the chair as he charged toward her and grabbed her by the shoulders. "You make me sick; do you know that? You think you're so much better than everyone else." Suddenly, he let go of her and stood up. "I was going to do another one, only this time I was going to put the head right outside that pathetic little flat of yours, and the rest of the parts all over Cumbria, so you'd know this was all about you."

Jillian felt her heart skip a beat at the mention of her flat. Knowing that he knew where she lived made her feel ill. She knew that, given what was happening, it was silly, but she felt it nonetheless.

Moving around the room again, Davies said, "Then I heard that moron Milston had given you some information at SCD9. So, I thought I'd give you a little scare, make you think twice about being such a clever clod. But *no!*" he said, throwing his arms up and turning back to face her,

"I heard you talking about my father and I knew . . . I knew you were getting close . . . No no no . . . that just wouldn't do, would it?"

Now he stood in front of her again, and the menacing look on his face sent shivers down Jillian's spine. "That's when I decided the next one would be you."

Jillian could feel her heart racing. Trying to keep her voice even, she said, "Look Paul . . ."

Anger shot out of him like a lightning bolt. His hand swept across his chest, then swung back in a great arc that hit her across the side of the face with such force that it knocked her body up slightly. Then she tipped onto her side and struck the hard cement floor.

The metallic taste of blood filled her mouth and spilled out the side, dripping down and pooling slightly by her lips on the floor. Her eye was already beginning to swell and her head throbbed. It wasn't like in the movies. When someone hit you or kicked you, it bloody well hurt. She wasn't sure just how much more her body could manage.

Davies tilted his head sideways and stared down at her. His voice was calm once again. He said, "I know what you're trying to do. Don't you dare try to use police techniques on me. I wrote those stupid manuals, you pathetic little bitch."

Straightening up once more, he said, "Now then. I'd best make sure my father goes to bed and sleeps well tonight. Perhaps a little something in his evening cognac. You and I are going to spend a lot of time together later this evening."

As he turned to go, he stopped at the doorway and turned back. His face was impassive, but there was something about the way he looked at her. His eyes were devoid of anything. Jillian realized in that moment that he was truly and completely mad, even before he said anything more. His next words, however, chilled her to the bone. "You know, I did her head first. With Vicky I mean." He paused slightly, then finished, "But with you I think we'll do the arms and legs so you can see how much pleasure you're going to bring me after all."

And with that, he walked out of the room and into the night.

CHAPTER 14

Jillian yearned for the warm embrace of her bed with its down comforter and soft pillows. Every fiber of her being ached as her head lay on the cold, hard floor. She tried not to breathe too deeply, for the pain that came with such a simple act was almost unbearable.

Sleep was calling her with increased intensity, and it would be so easy to just give in. To fall asleep and rest. That, however, was not an option. She knew if she allowed herself to sleep, she would die in this musty, godforsaken room at the hands of a madman. More than that, she wouldn't be asleep for long. She would be subjected to a pain far worse than anything she was feeling now.

Davies had left, starting his car and driving off, who knew where or for how long. Jillian tried to move her left arm and found, surprisingly, that it moved. Not much, but it moved further than she had been able to before.

Feeling around with her bound hands, she found that her crash to the floor had broken part of the back of the chair. If she could move her body a little . . .

Every movement sent fresh pains down her back. The only good news was that since everything hurt, she was becoming more or less numb to the pain. *When all you can feel is pain, you worry less about it*, she thought. Her ribs made things uncomfortable, as the stabbing pain from each breath was difficult to ignore, but if she was careful, it was manageable.

Inching her torso up first, then down a little to the left, she tried with slight, wincing movements to disconnect her bound wrists from the back slat of the chair. She could feel where it was cracked and kept applying pressure until suddenly, with a soft crack, it broke in two and her hands pulled free.

Inching on her side like a worm, she managed to get free of the chair. She laid her head back down, focusing on taking small breaths, trying to regain her strength. She dared not close her eyes for fear that she might

69

not open them again, and so she continued staring at her goal, knowing that sitting up was going to be brutal.

Slowly, with muffled cries through gritted teeth, she rolled onto her knees, her forehead pressed to the floor. Her hands were still bound behind her. Breathing through her nose, with her mouth firmly clenched from the pain, she counted down from three.

Her stomach muscles protested, and her ribs sent shockwaves down her nerves as she pulled herself up into a sitting position on her knees. She hadn't tried to stay quiet that time. The scream that echoed off the walls was piercing and loud. Sitting up, she felt dizzy, and the room blurred for a moment. Fear, and fear alone, kept her from toppling over.

Slowly, she began inching forward on her knees, grimacing with each unwanted movement that jarred her ribs, until she reached the chain saw lying on the ground near the end of the table. She moved next to its long, extended blade with its belt of sharp teeth and lowered her hands behind her onto it.

Slowly, she began moving the plastic zip ties back and forth across them. There was no way she could stand without her hands. She had to get them free, but how much time did she have left?

***

The twin engines of the AS365 Dauphin helicopter powered the craft through the night sky at blazing speed, its nose titled slightly forward. The medic was crouched over the map with Kara while Mark sat helplessly, unable to communicate or provide input without a headset. It was not a feeling he was used to.

Kara had taken a screenshot of Google Earth's image of the Davies family estate. There was plenty of space to land the helicopter among the five acres of land behind the main house. The question was how to find it in the dark.

The estate was near the town of Flitwick, just over an hour's drive north of London. They were flying over the M1, which thankfully was close to the town. The estate itself lay between a small lake and Woburn Forest, just off Wordfield Road.

Although the forest and lake would give them a general location, finding the estate itself would be tricky in the dark. Jackson, the medic, was searching for some landmark or other means of helping them find the estate.

They were getting close.

***

One moment, Jillian was moving her hands back and forth over the chain saw's teeth, and the next, her hand was free. One of the zip ties had opened. The other was still on her wrist, but that didn't matter. The relief at not having her shoulders pressed back was enough to bring a small smile to Jillian's lips.

She leaned forward, massaging her wrists, which were rubbed raw and bleeding a little from where they had caught the saw's sharp teeth.

Reaching up, she grasped the edge of the table, and slowly, with breath-catching jolts of pain, she pulled herself up to her feet. Leaning against the table, she fought the urge to be sick. Her legs were a bit wobbly, but she stayed standing.

Her heart, already pounding, stopped short when she heard the car approaching.

***

The weather had turned foul the further south they flew, and it was now beginning to rain. Clouds, though thankfully not heavy with lightning, were obscuring what little moonlight there had been, and now the light rain was making the visibility even worse.

Jackson had moved from his seat to kneel beside the stretcher that took up most of the cabin. He opened the side door of the helicopter, which created swirls of wind inside the cabin and let in some of the rain.

Kara had joined him, clinging to the side of the locked-down stretcher as they looked out the side of the craft into the dark landscape below.

***

Jillian looked around the room in panic. Moving to the other side of the door with adrenaline-fueled fear , she found some garden tools. Spades, a hoe, even a pickax for digging up stubborn roots, all of which would make great defensive weapons, but she knew she'd never be able to lift them with her ribs now surely broken.

The wind was picking up outside, and she could hear rain falling as she took small breaths, the sound seeming loud in the enclosed space. The lightest of the tools was a metal rake. Wrapping one arm around it, cradling it next to her body, she grabbed hold of the workbench with her other hand.

The door opened wide as Paul Davies stepped quickly inside out of the pouring rain. Swinging her body, Jillian used herself as a fulcrum, despite the pain in her side, to give as much leverage as she could to the rake. She pinned the wooden handle against her side as she arched and whipped the metal teeth toward his head.

Although she swung the rake with enough force to propel it upwards, she couldn't keep the head from spinning, and thus it was the back of the teeth that connected with Paul Davies's skull. The clang of metal against bone rang out loudly in the enclosed building.

The blow threw Davies back against the doorjamb. His arms flew up in protection, as though he expected a second blow was imminent.

Unfortunately, Jillian had used every ounce of her strength to swing the rake, and the reverberations from connecting with his head had jarred it from her grip. It clanged uselessly to the floor.

Davies was bent over in pain, cursing, but his body half blocked the doorway, effectively preventing her escape. Looking around, she sought for something, anything, to help in her defense.

Picking up the rake by the metal end, Davies swung the wooden end, connecting with Jillian's shoulder, the force of which sent her sprawling, her head banging against the floor. The impact once again sent waves of nausea and pain up and down the length of her body and set her head pounding.

She watched as Davies, bleeding profusely from the head wound she had inflicted, stood up to his full height and turned the rake around so that the teeth were now menacingly close to her face as she lay helplessly.

Davies seemed to enjoy her fear, a thin, sadistic smile spreading across his face as he stepped closer and closer. Her head was throbbing, and the throbbing was getting louder and more intense.

Jillian pulled her knees into her chest and held up a hand in defense, looking frightened and vulnerable. Davies's smile grew even wider as he stood beside her, drawing the rake back with both hands on the handle, about to plunge it down onto her face.

With every muscle taut, Jillian was prepared, and as his arms pulled all the way back with the rake, she kicked her legs out, as though releasing the catch on a coiled spring. Her heel connected with the center of his right kneecap. She heard a sickening sound of muscle and bone tearing and snapping in two.

Davies let out a bloodcurdling scream as he fell backward, his leg bent at an impossible angle.

If she thought he'd been angry before, it was nothing compared to the screaming, threats, and vitriol that spewed from his mouth as he lay writhing in pain. His arms flung in every direction as he screamed, calling her every filthy name imaginable. He shouted at her with increasing malice about what he was going to do to her. His flailing knocked about all manner of gardening pots and trays from the shelf behind him.

Jillian didn't have the energy to stand and simply lay there watching him, trying to breathe slowly, trying desperately to regain her strength. Perhaps it was her silence, or simply how she stared at him, unfazed by his onslaught of insults, but he suddenly gripped a pair of pruning shears in his fist, and with surprising speed, bent forward and jammed them into her thigh.

The pain was excruciating. Blood immediately began pouring from the wound. The shock of seeing the shears sticking out from the front of her leg, the blood, and the unbelievable pain, was almost too much. Jillian's vision blurred as she gasped for air. She could not get it in fast enough. With each scant breath, she leaned ever lower, until finally she was lying flat on her back in a torrent of pain she never thought she could be capable of feeling.

As Jillian lay helpless, every ounce of energy having left her, she watched incredulously as Davies used the rake to help himself to his feet. He hobbled over to the bench, using the rake as a makeshift crutch, and picked up the chain saw.

She hadn't noticed before, but it was a battery-powered saw he could start easily by pressing a switch. Still leaning on the rake, he pulled the trigger, and the saw roared to life.

***

Kara squinted against the rain. Suddenly, Mark was by her side, trying to say something. She took off one side of her earphones. "What are we looking for?" he yelled.

Kara held up the photo of the estate. Mark simply nodded and began helping her search.

It was hard to see in the dark, with wind battering her face and rain stinging her eyes. She was betting an awful lot on a hunch, and she knew this could very well be the end of her career. This had already taken things much further than DS Halloway was comfortable with and without his approval. God only knew what the chief superintendent was going to say about requisitioning an EMS helicopter.

If she was wrong about the location, if Scotte wasn't there . . . she never finished the thought. Suddenly Mark pointed. Jackson immediately directed the pilot, who dropped altitude and banked the helicopter.

The helicopter landed hard; the ground having come up quicker than expected because of the shadows caused by the rain and the night. Jackson hopped out first, holding his arm back to help Kara and Mark, who dashed out from under the wash of the rotors, which were beating against the wind and the rain.

"Now what?" Mark screamed, looking from one side to the other. In one direction lay the big house of the estate. In the other was a small stone building with a car in front of it.

Then Kara heard a noise. What it was she couldn't be sure, but without a word, she turned and ran. Sprinting as fast as her legs could carry her through the wet grass and the wind and the rain, she ran for all she was worth.

***

Davies revved the chain saw like some crazed lunatic, which Jillian supposed by now that he was. She was so tired, in so much pain. There was nothing she could do. This is where she was going to die. Although she was terrified, that wasn't her next thought. The thought that entered her mind surprised her and unexpectedly brought tears to her eyes, but she didn't have time to process it.

Davies held out the chain saw above her leg, which still had the shears sticking out of it. Jillian couldn't have moved it if she tried. He revved the saw to its maximum RPM, the sharp teeth glittering against the light as they spun their deathly circuit around the blade, then raised it slightly and angled it straight down.

A shadow crossed Jillian's face. It was dark, blocking out all the surrounding light. It moved so fast she barely saw it. Davies and the saw flew backward as if pulled back by strings. The saw clattered noisily against the floor, sparks flying momentarily as the spinning blade hit the concrete but stopping almost instantly once Davies released the trigger.

As for Paul Davies, he lay flat on his back, out of breath for once, with PC Devanor on top of him, all her weight resting on her knee in the middle of his chest as she struggled to breathe herself, her chest heaving.

Into this incredible scene, Mark Halloway came sprinting and skidded to a stop. He looked down at Jillian and then over at Kara, his mouth agape.

Kara, looking over her shoulder, said, "Here"—then after a breath— "Take him."

Seeing the shears sticking out of Jillian's leg, he hesitated; then seeing the look Kara was giving him, he ran over to her and put his own considerably heavier weight on Davies. Kara quickly scrambled over to Jillian.

Jillian, too bewildered and in too much pain to say anything, just stared as tears streamed down her face.

At this point, Jackson came through the door in his orange EMS suit, and Jillian began thinking she was in some sort of impossible dream.

Jackson looked from Jillian's bleeding leg to the implausible angle at which Paul Davies's leg was bent back to his side.

Kara, seeing where Jackson was looking, said loudly, "*Sod him.*" She motioned back to Jillian. "She goes in the helicopter." Turning back to Davies, she added in a tone that left no room for doubt, "That bastard can wait for the ambulance."

CHAPTER 15
(EPILOGUE)

A butterfly. *That's* what she was.

It finally hit Jillian that she was a butterfly . . . Okay, well, maybe not yet, but soon. She was still in the cocoon, but she was transforming. It wouldn't be easy breaking out, but it would be worth it. She started trying to break free. It was much harder than she thought.

She punched and then kicked at the shell, but it wouldn't give. Her leg hurt from kicking. It was *really* hurting. The pain was intensifying, and she was having trouble breathing; she couldn't take in a breath.

Then she woke up.

Sort of.

She tried to open her eyes, but one of them was completely shut and it hurt to even try to open it. The other eyelid fluttered. It was dark, or maybe just a little dark. Pain was everywhere. A shadow moved over her head and suddenly she was frightened, though she didn't know why. Everything was blurry. There was noise, but it sounded to her like she was underwater. She couldn't understand the words . . . then darkness.

Much later, she heard beeping. She tried to breathe, but it was hard, and her chest hurt, or somewhere near her chest, but lower. She wanted to open her eyes, but she could feel something covering one of them. Was she dreaming? It was hard to tell. Slowly, she opened the other one.

A nurse smiled gently and pushed something behind Jillian's head. A doctor in a white coat stepped in front of the nurse.

"Hello," he said. His voice was soothing and gentle. "My name is Dr. Anstel. Can you tell me your name?"

"Jillian," she said, though her voice was garbled, and her throat hurt.

The doctor nodded and smiled. "Good." Then he reached up over her head and touched something, and there was a beep. "You've been through a lot, so I'm going to let you rest some more, and when you wake up we'll have a good talk, okay?"

She wanted to ask him what he meant. Why was she in a hospital? Why did she need rest? But then she felt something warm in her arm and . . . darkness.

Voices. She could hear soft voices. The beeping was still there. So was the slight pressure on her eye. She slowly opened the other one. The voices were to her left. The voices stopped. She heard movement, then Kara's face came into view.

Kara smiled as wide as her face would allow. "Hi there," she said, gently taking Jillian's hand.

A nurse came in and began talking, asking questions, and writing things on a chart. Finally, she turned to someone behind her and said, "Okay, you can visit, but not too long. She's still going to need more rest."

No, I'm not, Jillian thought. She was tired of sleeping.

The nurse turned and Kara came back into view, along with Detective Chief Inspector Maryanne Sanderson. Kara fussed a little, making sure Jillian was comfortable, asking if she wanted anything.

"Water."

Kara gave her a straw to sip from a cup, and cool water trickled down her raw throat.

After a few moments, Sanderson turned to Kara and said, "Can you give us a few minutes?"

Kara nodded, said she would fetch some tea, and quietly left the room.

Sanderson pulled a chair close to the bed so she would be in Jillian's line of sight. "She hasn't left your side," Sanderson said, nodding to where Kara had just gone. "She's been here every night."

"How long," Jillian said hoarsely.

Sanderson pursed her lips, then said, "You came in three days ago. Your surgery lasted most of the night. You've been out two and a half days."

Jillian blinked. She certainly felt like a truck had hit her.

Sanderson went on, "She slept on that couch. She refuses to leave until . . ." She stopped.

Jillian opened her mouth to ask *Until what?* but the DCI cut her off. "How much do you remember?"

Jillian closed her eye, then opened it slowly. "All of it."

Sanderson nodded. "Well, he was taken to hospital," she said, then quickly added, "Not this one."

Jillian smiled weakly.

"He was in surgery almost as long as you were, then put under guard on a ward." Sanderson waited a beat, then said, "Your PC said she wasn't leaving your side until he was behind bars. She can be a right stubborn bitch, to be honest."

That made Jillian smile even more.

Then Sanderson surprised her. "If you don't watch out, I might steal her from you."

"Try it, mum," Jillian said slowly, every word an effort. "And I'll kick your arse."

This time, it was Sanderson who laughed. Then, turning serious, she said, "Are you up for walking me through it?"

Jillian nodded ever so slightly.

"What made you suspect Paul Davies?"

It took a long time, given how slowly Jillian needed to talk.

"DS Rob Milston, SCD9, sent me some files on Dominic Lesther, Sarah Longwood's boyfriend. Turns out he was more pimp than boyfriend, though probably a bit of both. Kara actually found several things that were odd, and when I started looking at his history, and hers, Davies's name kept coming up. He'd arrested them both years ago, back when he was a DI. As he moved up in rank, his name just kept coming up on major operations that involved one or both of them. There were too many coincidences."

"So, you came down to Thames Valley, but why?" Sanderson asked.

"I wanted to check his work history, his schedules. I knew if I accessed it outside of the station, he might notice, have a flag on his name or what have you. But inside, especially in . . ."

"The admin section," Sanderson said, smiling. "He'd never question it."

Jillian nodded. "I also needed his number plate, which I gave to Kara, but it hadn't left the area on any of the dates."

"That's when you called me," Sanderson said.

"Yes. There was no way I could run the check out of Kidlington station. Too risky."

"When you called asking me to track registrations and number plates for any vehicles listed to a Robert Alan Davies, it never occurred to me it was Paul's father you were looking at."

Jillian smiled. "I was hoping it wouldn't."

"You should have told me," Sanderson said sternly.

"You wouldn't have believed me," Jillian responded, equally sternly.

Sanderson said nothing.

"What I can't quite figure out is how he cottoned on to me."

"Ah, I can help you there. Turns out, while you were at Kidlington fiddling with the admin searches, he was with DS Milston and the SCD9 team on a major drug enforcement operation. He asked the DS about the case and your being in town a few days prior, and Milston let slip that he'd sent you those files. No reason for him not to, really."

Jillian winced, but she had to admit that she was right.

"Davies simply feigned that his phone battery was dead and asked to borrow Milston's. He sent you the text, then deleted it from Milston's phone, and there you have it."

"I feel quite the fool," Jillian said, sighing.

"Don't," Sanderson said, and this time she was forceful. "There was no way you could have known he would have had that conversation with Milston. I only wish you would have confided in me and let me help."

"I wasn't sure. I still needed proof," Jillian said in her defense.

Sanderson just pursed her lips again.

Jillian suddenly had a thought. "How did they find me?"

"Ah," Sanderson said. "Well. When you were talking to your PC and your phone dropped—we found it under your car parked at the café, by the way. Anyway, your PC was worried. She ran the plate you gave her and there he was, driving all over the bloody Kingdom happy as you please, his stupid mug on ANPR."

Sanderson's eyebrows rose and fell. Then she said, "So your young PC calls her DS. They have a chat and call your chief super, who blew it, I'm afraid, and told them not to pursue anything until they heard from you." Then she added, "He's none too pleased with himself, I can tell you, and I'm afraid some of your team are going to bear the brunt of his wrath."

"My team?" Jillian asked. "Why?"

"Oh, just wait till I tell you," Sanderson said, her eyebrows rising again. "Your constable, thinking rightly that if Davies was using his father's car, then maybe he was using his father's place." It was Sanderson's turn to pause. "What made you think of his father, by the way?"

"Something Denise said." Then, seeing the frown on the DCI's face, she added, "My friend in the admin/comms section. Anyway, she said something about Davies taking time off to go help his family clear down some dead trees on their estate."

Sanderson whistled. Then, after a moment, she continued her story. "So, your PC calls me."

"You?" Jillian said incredulously.

"Yep. She pleads her case, tells me she's worried sick something's happened to you, that she had called in a report on your car to a local nick by the café, and they'd found your car but no sign of you."

Jillian smiled at the thought of her smart young PC and how she should thank her. Sanderson cut into that little thought with, "Then she hits me with a request to appropriate the EMS helicopter from Cumberland Infirmary in Carlisle."

This time it was Jillian who raised her eyebrow and whose jaw dropped speechlessly.

Sanderson just smiled and nodded. "She wouldn't take no for an answer. Told me if something happened to you, it would be on my head and she'd tell it to anyone who would listen."

Jillian laughed out loud, then winced in pain.

"Told you she could be a proper bitch," Sanderson said. "I ordered her to go home to Cumbria last night on the phone when she called to tell me you'd woken up the first time."

Jillian waited for the punchline.

"I showed up this morning, and she was asleep on that damned couch," Sanderson said, half-heartedly nodding across the room.

Jillian thought for a moment. "I want her promoted to detective constable."

Sanderson laughed, then seeing that Jillian was serious, looked straight at her. "She's only been a PC for just under a year, and in training at that."

Jillian stared back, unfazed.

"Don't look at me," Sanderson said. "She'd have to go through the Detective Academy first, and then you'd need your chief super on board, which believe you me, after she went around him to me, he is as likely to recommend her for promotion as he is to grow wings and fly." Sanderson stood up. "You should get some rest."

As she pushed the chair back to the wall, Jillian said, "If Kara got a recommendation to the Met from the Thames Valley super, it might do it."

Sanderson stifled a laugh. "Last I heard, your leaving Thames Valley wasn't too popular with the super."

"No," Jillian said, "But Denise told me he's being promoted to chief super, and with DCI Davies gone, someone else will have to fill the super role." And with that, she looked Sanderson straight in the eyes and raised her eyebrow.

Sanderson frowned and shook her head. But Jillian could tell she was thinking about it. Then she walked out the door and Kara walked back in, all smiles. Jillian motioned for her to come closer, but she shook her head. "Someone's been dyin' to get in here to see you, but they wouldn't let anyone but us coppers in here."

Jillian frowned, and then Dr. Daniella Morales walked in, holding a huge bouquet of flowers.

A massive white flash suddenly went off inside Jillian's head. She was suddenly back in the brick building with Davies coming at her with the chain saw. She remembered being afraid, and being extraordinarily sad at the same time. The thought of never seeing Daniella again would have been the last thought she had before she died.

Daniella walked up to the side of the bed and gently took Jillian's hand, both of them smiling and crying at the same time.

DEATH
BENEATH THE
SURFACE

CHAPTER 1

Detective Inspector Jillian Scotte took her seat at the table by the window—a prime location in this up-and-coming restaurant in the heart of London—and accepted the menu from the well-dressed maître d'.

She was a few minutes early, which gave her a chance to peruse the menu and reflect on all that had happened over the past year.

Her recovery from the attack by deranged killer Paul Davies had been a long and painful road. On the plus side, she had worked hard on her physical therapy and recovery, such that she had become obsessed with getting into the best shape of her life.

Wary of putting stress on her repaired leg, she had taken to bicycle riding. She rode her bike to and from work almost every day, and at least one day of most weekends she could be found pounding out the miles across the countryside of West Cumbria.

She would never put herself in the position of being too weak to escape an assailant ever again. Not that there had been much danger of that lately. In fact, life as far as work was concerned, had become predictably boring.

Kara, now Detective Constable Devanor since finishing her Detective Academy course, seemed to be getting restless as well. Her recent ascension to detective constable had not been easy. Chief Superintendent Smalton, Jillian's boss and that of the Ravenstonedale station, had not taken kindly to Jillian going around him and over his head to get Kara the promotion.

Even Detective Sergeant Mark Halloway seemed put out when the news came, despite having seen from the front row all that Kara had done on the case, including saving Jillian's life. Maybe that was what had him bent out of shape; Kara had shown him up, and she'd been a police constable in training at the time, a complete rookie.

Jillian's thoughts were interrupted by the arrival of her lunch date. Superintendent Maryanne Sanderson walked up hurriedly, exchanging a kiss on the cheek with Jillian. "Sorry I'm late, bloody meetings never end on time."

Jillian smiled. "It's no problem. Just got here myself."

Sanderson, formerly the detective chief inspector from Norwich, was New Scotland Yard's newest superintendent and rising star. Although she had considered applying for the vacancy in Thames Valley that Jillian had suggested, she had waited, and when a position opened at the Met, she jumped.

Maryanne Sanderson was dressed in her black-and-white uniform, smartly fitted, with the crown denoting her rank on the epaulets. It was the same rank as a major in the British Army. She looked Jillian over with a wry smile.

Jillian, who was wearing a new gray and black skirt–suit combo she found at Zara, smiled back and took a drink of water as she looked over the menu she'd been holding for several minutes but hadn't actually read.

The two women ordered. Caesar salad for Maryanne, and salmon with wild rice for Jillian.

They talked for a while about life, catching up on rehab (Jillian) and work (Maryanne) until the food arrived.

As they tucked into their lunches, Maryanne swallowed her first bite, taken a sip of water, and dabbed her lips with her napkin before speaking. "I asked you down here to make you a proposition."

"Oh," Jillian said. She'd wondered if there was more to this lunch than just a catch-up. She and Sanderson had kept in touch, mostly via email and text, but had only seen each other twice since the first day Jillian had woken up in the hospital.

"Mmm," Maryanne said, eating a piece of fresh-baked bread. "How do you feel about the coast?"

Jillian stopped her fork mid-rise with a pierced piece of salmon on it. "Which one?" she asked before finishing her fork's journey and chewing on the salmon.

"Southern," Maryanne said. "You know, Dorset, Bournemouth, Isle of Wight and all that."

Now Jillian set her knife and fork down on her plate. She looked at Maryanne, who looked back, nonplussed, as if she were simply talking about the weather. "You're serious!" Jillian said. A statement, not a question.

It was Maryanne's turn to set down her cutlery. "Yes." She took a sip of her water and set the glass carefully back down. "There's been an uptick in violent crime in the southern part of England, from London to the coast. Especially the coast. We want to start up a Violent Crime Unit, independent from other agencies. You'd be reporting directly to New Scotland Yard. To me, in fact."

Jillian sat back hard in her chair. "Me? You're mad. I'm only a DI—they'll want a DCI or someone like you, surely?"

Maryanne leaned forward slightly, her forearms against the edge of the table. "Yes. They actually suggested I head it. When I said no, they threw out a few DCIs. I told them I want you."

Jillian didn't quite know what to say, so she just stared back.

Eventually, Maryanne set her fork and knife across her plate and moved it to the side. Placing her elbows on the table, she laced her hands together and tilted her head. "Look, you're the best DI we've had in decades. You're wasting away up there in that godforsaken part of the country, and I need you where you can do the most good. Right now, that's as the head of the VCU. You know I'm right, admit it."

Jillian held her gaze for a full sixty seconds, then a thin smile forced its way unwillingly across her lips. Maryanne nodded and smiled back.

Jillian took a big sigh. "I'm not saying yes just yet," she said carefully. "I need at least a day to think about it."

"Of course," Maryanne said. "You have until"—she looked at her watch—"one o'clock tomorrow afternoon." And then she smiled conspiratorially across the table.

Jillian laughed, but then her face turned a bit more serious. "*If*—" She made sure she had the superintendent's attention. "—*If* I say yes, I want to take DC Devanor with me."

Maryanne smiled broadly. Reaching down to her purse on the floor, she pulled out a manila envelope. "I thought you might say that." As she handed the envelope over, she added, "Here is the reassignment paperwork for both of you."

Later, sitting on the train back to Cumbria, Jillian couldn't stop thinking of her lunch with the superintendent. There was no doubt the offer had more upsides than downsides. One big downside loomed, however.. What the hell was she going to say to Daniella?

CHAPTER 2

There was a candle in a lantern just inside the door. It seemed odd, Jillian thought, given the text she had received on the train from Daniella: *When will you be home? We need to talk.*

Jillian had moved in with Daniella two months ago, since her place had more room and a much better view than Jillian's. The first month had been bliss. But in the last three or four weeks, something had changed. Daniella seemed distant, and to be fair, Jillian had spent more time away too. At work, out riding, anything really, to avoid the awkwardness that had descended on them.

So, a romantic candle in a home where neither of them went out of their way to buy them, seemed out of place.

Maybe her moving in had been too soon. Maybe Daniella regretted her offer or had changed her mind. Whatever it was, she was right—they needed to talk.

The hall lights were off. So were the lights in the small kitchen and living room. As she walked through, Jillian set down her purse and keys and stared at the living room full of lit candles. Daniella entered from the bedroom. "Hi," she said, smiling nervously. Something was definitely up, Jillian thought.

"Do you want a glass of wine?" Daniella said, reaching for a half-drunk glass on the kitchen counter.

"Sure," Jillian said. She was really too tired after her long train ride down to London and back in one day, but whatever this was, she might as well have a drink to go with it.

Daniella gave her a light kiss as she handed her the glass and then moved to the overstuffed chair. Jillian took the loveseat, slipping off her shoes and curling her legs up underneath her.

Daniella was fidgeting with her wine. After taking a large drink, she set the glass down on the coffee table and looked up at Jillian. Her eyes were shiny, like she was going to cry. "First, I want to say I'm sorry."

Jillian opened her mouth to speak, but Daniella cut her off. "Please, let me get this out." She swallowed hard. "A little over three weeks ago, I was accepted for a special research program at the University of Surrey. It's part of their Quantum Biology PhD program and they're working in conjunction with a university out of Austria." She said it all quickly, as though afraid that if she didn't get the words out right then, she wouldn't be able to say them.

Jillian raised her eyebrows, suitably impressed and simultaneously whirling at the news. Her lack of verbal response made Daniella even more uneasy, and she hurriedly said, "I never thought I'd be accepted when I applied, and that was almost a year ago. I mean we . . .you . . ." Suddenly tears formed at the corner of her eyes.

Jillian put her glass down and approached the chair, kneeling on the floor and taking Daniella's hands in hers. Daniella, having unburdened herself of her secret, had opened the floodgates. "It's a sixteen-week course . . ." she began between sobs, "and . . . I have to live . . . on the campus . . . It's so far . . ."

Jillian was smiling now. The reason for the awkwardness between them was becoming more apparent, and a flood of relief came over her. She had thought tonight was going to be an end, and instead . . .

Daniella, however, was still going. "I just don't want . . . I asked you to move in . . . and now . . . I'm leaving . . ." Her eyes got huge then, and she said, "Not forever, I mean it's just sixteen weeks, but . . ." Then she suddenly blinked hard several times and looked Jillian straight in the eyes. "I just don't want to lose you." Then, her face shifted, and she frowned and sniffed, wiping her nose with the back of her hand. "Why are you smiling?"

Jillian reached up and kissed her gently, then said, "Three things. First, I am *so* proud of you. Second, let me tell you about my day, and third, how do you feel about moving to the coast?"

***

The next few weeks became a blur. Daniella was busy packing up their things, getting ready for her course, and looking at her job prospects in the south of England. Jillian, having accepted Superintendent Sanderson's offer, began putting things in motion the next morning.

Her first order of business had been DC Kara Devanor. Jillian called her into her office first thing and asked her how she'd feel about a transfer to the southern coast of England. Kara was immediately hurt. "Have I done something wrong, mum?" she asked. "Whatever it is, I'm truly sorry, and I'll do whatever I have to do to make it right."

Jillian actually laughed out loud, which did nothing to assuage Kara's fear.

"No, Kara," she said, lowering her voice a little lest anyone from outside her office was listening. "I'm not shipping you off, I'm asking you to come with me."

It took a second to register, but when it did, Kara's face lit up like a Christmas tree. Jillian filled her in on what she knew, and together they began putting together a plan—the first part of which entailed Kara scouting out a location for the team.

It took a few days, but eventually she found a place. It was an old, abandoned factory that had been cleaned up and made ready for let just before the COVID pandemic had hit. Southampton had never fully recovered economically, so the building had remained empty. It needed a little customizing, but it had its own parking lot inside a fence, which provided some security, and was otherwise sound.

It was bigger than Superintendent Sanderson had been thinking for them, and the price was on the edge of the budget, but given the alternatives, it would be cheaper in the long run than some of the less expensive possibilities, which needed far more improvements.

After seeing Daniella safely to her university and sneaking a night together in her dorm room, Jillian drove the hour down to Southampton, ready for her first day on the job. She had "met" the other members of her team via video conference calls, one byproduct of the pandemic that made life easier all around.

Jillian would have liked to do proper interviews, but Sanderson had explained that there simply wasn't time, and with the sensitive nature of plopping down this team in the middle of other police districts, having members from those districts join the unit was one way to smooth things over.

Although that made sense to Jillian, she also worried about where loyalties might lie.

Her phone rang, and she hit the answer call on her car display. "DI Scotte," she stated clearly into the car's built-in microphone.

"Hello boss." Kara's voice rang out loud and clear. "How far away are you?"

"Not far," Jillian responded. "'Bout ten minutes, maybe less. What's up?"

"No rest for the wicked, I'm afraid," Kara said, her tone serious, causing Jillian's eyes to narrow. "They've found a body. I'll text you the location and meet you there."

CHAPTER 3

Social media had changed everything. People no longer waited for the news cameras to report what was happening. There was always someone—usually several someones—with a smartphone to capture what was happening and post it online for the world to see.

A group of such individuals were being held back by the local constabulary as Jillian pulled up to the address Kara had texted to her. Since she was new to the area, she flashed her warrant card to the uniformed officer, who nodded curtly and lifted the police tape for her to walk under.

She spotted Kara and one of her team, Detective Sergeant Stephen Listun, standing with a large man in a long rain jacket near the bank of the river Itchen.

As she approached, Kara turned and spotted her with an annoyed look and said, "Hello guv," causing the two men to turn around. The reason for Kara's exasperation was immediately evident when the man in the rain slicker said, "Ah, about time the TV star showed up."

Jillian didn't recognize him and decided to ignore him for the moment. Smiling, she extended her hand and spoke to her sergeant. "Hello DS Listun," she said, shaking his hand. "It's great to finally meet in real life."

Listun gave her a genuine smile. "Hello mum. Much better than video." The smile faded quickly as the man in the raincoat cleared his throat. Turning halfway toward him, Listun said, "Sorry. Detective Chief Inspector Walford, this is DI Scotte ."

"Yes," the man said gruffly, without bothering to offer a hand. "We all know who she is, Stephen." Motioning to the group of crime scene officers next to the water, he added, "Now that she's here, let's get on with it." He turned and began carefully descending the riverbank.

DS Listun looked awkwardly at Jillian, who simply motioned for him to follow. As soon as he had turned, she looked over at Kara, who rolled her eyes exaggeratedly and waited for her boss to go before following close behind.

Down by the riverbank, a police photographer was taking pictures of a body that had recently been pulled from the water. A man who looked to be in his late fifties, with grayish-white hair beneath his white protective overalls, was squatting close to the victim's head.

"What've you got, James?" the DCI asked in an indifferent tone.

Looking up and seeing DCI Walford, the man said with a deadpan expression, "She drowned." Seeing Jillian, he stood up. Looking at his gloved hands, he held them halfway up, facing out, as an apology for not offering a handshake. "I'm James Kolbern, Medical Examiner."

"Detective Inspector Jillian Scotte," she answered. "Pleasure to meet you."

"And you," he said before the DCI interrupted with "Yeah, yeah, get on with it."

Kolbern took a deep breath and looked directly at Jillian before slowly turning to regard Walford. "I won't know much more till I get her on the slab." Then he knelt back down to examine the body some more.

"Right," Walford said, already turning to climb back up. "That's that, then."

Jillian spoke up, looking directly at the ME. "Do you mind if I have a look?"

"Not at all," the doctor said, stiffly standing and pulling off his gloves. "I'm pretty much done anyway." He turned to the photographer. "When the inspector's finished, make sure you get close shots of both sides there and there," he said, pointing.

Once the ME and photographer had moved off a bit, Jillian knelt next to the body. The victim was a young woman, early to mid-twenties by the looks of it. Jillian didn't expect to find anything, and in fact she wasn't really looking for clues. Movies and television always showed detectives examining bodies and finding some obvious clues the ME had missed or other detectives had overlooked.

That rarely happened in actual police work and had never happened to Jillian. The reason she was kneeling next to the body was to take in the victim just as they'd found her, or in this case as close to where they'd found her as possible. Jillian wanted to spend a moment looking at her, remembering that she was someone's daughter, maybe a mother herself. Maybe someone's girlfriend.

Jillian would soon be running the investigation, and she always felt it was important to connect to the human side of the case before she did anything else. She closed her eyes for a brief second, making a silent promise to both herself and the victim that she would do her best. Then she stood up.

The DCI, sighing loudly, said, "Find anything there, Sherlock, or can we all move on now?"

Jillian finally made direct eye contact with him and held it for a pause. "After you," she said coldly, glancing up the bank.

When they reached the top , Walford said loudly, "Right, you two." He indicated DS Listun and DC Devanor. "Next time you take over one of my investigations, you'd better get my super's permission ahead of time. No more of this showing up like you own the bloody place, right?"

Listun and Devanor both looked at each other with equally confused expressions. Listun opened his mouth to say something, but Jillian cut him off. "Could you both give the DCI and I a minute?" She said it smiling, but Kara knew that tone and quickly turned to head back to her car. Listun followed.

Walford started to say, "Right, well, this is all yours now . . ." But this time Jillian cut him off. "Detective Chief Inspector Walford. I'm sorry if setting up the VCU down here feels like we're stepping on your patch, because I realize how difficult it must be." He opened his mouth to say something, but Jillian wasn't finished. "I know I'd be miffed if someone came in and set up shop in my back garden, especially someone junior." Pausing only for a breath, she looked directly at him and said, "However, if you have a problem with any member of my team in the future, I expect you to come to me directly. You will not address my team as though they work for you. They don't. They work for me."

"Now listen here . . ." he began.

"No, DCI Walford, you listen. Like it or not, we are here to stay. We may be based in Southampton, but we will be working much of Southern England, and I don't have time for your ego to get in my way. If you have a problem with that, I suggest you take it up with New Scotland Yard." Jillian left him standing with his mouth open as she walked away.

Listun and Devanor were both standing by a dark blue Mini. She would have thought that with Listun coming in at about six feet tall, he'd have a bigger car.

"Boss," Kara said exasperated, "He's the one who called *us* to tell us to take the case."

DS Listun nodded.

"Really?" Jillian said, shaking her head. "Why would he want VCU to take on a simple drowning? Did you work for him?" she asked Listun.

"Not directly, mum," he replied. "I worked out of Portswood Station. He's out of Southampton Constabulary."

"Portswood's closer to here, isn't it?" Jillian asked. "Isn't he a bit far from home?"

Listun nodded. They all noticed that the DCI was now talking to a dark-skinned woman with a camera on a tripod who was holding a micro-phone toward the inspector.

"Who's that?" Jillian asked.

"Used to be a reporter," Listun said. "Now she works for a digital-only news agency that split off from the papers and telly about a year ago."

Jillian nodded, then turned back to her team. "Okay, Kara, you head back to the office. Until we hear from the ME, let's do some basic back-ground stuff. Look for MISPAS that might be a match." MISPAS was police slang for missing persons. Turning to Listun she said, "Sorry to do this to you, but you know these coppers better, so can you coordinate some local door-to-door, see if anyone saw anything?" She didn't really pose it as a question. Normally, the roles for DS and DC would have been reversed, but Jillian feared that if she had Kara do it, Walford might make things more difficult than if Listun did the asking. Their brief from London indicated that local constabularies would provide on-the-ground support for investigations, but she could already see that it wasn't going to be that easy.

A few more camera crews had shown up, but they were just photogra-phers taking pictures. There wasn't enough here for the media to send full crews. She noticed the DCI heading off to his car and the digital journalist looking directly at her while breaking down her gear.

Jillian walked around the corner to a food truck parked across the street near a factory gate. After quickly getting two cups of coffee, Jillian returned and found the journalist picking up her camera bag and tripod. As she turned, she almost ran into Jillian.

Startled, she stopped as Jillian stood in front of her with both cups of coffee.

"Hello, I'm Detective Inspector Scotte." Jillian offered one of the cups and said, "Can we talk a moment, off the record?"

The woman put down her gear with a wary expression and slowly reached for the coffee. "Amelia Hamza," she said, taking the coffee and tilting her head slightly to one side.

She was a striking woman, Jillian thought, her dark skin smooth and her eyes a deep green, with jet-black hair that she wore straight. Her outfit, jeans with short dark brown boots and a puffy black jacket over a purple jumper, was more for comfort than style. Being part of a digital team likely meant she worked as much from home as in an office, Jillian thought.

"Look," Jillian said, getting straight to the point. "We don't know each other . . ."

But the woman cut in. "I know who you are."

That stood to reason. Hamza was a journalist, and Jillian had been in the news, in a major way, twice in the span of just over a year, not to mention whatever DCI Walford had been saying about her just now. Hamza went on. "I also know that you're here leading up a new Violent Crime Unit."

"Did DCI Walford tell you that?" Jillian asked, but Hamza just stared blankly back. It didn't much matter; it wasn't really a secret. They just hadn't announced it publicly because things were still very much in the early stages. The damned office wasn't even fully ready yet.

Jillian took a deep breath. "What I wanted to say was this. You and I both have jobs to do. I don't know you, and while you think you may know me from the press, you don't." At that, Jillian made it a point to look directly into the woman's eyes.

Continuing, Jillian said, "While many of my colleagues don't like members of the media and are often at odds with you, I am not them." Hamza's eyebrows went up questioningly. Jillian kept going. "I'm not saying we need to be friends. There will be times when you want something from me that I can't give you. And there will be times when you have to put something out to the public that I won't want you to have done; that's part of our jobs."

Taking a sip of her coffee, Jillian said, "However, I think both of us can do our jobs better if we understand each other and work, as best as we can, for the betterment of our community." Jillian saw the woman take a deep breath and knew what was about to come, so she held up her hand. "That doesn't mean I get to tell you what you should and shouldn't write."

"What then?" Hamza said defensively.

"It means we respect each other and the jobs we have to do," Jillian said sincerely. "I will always keep the victims and their families first, along with the safety and well-being of the community. I know your job is to report what's going on, and your priority is to inform the public as best you can. I simply don't see why those two things must be mutually exclusive."

Hamza continued listening, her brow furrowing slightly.

"As I say, I know we won't always see eye to eye, but if we can work together when we can, I think we can accomplish both of our goals much better without being at war with one another."

"What you're asking for is trust." the journalist said skeptically, folding her arms while taking care not to spill her coffee.

"Yes," Jillian said. After a moment she added, "Give me your mobile number."

Hamza frowned. After a moment's hesitation, in which she was obviously trying to figure out why Jillian was asking for something she could find online, she gave it to her.

Jillian pulled out her phone and tapped away until finally Hamza's phone buzzed.

"There, now you have the direct mobile number of the head of the new Violent Crime Unit." Turning away, she looked back over her shoulder as she went. "How's that for trust?"

CHAPTER 4

Plants greeted Jillian Scotte when she walked into the entryway of the converted factory building that was now the office of the VCU. Unlike a proper police nick, there was no desk sergeant or waiting area. It had a simple vestibule with two chairs and a window looking out onto the parking lot, with a door that required a key card for access and a phone to pick up if you somehow wandered in or were delivering something.

They didn't expect many unwanted visitors.

Someone, however, had decided to liven the room up a bit with a large box planter and tall green plant, the origin and species of which Jillian hadn't a clue. Along the windowsill were five smaller succulent plants. It all made Jillian smile. Someone cared enough to make it look less sterile. It was a good sign.

Jillian used her access card. The door buzzed loudly as the lock clicked open, and she walked into the large room that served as the team's primary office. She'd been in over the weekend trying to get her own office sorted, which was halfway down on the left. The open floor plan meant there were only a few closed-off areas, her office being one. The large conference-style room being another which was in the corner of the large space. Now absent an actual conference table, this was where they would gather for private conversations and team meetings.

Workers were still installing the finishing touches to two interview rooms, and they had one holding room, not quite a cell, but built sturdily enough to keep someone should the need arise. There was also an IT crew from London milling about, installing cameras and additional security systems, as well as making sure all the computer equipment was working correctly.

It was into all this hubbub that Jillian walked, and the members of her team stopped what they were doing and turned as her presence became known. She approached each of them in turn, shaking hands and saying hello properly.

After eventually heading into her office, she called DS Listun to follow. Setting down her bag and coat, she asked him to gather everyone into the incident room, which is what she wanted the large conference room called, in ten minutes. He nodded, and she said, "Why do you think Walford called us for this? Seems odd to call us for a drowning, doesn't it?"

Listun seemed a bit nervous, shifting from one foot to the other. Finally, he said, "I talked to some of the coppers, guv, and . . . well . . ." He clearly was not comfortable.

"Just say it," Jillian said.

"Well, the body was found hours before they called us. Took a while to get her out of the river. Wasn't till the M.E. showed up that he called."

Jillian was not pleased, but it still didn't answer the question of why.

The day was mostly spent getting everyone settled, organized, and familiar with one another, until Listun came into her office at about four o'clock. He knocked on the doorframe as he entered, and Jillian looked up from her desk. "ME sent over a preliminary on our victim," he said. He was holding a file folder.

"She was alive when she went into the water, but there are signs of assault, blunt force trauma behind her right ear, broken femur, and severe bruising up and down her torso. Also, signs of sexual assault. Officially, he'll say the cause of death was drowning, but I think we can rule out suicide."

Jillian asked, "Could they have been caused by the river, or a fall into it?"

Flipping pages, Listun said, "Doesn't look like it. Says most of them were likely days old."

Jillian nodded thoughtfully. "Where are we on the victim?"

"Just came in, mum," he answered, pointing to the report and handing it over to her, "but I've got DC Devanor looking into it now. Her name is Victoria Lessings, aged 24."

Kara walked in at that point. "Got her parents' address, they live up in Hursley. Also, she shared a flat with two other girls. Just got off the phone with one of them, who says they haven't seen Victoria for over a week, which is unusual, but they didn't report it."

"Right," Jillian said, standing up. "Stephen . . ." It was the first time she'd used his given name, and his eyebrows rose slightly. "Get someone to do a full workup on her. Work, school, friends, the lot. Then I want you to head over to her flat and talk to the roommates. I'll go talk to the parents. Kara, you're with me."

Everyone scattered, and soon Kara was driving Jillian through the streets of Southampton up to Hursley. Informing the families was one of the worst parts of the job, and one that, whenever possible, Jillian felt a duty to do herself.

The Lessings lived in a moderate, semi-detached home in the small village across the road from the large IBM facility. Margery and Holace Lessings sat in their small but comfortable sitting room in shock. Margery was openly weeping; her husband, with his arm draped around her shoulders, tried to comfort her, but he seemed too numb to put much effort into it.

They went through the preliminary questions: When was the last time you saw your daughter? Did she have a boyfriend or girlfriend? Did she talk about any troubles? Can you think about anyone who might want to harm her?

The last question sent Margery Lessings into a new fit of grief. Holace Lessings looked over at Jillian. "We adopted her when she was just a wee child. Three years old. Her mother had died, and she was taken in by the council welfare services. No father, you see. We took one look at her, didn't we, mother?" he said, squeezing his wife's shoulders as she nodded vigorously while wiping her eyes with a tissue. "One look, and we knew we wanted to bring her home with us."

Kara was sitting in a chair nearest the family and offered another tissue to Margery, who couldn't stop herself from sobbing. Jillian sat across in a chair Holace had brought over from the dining table for her.

They spent another half hour with the Lessings, but there was little they could glean from them. Jillian said they would be in touch, and as they pulled away from the house, her phone rang. It was DS Listun.

"DS Scotte," she said automatically. Hitting the speakerphone button, she held out her phone so Kara could hear.

"Hello guv, just finished talking to the roommates. We're bagging up her computer and a few things from her room, but not sure we'll find much. Bit of a mess, really, the whole place."

"Anything from the roommates?" Jillian asked.

"Both roommates are friends from uni. Put an advert in for a third to help with rent costs and Victoria answered. They said she was all right, but they'd only known her for about six months. Seems she broke up with an ex-boyfriend she was living with when she moved in with them."

Waiting a beat, he went on. "They said the ex, a Royce Jones, was always calling and bothering her. They didn't have an address or number for him. Hoping we'll find something on her laptop. We didn't find a phone," he added, anticipating his boss's next question. "They think he might have worked in construction. We'll start looking when I get back."

"Okay," Jillian said. "We didn't get much from the parents. Sounds like a typical family, mostly."

"There was one other thing, guv," Listun said. "One roommate said Victoria had seemed excited about two months ago because her biological father had contacted her."

Kara looked over at Jillian and raised her eyebrows. "Any details on the father?" Jillian asked.

"No," Listun responded, "just that Victoria seemed excited by it."

"Get that laptop to the tech team as quickly as you can. We need to find the ex and this father as soon as."

"Yes boss," Listun said. "Also, got a call from Stacey." Stacey Alston was the administrator they'd been given from London. It was she who was running the organization and setup of their VCU headquarters. "She said we just received ten cases from London."

"Ten?" Jillian said, surprised.

"Yes mum, 'unsolves' mostly from the past year."

Jillian sighed loudly. After hanging up with her DS, she sat staring out the window on the first day of her new post. So much for settling in quietly.

CHAPTER 5

The lockup was a corner unit of a Big Yellow Self Storage location off Nuffield Road in Poole. Detective Inspector Jillian Scotte stood with two members of her team flanking the padlocked door.

It had been a long trek to this point, not simply because of how far apart Southampton and Poole were, but also the long journey on the case that had led them to this moment.

***

Jillian's mind flashed back to her first day and how it had ended. She'd driven back to her hotel room, as her rented flat wouldn't be available for another week. She didn't want to find somewhere more permanent until they knew what Daniella's situation would be in a few months' time.

She'd just poured herself a glass of well-deserved red wine when her phone buzzed. Picking it up, she saw a new text from Amelia Hamza, the journalist she'd spoken to . . . Good grief, had that only been this morning?

The text read simply, *why me?*

Jillian sipped her wine for a moment, then composed her reply.

Call it a hunch. You left traditional media for digital, which means you're smart and see the writing on the wall as to the future of your craft. They let you go when clearly you have the look of an on-air personality, which means they're either stupid (possible) or something happened with your former employer (more likely). Either way, were I you, it would piss me off, which means you've got something to prove.

The response wasn't long in coming.

Who ARE you? Sherlock bloody Holmes? How could you possibly know that?

Jillian laughed, then tapped her reply. *I'm a detective. Also, I know how to use Google.*

There was no response.

The next day, the team was well into it by the time she arrived at the "Tof," the nickname her team had coined for their space. It was spelled with only one *f* but pronounced as though it had two. Team Office Factory—Tof. She liked the sound of it, and it felt better than saying "office" since it wasn't a proper nick.

Listun was busy getting everyone organized into teams to handle the new (old) cases while Kara was working on the Lessings case.

Jillian took a phone meeting with her new colleagues at the Met, filling them in on how she was settling in. She didn't mention her concerns about Walford because she knew Superintendent Sanderson would want to get involved, and she didn't need that right now.

Just after lunchtime, Kara knocked on her door. "Mum, we've just heard from the techies. They said Victoria's laptop was dead easy to get into . . ." Then, realizing her poor choice of words, she gulped and apologized. "Sorry, didn't mean to put it that way."

Jillian waved her on. "It's all right, I know what you meant. Did they find anything?"

"They're still getting the data pulled, but I've asked them to put a priority on getting anything possible on the ex and her father."

"Good," Jillian said, thinking that Kara was finished.

"I did manage to find some things on her social media accounts, though?"

Jillian looked back up.

"It turns out that Royce Jones is quite a popular name, who knew? So, I went back and started looking for photos of her and a male and found several that match the time frame. I then did a reverse photo lookup on Google and found him, then cross-referenced him on three social media platforms, and there are pictures of them both on all three." Looking down at her notebook, she said, "He doesn't come up on our system, but I've got an address from the tax registry ."

Jillian couldn't help but smile. Getting up, she grabbed her coat and called out, "DS Listun, care to join us?"

Listun grabbed his coat and ran after them. Kara filled him in on the way, and within fifteen minutes they were knocking on Jones's door. A tall, fit black man warily answered.

Jillian held up her warrant card. "Royce Jones?" she asked.

Jones looked at her card, then at the other two, and said, "Yeah, what's this all about?"

"My name is Detective Inspector Scotte. This is DS Listun and DC Devanor. May we come in?"

Jones hesitated, but then stepped back into the narrow hallway of his flat, leaving the door open. The trio followed him into a well-kept sitting room with a large-screen television and what looked like a relatively new sofa. A simple but elegant coffee table completed the small space.

Royce Jones sat on the sofa and leaned forward on his knees, looking up expectantly.

"Mr. Jones," Jillian began. "We understand you are the former boyfriend of Victoria Lessings. Is that true?"

Jones hung his head. Then, looking back up, he dejectedly said, "Yeah. Look, did she complain or summint? Cause I didn't mean nuttin' by it."

"By what, Mr. Jones?" Listun said pointedly.

"They was just phone calls," he said defensively. "I just wanted to talk to 'er didn't I? I didn't mean to yell, and the messages . . . I mean, I regretted leavin' 'em as soon as I hung up."

Jillian said nothing and just looked down at him. He looked at her and, getting more agitated, said, "Honestly, I didn't mean what I said . . . She just wouldn't return my calls and I was angry. That's not a crime, is it?" He said the last part more as a statement than a question.

"Mr. Jones," Jillian said as gently as she could. "I'm sorry to have to tell you, but Victoria is dead."

Jones sat looking at her for several seconds, unblinkingly. It was as if he hadn't heard her because he frowned, tilted his head slightly, and said, "What?" He paused before adding, "What did you say?"

"Her body was found yesterday by the river Itchen," Jillian said, keeping her voice even.

"No," he said, shaking his head. "No, no, no. Can't be." Then he looked over at Listun. "She can't be dead. I just spoke to 'er a few days ago."

Taking out his notebook, although Kara had already been taking notes on hers, Listun said, "When exactly did you last speak to her, Mr. Jones?"

Royce Jones sat back, the finality of what they were telling him finally sinking in.

"Mr. Jones?" Listun prompted.

Jones looked up at him, his eyes watering. "'Bout a week, maybe a week ago yesterday. S'why I was getting so worked up callin' when she wouldn't . . ." He couldn't finish the sentence.

"Can you tell us your whereabouts two nights ago?" Listun asked.

"Me?" Jones asked, clearly understanding the meaning behind the question. "You think I had somethin' to do wid it?" he said, getting angry. "You think I could kill Vic?"

Jillian cut in, making him change his focus from Listun. "We have to ask, Royce. It's standard procedure, so we can eliminate you from our inquiries." She said it gently, and although Jones seemed to calm down a bit, he was still agitated.

"I was workin' wasn't I?" he said, giving Listun a nasty look.

"And where do you work, Mr. Jones?" Listun asked, ignoring the tone and look. He'd done this plenty of times before.

Jones told him the name of the construction firm he worked for and that he'd worked until nearly ten o'clock that night.

"Bit late to be working construction, isn't it?" Listun asked, the sarcasm heavy in his voice.

"I do walls and plaster. I like to work at night 'cause it's cooler. Boss doesn't mind s'long as the work gets done," Jones responded tersely.

Jillian asked a few more questions, but without the background of any correspondence he had with the victim, she didn't want to dig too much. She'd have to wait for the techies to get the data to them before she could go down that road.

The trio left and got back into their car to return to the Tof.

Amid the silent thoughts of each member in the car, Kara spoke up. "He seemed genuinely surprised to hear she was dead."

"I've met better liars before," Listun said. "Besides, I still think there's something off about working on construction till ten at night when it's dark and no one's around to corroborate if you're there or not."

Jillian let them talk it through. She had similar thoughts but wanted them to form their own opinions, not following those of their boss because of who she was.

***

The next morning, the techies sent over masses of information from the laptop, including voluminous records from the victim's emails, chat sessions, and even a few videos. Stephen and Kara split up the data and began going through them.

They had not, however, found anything on Victoria's father.

During the morning brief in the incident room, one of the team suggested looking for the adoption records.

Jillian and Kara soon found themselves at the Southampton Crown Court off London Road, where they were directed three times before finding themselves in the tiny office of a Mr. Nicolas Fendby. He looked like he'd been at the Crown Court for some time by the state of his office, which was overflowing; there were piles of folders and paper on every conceivable surface of his desk.

Pushing his black-rimmed glasses up onto the bridge of his nose, he asked how he could help.

Jillian flashed her warrant card, hoping to clear her way through the bureaucracy. She told him they were investigating the murder of a Victoria Lessings, who had been adopted some twenty-one years ago or so, and they wanted to find the biological father.

Mr. Fendby stared at Jillian blankly for a few seconds, looking like he had swallowed a fly. Then he actually swallowed loudly and said, "But we don't have those records here."

Kara, somewhat surprised, said, "But surely, an adoption would have to be registered by the court?"

"Registered, yes," Fendby replied, "but the records aren't kept here. All adoption orders are sent to the GRO, General Registry Office, who then enters the adoption into the Adopted Child Register."

"So, we can find the father in that register?" Kara asked hopefully.

"Well, no," Fendby replied unhelpfully. "That would be the Adoption Contact Registry, also kept at the GRO, which is in Southport, Merseyside."

"Right," Kara said slowly, getting annoyed. "So, we can find the father's information in the Adoption Contact Registry, then?"

"It depends on whether he's given permission?" Fendby said, looking somewhat pained to have given yet another unhelpful answer.

"You're joking," Jillian and Kara said together.

"I'm afraid not. All adoption information is strictly guarded. Both an adopted child and birth parent can register a veto if they do not want to be contacted by anyone regarding the adoption. There are two types of veto, an 'absolute veto' and a 'qualified veto.' Now an absolute veto . . ."

Jillian cut him off, leaning forward on his desk with both arms. "Mr. Fendby, we are investigating a murder inquiry," she said, making direct eye contact with him. "The adopted child in question is now dead. I would like to contact her father. How do I do that?"

Perhaps it was something in her eyes, or the tone of her voice, but Fendby suddenly became quite nervous. Standing up and turning around to a row of filing cabinets, he pulled out two pages and passed them to her over his desk. "If you fill these out, Inspector, we can send a request on your behalf to the GRO."

Jillian handed the forms over to Kara, who immediately began filling them out.

***

Her mind snapped back to the present at the Big Yellow Self Storage unit. Jillian nodded to DS Listun, who placed bolt cutters around the padlock on unit number 214 and snapped the lock, which made a loud cracking sound as it bounced on the cement floor.

Whatever they might find in the storage unit, she was sure it would lead them to their killer.

DS Listun grabbed the door handle and opened it.

CHAPTER 6

The sound of the cut padlock hitting the cement floor echoed like a gunshot down the tiny corridor of the Big Yellow Self Storage unit. As DS Listun opened the door, he and Jillian peered into the darkness inside.

At first, they couldn't see anything, and then the light sensor kicked in and the overhead fluorescent lights flickered on, casting a soft white glow over the contents of the room.

Jillian's thoughts returned once again to the path that had brought them here.

***

On the second night in her new role, Jillian had wearily opened the door to her hotel room, dropped her bag, coat, and key onto the small dresser that doubled as her television stand, poured herself a glass of wine, and collapsed on the bed.

Thirty minutes later, she was on a video call with Daniella. It was good to see her and hear her voice. It felt like it had been an eternity instead of just a few days. Daniella said she was getting settled into her course and making friends. She filled Jillian in on all the details, then asked how things were going at the VCU.

Jillian sighed heavily and then gave her the basics, careful not to get into too much detail about the case. It helped that Daniella was a medical examiner. She was used to the lingo and enjoyed talking things through with Jillian.

They spoke for a while, and when they ran out of things to say, they just said nothing and looked at each other through the screen, neither wanting to end the call. Eventually, it had to be done, and Jillian, exhausted, lay back on her bed and fell asleep, still wearing her clothes.

Jillian stopped the next day at Southampton Central Police Station, hoping to prod the techies in their data search of the victim's laptop. They said they had just sent their findings over to her office, which, had she read her email, she would have known.

Frustrated at the waste of her own time, Jillian turned to leave, only to find DCI Walford striding toward her. Just what she needed.

"DI Scotte," he said, louder than was necessary. "A word!" It was not a request.

She followed him back to his office, with many heads turning her way as she went. He slammed the door shut behind her. "What do you think you're doing marching in here wasting my technical staff's time?"

"I was following up on their progress of my case , sir," she added, hoping her respectful tone toward his rank would help defuse his growing antagonism.

"We've got plenty going on at the moment, DI Scotte, without you treating this station like your own personal department where people jump every time you say boo."

Jillian opened her mouth to say something, but Walford cut her off. "Seems to me you've got plenty going on with your own growing caseload. Why don't you get to work cracking some of those cases instead of running around wasting everybody's time searching for long-lost parents?" Walford walked back to his office door, yanking it open to show his tirade was ending, but not before he said, again louder than necessary, "Honestly, I don't know what the fuss is all about with you. Now let us get on about the business of policing Southampton, if you don't mind."

There were plenty of things she could say. Plenty of things she wanted to say, but there was little point in a public fight with this blowhard, and she did indeed have plenty of other things on her mind at the moment. As he held the door, she simply stood and stared at him, level in the eye.

Something about her look made Walford visibly stiffen. Eventually, he looked at a bookshelf behind her. "Sir" was all she said as she walked out of his office and back through the department toward the exit.

She was oblivious to the stares she received. She wondered, not for the first time, what she had done to Walford that made him so angry and antagonistic to her.

If her morning hadn't been frustrating enough, her temper grew as she arrived at the Tof. She walked stiffly through the bustling room as her team busily went about their work. She put down her bag and coat, picked up her phone, and texted DC Devanor: *Ladies loo, three minutes.* Then she walked out of her office to the ladies' lavatory and waited.

Kara opened the door and peered warily around the privacy wall at the entrance. "Mum?" she said cautiously. Jillian had already opened each stall door and now stood by a washbasin with her hands on each side of her head, staring at the mirror.

Straightening up, she turned to Kara, and half smiled. "I don't have time to fully explain, but in a few moments, I'm going to call the team into the incident room, and I need you to do something for me."

Kara stood still and nodded once.

"I don't want you to take a seat. I want you up against the side wall with your notebook, as though you just feel like standing, but it's important that you can see everyone in the room, got it?"

Kara frowned, but nodded once more.

"You'll know why as soon as I start, but I need you watching the room, not me."

With that cryptic message, Jillian walked past Kara and out of the lavatory. Kara stood still for a full minute before washing her hands out of habit and then leaving.

Jillian called DS Listun into her office and told him she wanted the entire team in the incident room straightaway. "Everything all right, mum?" he asked, sensing her tension.

She didn't even look up from the papers she was mindlessly rearranging on her desk. "Just get them in there now, please, Stephen."

Once everyone was assembled, Jillian noted Kara against the wall out of the corner of her eye and got straight to the point. "Each of you has been assigned to this team because of what you bring to it. You each have a skill, a background, a role to play as part of the team. We will be successful only if we are all rowing in the same direction."

Her tone was harsh; she wasn't trying to motivate them. "One of you has been reporting information from within this office back to the Southampton Constabulary ."

She paused long enough to slowly scan the room , looking at each member of the team one by one, Kara included, though she was happy to note that Kara was not looking back at her but at her team, with an intense gaze.

"If I can't trust you, if *we* can't trust each other, then we are not a team. I know we've only been together for a very short time, and I don't expect you to blindly trust everything I say just yet, but I cannot and will not have you undermine the rest of the work your colleagues are doing. If you have the courage to come and see me about this, do so immediately. If I have to come to you, it will not end well."

With that warning, she strode out of the room and back into her office, slamming the door.

A few moments later, DS Listun knocked. She nodded for him to come in. As he entered, he half turned to close the door behind him, and Jillian caught Kara's eye as she made her way back to her desk. Jillian locked eyes with Kara, then flitted her gaze from Kara to Listun and back. Kara briefly shook her head from side to side almost imperceptibly.

Listun turned back toward Jillian. "Mum, I'd like to speak openly."

"Please do," Jillian said, leaning back in her chair. Listun stood before her desk, not taking a seat.

"As the ranking DS, I feel you should come to me first before going after the team like that. I'm trying to build us into a working unit, and I can't do that if you undermine my efforts like I'm . . ."

Listun stopped short, noting the look in Jillian's eyes. They stood staring at each other for a few moments. Jillian said nothing, just staring back harshly.

Listun lifted his chin, the realization hitting him. "You think I might be the mole." It was a statement, not a question.

Jillian let his statement linger for a moment before answering. "I just came from Southampton Central, where DCI Walford said some things that only members of this team would know. I know I didn't say anything to anyone, and I'm quite certain DS Devanor didn't. Beyond that, I couldn't say with any certainty."

Listun was visibly hurt, but there was little he could say.

"Who do you think it might be?" Jillian asked.

"I have no idea," Listun said reflexively.

Jillian leaned forward and stood up slowly, emphasizing her point, "Neither do I, Stephen. Stop taking this as an affront to your standing and help me find out."

Looking out her window, she beckoned for Kara to come in.

"Well?" Jillian said simply, once Kara had closed the door behind her.

Looking uncomfortably at Listun, then back to Jillian, Kara said, "There were two people who looked down the moment you said it. Stella Dawson and Rick Genaly. Dawson was fidgety, but Genaly looked . . . I'm not sure how to put it, mum, but there was something off about his reaction."

Dawson was a police constable; Genaly was one of their administrative researchers. Dawson had come from Portsmouth. Genaly had been assigned from Southampton.

Listun looked at Kara and then turned his gaze to Jillian. "I'll look into it."

"Thank you," Jillian said, and both her detectives left the office.

***

Three days later, Jillian was meeting with Listun in her office when Kara came in. "Mum, I just got off the phone with the GRO at Merseyside. They said the request we put in just got to them . . ."

Jillian banged her desk in frustration. "God damnit, we asked for that four days ago!"

Kara waited a beat, "Yes, mum. I, uhm, did mention that to them, but they claim it only just arrived. I did, however, press them on the urgency of our request, and they were quite helpful. In fact, we have the name of the father."

Listun leaned forward in his chair. "And . . ." he prompted.

Kara smiled slightly. "Francis Billings. Research are digging into him now."

Jillian turned to Listun. "Top priority, Stephen. I want to talk to Mr. Billings today."

Within the hour, they had an address and place of employment on the docks. After pulling up, Listun and Jillian got out of their car and walked into the manager's office.

"Frank? Sure, he's around here somewhere," the dockmaster told them, and soon they were brought to a tall, thin man in his early to middle fifties, wrapping up large coils of boating rope near the dock's edge.

"Frank Billings?" Listun asked, as both he and Jillian flashed their warrant cards.

Billings straightened up with a frown. "That's me," he said simply.

"We'd like to ask you a few questions about your daughter."

"I don't have a daughter," he replied, dropping the rope onto the dock.

"The daughter given up for adoption, Mr. Billings," Jillian said, forcing him to turn and look at her for the first time.

Something swept over his eyes, and then he lowered his voice slightly. "That was a long time ago."

"I'm sorry to tell you this, Mr. Billings," Jillian said, "but I'm afraid she was found dead a few days ago."

"S'got nothin' to do with me," he said gruffly. "Her mum and I split fore she 'as born."

"We understand you recently reconnected with her," Listun said into the silence.

Billings looked up at him, confused. "What you on about?"

"Her roommates told us you recently contacted her and that you wanted to meet her."

Billings stood still, looking at DS Listun as though he's spoken another language. "Are you mad?" he said. "I've got a family of me own now. Wife and two sons I can barely manage. I'm working myself to the bone just trying to keep 'em all fed. Why on earth would I want to go an' talk to some baby I never knew?" Placing his hands on his hips, he said, "I don't even know the damn girl's name."

Once their questions were finished, Listun and Jillian climbed back into their car. Listun's phone rang. After looking at the caller ID, he answered and put it on speaker. It was Kara.

"Hi Sarge," Kara's voice rang out. "Is the boss with you?"

"You're on speaker with both of us," Listun said.

"Research have been digging through the data from tech. Nothing much, I'm afraid, though they did find a reference on her calendar to a storage unit in Poole."

"What was the reference?" Listun asked.

"Only that she had it down in her calendar nine days ago."

Jillian and Listun shared a look.

"I want a warrant for that lockup," Jillian said, and then her mind turned to the question both she and DS Listun were thinking. If Frank Billings hadn't been in contact with his daughter, who had?

CHAPTER 7

Weather was the ever-fickle mistress in England. As the light sputtered on inside the lockup, lightning flashed and thunder clapped. The pitiful fluorescent bulb overhead flickered on the verge of going out altogether.

Detective Inspector Jillian Scotte, Detective Sergeant Stephen Listun, and Police Constable Stella Dawson all peered into the space.

It was full of boxes down both sides, with more in a wide row in the middle, creating an aisle on either side. Many of the boxes were open.

All clad in blue latex gloves, the team went in. Listun and Dawson went down each side, while Jillian went straight to the middle. In the open boxes, she saw what appeared to be old baby clothes, some plush stuffed toys, and a few odds and ends.

As she went from one box to the next, she saw photo albums with pictures of a couple in their mid-twenties. Photos of picnics, of a flat with simple furnishings, of dinners out. As Jillian turned the pages of the book, she saw that the woman was obviously pregnant. Then further still, a brand-new baby girl appeared, dressed in one-piece outfits with little socks and hats.

"Boss," she heard Listun call out.

Leaving her box of treasures, she headed down the left side to the back of the lockup. Listun had taken some of the top boxes down, and they now lay open on the floor to reveal sheet sets and old anoraks and clothes.

"What is it?" she asked, coming to a stop a few feet away.

"The lower boxes," he said, pointing down.

"What about them?"

"They're empty."

Jillian frowned. "What do you mean *empty*?"

Listun showed her. Some contained maybe one piece of Styrofoam to help hold the boxes above, but otherwise, they were empty. They both turned toward PC Dawson, who was already removing a few of the top boxes near her. Sure enough, the same was true on her side.

Jillian walked halfway back to the front and kicked a box at the bottom of the middle section. It too felt hollow.

Turning back to Listun, she said, "Get a team in here and catalog all of it."

Listun nodded and pulled out his mobile.

Jillian felt a knot forming in the bottom of her stomach. Far from leading her to the killer, the lockup was raising more questions than it answered.

Leaving her sergeant to the task, she headed back to her hotel. It had been a long week and she needed a break. That break should be waiting for her in her room.

When she opened the door, she knew before she even stepped in that Daniella was there; she could smell her perfume. With the next day free from studies, Daniella had sped down after her courses and would return late the next night, or perhaps, if Jillian had anything to say about it, not until early the next morning.

Ignoring her buzzing phone, Jillian ran up and wrapped her arms around Daniella, kissing her passionately.

Holding her tight, Daniella looked at her, smiling once they broke the kiss. "Hi yourself."

Jillian leaned her forehead against Daniella's. "Been a long week."

"I can see that." Releasing the embrace, she pointed to the hotel information on the coffee table. "Doesn't look like much to eat here. What have you been doing for food?"

Jillian shrugged.

"Not eating is *not* how you keep yourself healthy in my absence," she chided gently. "Have you been riding?"

"No time," Jillian said, plopping down onto the bed and immediately lying back to stare up at the ceiling. "Let's head down to High Street. There's a Turkish place called the Ottoman Kitchen that looked good."

Suddenly Daniella climbed up onto the bed, straddling Jillian and looking down at her with her hair falling down both sides of her face. "I was thinking of something that looked good too."

It was later that they pulled up for dinner at the Ottoman Kitchen. After a wonderful meal, lots of laughter, and catching up on both their weeks, they walked out arm in arm to their car. "Oh shit," Jillian said, looking ahead.

Daniella followed her gaze. "Who is it?" she asked, noticing a woman who was standing with her arms crossed, looking straight at them.

"Give me a minute," Jillian said, taking out the car keys. "Wait for me in the car and I'll tell you once I've spoken to her."

Daniella frowned, but took the keys.

Jillian strode up to a woman, who was wearing dark blue jeans and a black leather jacket. A motorcycle helmet hung from one arm. Amelia Hamza.

"Hello Amelia," Jillian said.

"Who's your date?" Amelia asked.

"None of your business. Following me?"

"Yes," she responded, surprising Jillian. "I've been texting you all day and you've been ignoring me."

Jillian sighed. "No. I've been ignoring my phone and all its texts," she said truthfully. "It wasn't just you."

Amelia didn't look convinced. "My boss wants me to run a story on the victim being adopted and your interest in her relatives."

This was the second time in a week that someone had gotten this information. Jillian could already feel her blood pressure increasing.

"I'd rather you didn't," she said between clenched teeth.

Amelia kept her game face on. "Too bad. My job is to report the news, and so far, that seems to be the latest news in this case. Unless you have something else to give me?"

Jillian took a deep breath. "Amelia, if I had something to tell you, I would. Right now, we're just getting into this case, and if you go out and report what we're working on, it could jeopardize what we're doing."

"And just what *are* you doing?" the journalist asked.

Jillian said nothing. Amelia pressed on. "Do you have any suspects? Is the father one of them? Friends? Other family? Is this a serial killer?"

Jillian frowned slightly. Then, sighing loudly, she turned and looked back at the car where Daniella was sitting, watching them intently. "No, we don't have a prime suspect yet. We have few leads, and those keep turning up dead ends or leading us deeper into the labyrinth."

Amelia threw up her hands. "Well then. Guess I'll go with what I have."

Jillian didn't like the way this was going, especially since she felt powerless to stop it. Finally, she asked, "Is there anything I could say to change your mind?"

Amelia considered her for a moment, her finger drumming against the helmet she now held in front of her like some sort of shield. Pursing her lips and narrowing her eyes, she straightened up a little and said, "Let me do a piece on you."

"Me?" Jillian said, surprised.

"Yes." Amelia's eyes lit up a little. "Famous Scotland Yard rising star gets assigned to new VCU team in Southampton. I can easily get all the background stuff from the press you've gotten over the years. All I would need is some personal stuff, a quick interview, maybe some B-roll."

Jillian hated being in the public eye and this went against every fiber inside of her, but she needed Amelia to hold off on running her story. Jillian nodded her head back to her car. "She stays out of it." She said it with finality, making her point clear.

She could tell Amelia didn't like it, but she nodded once.

"Tell me where, and I'll give you fifteen minutes tomorrow morning, no more," Jillian said stiffly.

"Fine," Amelia snapped.

Too quick, Jillian thought. Dammit, she probably should have said five minutes. Jillian got back in the car and, with a heavy sigh, told Daniella all about Amelia Hamza.

***

Jillian gave her fifteen-minute interview the next morning before returning to the hotel to grab Daniella and head out on a drive through the New Forest for a picnic and some local sightseeing.

Hamza had grilled her hard for the full fifteen minutes, getting as personal as she could without talking about her love life. It wasn't as bad as Jillian had feared, but she already knew she would not like the piece when it was published.

She had convinced Daniella to stay until the next morning, though to be fair, she was already saying yes before Jillian fully asked the question. They got up early, said gentle goodbyes, and Jillian headed into the office to start the week.

She hadn't expected the article to run so quickly, but apparently it had been published in the Daily Coast, the online digital news site that Hamza worked for. The photo, taken during her interview, was, at least, not horrible, Jillian thought, but she had been right—as she sat at her desk watching the video, she hated it.

It wasn't that it was bad. It was very well done; Hamza had stuck mostly to the facts about Jillian's previous success, doing walk-and-talk style commentary interspersed with news footage and generic police B-roll. Jillian's interview was inserted here and there, and she was glad she hadn't been taken out of context. She was surprised to see Kara mentioned from the Paul Davies case, and somewhat unnerved that she was referred to as a close confidante whom DI Scotte had brought down to the VCU with her.

Never mind that she was right; it wouldn't help their working relationship with the rest of the team. Worse still, there was mention of another "close friend" from Cumbria whom DI Scotte could be seen with from time to time. She hadn't mentioned Daniella by name, but Jillian was going to have a word with Ms. Hamza about what the term "off limits" meant.

Kara knocked on her office door and came in, her cheeks looking a little flushed. Clearly, she had seen the story and was far from bothered by being labeled a close confidante.

There was nothing to be done, so Jillian just let it go. "What's up?"

"Just finishing up the list from the lockup, mum."

DI Listun walked in at that point and stood silently off to one side. Kara continued, "Nothing of note, other than there were no fingerprints."

"What, none?" Jillian asked, surprised.

"No mum. Everything had been wiped down or handled with gloves."

Looking at Listun, she asked, "Anything on who's been renting it?"

"'Fraid not," he said, consulting his notebook. "It's been rented for a little over three years, paid in annual amounts, in advance. Name of Jarred Norwin."

When he didn't continue, Jillian said, "And what do we know about Mr. Norwin?"

Listun took a deep breath. "He died four and a half years ago."

Jillian threw her pen down on her desk in frustration. "What about the contents of the lockup?"

"Just old sheets, clothes, some pics, some mementos you can find at any boot sale or market."

"So, we're no further along then?" Jillian asked, exasperatedly.

Listun spoke up, clearly sensing her frustration. "We're checking into the father and the ex-boyfriend. Going through alibis, work records, banks, et cetera. . ."

As they turned to leave, Jillian suddenly remembered something. "Oh, I was talking to"—she almost said Amelia Hamza's name but caught herself just in time—"someone the other day, and they asked me if our killer was a serial killer."

Listun and Kara looked at her blankly.

Looking at Listun, she said, "Do you remember any other murders that look like this one? Maybe murder victims in the river Itchen that resemble Victoria Lessings's?"

"Quite a lot of bodies get dumped in the Itchen, boss. Feeds into the Channel, doesn't it," he said by way of explanation, and he and Kara walked out of Jillian's office.

Jillian turned and looked out of her window. Of the eleven cases they'd been given, only four were actively running, the Lessings case included. While most of the other cases were still in the organizational stage of assembling all the documentation together and starting up proper case profiles, she almost felt they were further along than this case. Every time she thought she was going forward, she seemed to take three steps backward.

CHAPTER 8

Time stood still. At least it did for the detective inspector in charge of New Scotland Yard's new Violent Crime Unit.

To say that the Lessings case had come to a grinding halt would be an understatement. Jillian's team knew someone had lured Victoria to a lockup with what looked like the belongings of a family with a baby girl, but in fact, it was all fake, made up of photos from the internet and used clothing from junk shops and markets.

Frustratingly, although the clothes contained DNA from various people, it was likely from previous owners. Neither the photos and cardboard boxes nor any of the mementos had fingerprints on them. They had been wiped clean. Every. Single. Item.

The team had gone through every box, cataloging everything and sending off samples for DNA testing. It had taken more than a few days and so far had resulted in nothing that would lead them to their killer.

Jillian's handlers at the Met weren't quite banging on the door, but they were asking about results. To make matters worse, her Southampton nemesis, DCI Walford, was telling anyone who would listen how appointing a DI to head up the VCU had been a big mistake despite her overinflated ego from previous cases and all the attention she received in the press.

That part was virtually a quote from the piece that had run on the late-morning news.

Was he miffed that he hadn't been given the job? Was that his problem? Jillian wondered as she looked out her office window. She didn't have time for him or his grievances.

She turned around to a knock on her door, and DS Listun came in. "Morning, boss. Just wanted to update you on where we are with the Lessings case."

Jillian raised a skeptical eyebrow.

"We finally got her mobile phone account access," Listun said, which made Jillian sit up a little straighter. "We were able to access her voice mailbox." Although it was very difficult to reach back and grab text messages or other app information without the phone, the one thing that lived in the cloud and not the device was voice mail. With a flourish, he laid some papers on her desk. "Mr. Jones was quite prolific in his messages."

Indeed, most of the voice mails were from Royce Jones, and they made for quite interesting reading, though Jillian imagined they had not been pretty to listen to. Jones mostly professed his undying love for Victoria in various ways. He clearly had a problem and was overbearingly distraught about losing her. *Probably why she left him*, Jillian thought as she continued to read.

Jones's messages became more desperate as time went on, pleading, shouting, and then turning angry to make several threats, including "I'd rather jump off a bridge with you than lose you to someone else . . ."

Jillian looked up from the pages.

Listun pointed to the last sheet. "Keep going," he prompted.

Pulling up the last sheet, she started reading, then frowned. After reading it twice, she looked up at Listun. "Do you think she told him?"

"No way to know unless we ask him," Listun said.

Jillian nodded. "Bring Mr. Jones in for a little more formal chat."

Listun turned and left her office. Then, looking down at the page, Jillian reread the transcription of his voice mail: "Is it because you found your bio dad? Is that why you're ignoring me?"

She read through the page once more and then grabbed her coat and bag from the hook on the back of her door and called out, "Kara, grab your things!"

Kara, accustomed to her boss's unpredictable needs, sighed, threw her pen down on her keyboard, grabbed her things, and half walked, half ran after her down the hallway.

The two detectives arrived once more at the Crown Court building near the Ransom Memorial Fountain. Making their way back to the clerk and records section, they found Mrs. Kassal, the head clerk, along with Mr. Fendby. They were talking in the hallway.

"Hello Inspector," Mrs. Kassal said. "To what do we owe this unexpected pleasure?" She looked anything but pleased to see the two policewomen.

Unfazed by the veiled insult, Jillian said, "I was wondering if Victoria Lessings had ever come in search of her biological parents in the time leading up to her death."

The head clerk pursed her lips and turned to her records-keeper, who said, "Yes, I believe she did."

The sheer incompetence of government bureaucrats never ceased to amaze Jillian, and she felt her blood pressure beginning to rise. Breathing deeply, she looked at Fendby. "You didn't think to mention this the last time we were here?"

Fendby looked affronted and replied, "You didn't ask."

Kara, sensing her boss was about to explode, cut in. "Can you tell us when she was here?"

Mrs. Kassal, not wanting to be ignored, said, "If she made a request for records, it'll be in the log, won't it?"

She looked at Fendby, who nodded and then added, "I remember it was a Monday, two, maybe three months before she died."

Everyone looked at him, surprised. "Well," he said, nonplussed, "I remember because of the great fight she had with that bloke who turned up."

"Ohhh yes!" Kassal exclaimed, "I remember that too. You never heard such language."

"Who was it that turned up?" Kara asked.

"A former boyfriend, I think," Fendby said. "At least that was the impression I got." Mrs. Kassal was nodding vigorously in agreement.

Pulling out her phone, Kara scrolled through social media until she found a photo of Royce Jones. Holding her phone out so both clerks could see, she asked, "Was this him?"

Both of them nodded in unison.

They returned to the Tof right as Listun was escorting Mr. Royce into the just-finished interview room one.

"Do you want to talk to him or shall I?" Listun asked.

"We'll both go," Jillian said, impatiently throwing her things into her office. "Kara, you go behind the glass and watch. Interrupt if you think of anything important."

Finally, with something and someone to focus on, the trio walked toward the interview suite with a purpose in their steps.

CHAPTER 9

Everyone always assumes there's a book, Jillian thought as they approached the interview room. There isn't a one-size-fits-all manual, a "how to" on doing interviews, because each one is unique.

Although the Sergeant's Academy devotes a significant section of training to interview skills, there are many more conference workshops and courses a copper can take to learn the intricacies and nuances involved in interviewing various suspects.

Having been cautioned by Listun, Royce Jones denied calling a solicitor, defiantly announcing, "I've got noffin' to hide, have I?"

Jillian started the recorder, announced herself and DS Listun, then jumped right in. "When did you know Victoria had been contacted by her biological father?"

Jones shifted in his seat uncomfortably before answering, "I followed her one day when she went to search court records."

"In fact," Jillian said, looking down at her yellow pad of notes, "You did more than follow her. You had a proper row with her in front of several witnesses."

Jones chewed on his lower lip. "Yeah, well, I was frustrated. She wouldn't return my phone calls or emails. I just wanted to talk with 'er and she wasn't 'avin' it, so I lost my temper."

"Is that the reason she broke up with you, because of your temper?" Jillian asked pointedly.

"*No,*" he responded, but his answer had been too quick, too defensive.

"Speaking of messages," Jillian announced, quickly changing the subject to keep him off guard. She opened a folder and pulled out the transcriptions of his text messages, laying them out on the table before him. "Would you care to explain these?" She pointed to the rather inflammatory messages that had been highlighted.

"I tole you." Royce Jones looked up quickly after he saw what they were. "I tole you about these the first time you came messin' me about."

"No," Jillian countered. "Actually, you didn't. You asked if we were there because of messages, but you never told us they were so violent."

"I didn't mean any of it," he said sharply. "I loved Vic; I'd never 'ave harmed a hair on 'er 'ead. Why can't you believe me? She meant everyfin' to me."

"What I can't understand, Mr. Jones, is that after giving you the shove, for months, you've been after her, obsessing about her, stalking her, following her." She paused, as Jones was just shaking his head from side to side at each point. "All that time, she's still giving you nothing. No contact, no return messages, effectively telling you to bugger off." Again, she paused, then said, "So what was it that finally pushed you over the edge?"

Jones slammed his fist on the table, causing Listun to half come out of his chair. "I didn't kill her!" he shouted.

Jillian waved DS Listun back to his chair. Waiting for Jones to calm himself, she took a slow, deep breath. "Right. Let's start with when Victoria broke off your relationship. Tell me how it happened. "

And so it went. For two and a half hours, Jillian and Listun went back and forth, going over and over each question from different angles. At one point, Jillian left the room to get tea for each of them, more as a ploy than because she or Listun was thirsty. Stephen then tried being the male friend.

"Look, Royce, you clearly fancied her . . ." he began, but Jones was adamant, turning on him and leaning heavily on the table.

"You're not listening!" he said forcefully. "I didn't just fancy 'er. I. Fucking. Loved. Her." He made a point of punctuating each word.

As they neared the three-hour mark, Jillian changed tactics. "In order for us to understand your relationship with Victoria fully, we'd like you to submit to a DNA sample and voluntarily give us your phone."

Astonishingly, he reached for his phone and placed it on the table, his hand beginning to push it toward her before pausing. He looked from Jillian to Listun and back again. "I fink I should call my solicitor."

Damn it! Jillian thought. They were so close. She tried to make herself as nonthreatening and neutral as possible. "I'll have DS Listun here," she said, nodding at Stephen, "give you a proper receipt for the phone, and you'll have it back as soon as we've finished looking at the correspondence between you and Victoria."

She had no intention of giving his phone back, but he wasn't to know that. "And," she said quickly, sensing his hesitation and seeing a frown cross his face, "he will then take you to call your solicitor straightaway."

Nobody moved a muscle. She and Listun stayed perfectly still. Jones still held his hand over the phone. "I need my phone," he said wearily. "How long till I get it back?"

"Not long," Jillian lied, keeping her face as impassive as possible.

Listun slowly reached his hand, palm up, across the table. "If you can also write down your code in case it gets locked while we're going over the messages. You can quickly change it later."

Amazingly, Jones took his hand off the phone.

Listun quickly snatched it and set off to get the receipt and have the team go through it.

The solicitor, a large man with a heavy Slavic accent, was not at all happy about the phone, but after several attempts at retrieving it, he eventually conceded that they had broken no laws in obtaining it, as Jones had volunteered it when they asked.

The solicitor tried demanding that they return the phone that evening or the next morning at the latest. Jillian said they would do their best, not meaning a word of it, which he rightly scoffed at.

With nothing substantial in the way of proof to hold him, the solicitor demanded that Royce Jones be allowed to leave, which Jillian reluctantly agreed to.

When they regrouped in her office nearly five hours after they had started, she asked Kara and Listun what they thought.

Listun said, "Techs are going through the phone and cataloging everything. Should know what we've got either tonight or early tomorrow."

Kara was chewing the end of her pen cap. Jillian looked at her, and it took a minute for Kara to notice that the focus had shifted to her. 'Oh, sorry," she said automatically. "It's just that something's not right."

"Why give us the phone, you mean?" Jillian prompted.

"Well yes," Kara said. "That was odd. I mean, if you've just killed someone, let alone your ex-girlfriend whom you profess your unending love to, the last thing you'd want is the constabulary going through your life, right?

"Also, that message about jumping off a bridge . . ."—she pulled a face, trying to make sense of her own words—"I mean, he sent it the day we found her body. Later that morning."

"Maybe guilt. Trying to justify himself to her, even if only by text?" Listun posited.

"Well," Jillian said, already feeling the adrenaline of the day waning and the heaviness of exhaustion seeping down onto her shoulders. "Let's see what tomorrow brings, shall we?"

Jillian picked up a takeaway on her way home with a large chocolate shake. She sat in her car eating it, too tired to bother driving home first.

Back at her just-moved-into flat, her temporary home until she and Daniella decided what to do, she fell asleep almost instantly. Her dreams were scattered, making for restlessness as she tossed and turned.

The sound of her phone vibrating felt a long way off in her dream state. After the third round of incessant buzzing, she swore out loud and reached for the phone. Her barely open eye took in the time from the alarm clock: half-past two in the morning. *This can't be good*, she thought.

"DI Scotte," she said groggily.

"You've been a busy bee, haven't you?" The voice said, and Jillian was instantly awake.

It was a computer-generated or modulated voice. "Victoria had a choice to make, and she chose someone else over me."

"Who is this?" Jillian said, mostly to be saying something as she tried to wake her muddled, sleep-filled brain.

"I'm the one who's giving you a choice of your own now."

Jillian frowned and was about to speak when her phone buzzed from a new text message .

"Open it," the voice said.

Jillian felt herself go cold. Tapping on her screen, she pulled up the message. It was a picture.

The picture was of Daniella and Kara.

They were neck deep in a river, the water up to their chins.

"Time to get moving," the voice said. "If you hang up, they die. If you don't do exactly as I say, they die."

Jillian couldn't stop staring at the photograph. Her heart was racing.

"You're wasting time. With all the rain and the storm that's raging tonight, I'd say they have less than fifteen minutes left. You'll want to head down toward Kemps Shipyard."

Jillian's mind finally focussed. She threw on shoes, still in her pajamas. She grabbed her coat and was soon driving wildly through the streets, guided by the computer voice as she got closer. Finally, the voice instructed her to park off to the side and walk down to the water's edge near Northam Bridge.

The rain was pouring down nearly sideways in the raging storm, making it difficult to see, until she got to the edge and looked under the bridge. There, several feet from shore, were Kara and Daniella. They were blindfolded, barely above the water as they strained their heads back to keep breathing through their noses as water began to wash over their mouths, which were taped over with waterproof duct tape.

Then she noticed the tripod with a camera pointed at them. The voice from her phone said, "Looks like minutes now."

Jillian's heart sank.

The voice continued, "There's a gun on the ground by the camera."

Jillian walked to it, feeling as though her legs were not her own.

"There's one bullet in it. You don't have time to save them both. Time to choose! Drowning is a horrible way to die. You can put one of them out of their misery. Your choice."

The call ended.

Jillian stood with the gun in her hand, looking into the river. She was soaking wet. Her mind felt as though it were stuck in the mud of the river bottom. She couldn't imagine how cold Daniella and Kara must be.

There was no time to call Listun.

There was no time to do anything. Forcing her mind to calm itself, she kept her gaze on the two people she cared the most about.

One bullet.

One choice.

Sprinting back up to her car, she yanked the passenger door open, reached inside, then half ran, half fell down the soggy grass embankment, coming to a halt at the bottom. She felt her legs shake from cold and fear as she stumbled back under the bridge to the water's edge.

Through blurry eyes, she raised the gun. Her arm shaking.

Willing it to steady, she blinked the rain and tears out of her eyes.

Despite the raging storm, the shot echoed loudly under the bridge.

CHAPTER 10

Pain was something Jillian knew all too well. After what Paul Davies had done to her, she never thought she would feel so much pain again. She was wrong.

This was a different kind of pain. The most excruciating kind.

"Looks like minutes now," the voice said, but it sounded strange—almost in stereo. She looked back over her shoulder briefly. The camera had a small screen attached to it, and she could see herself looking back over her shoulder as the screen projected the camera's view. That's where the sound was also coming from: not just her phone, but from the small screen, which had a tiny speaker built into it.

She turned back around, seeing the two women in the river, blind-folded, shivering, near to drowning.

Jillian's heart sank.

The voice continued, "There's a gun on the ground by the camera."

Jillian walked to it, feeling as though her legs were not her own. She picked it up and stood before the camera, gun in one hand, her phone still pressed to her ear with the other.

"There's one bullet in it. You don't have time to save them both. Time to choose! Drowning is a horrible way to die. You can put one of them out of their misery. Your choice."

The call ended, but she still saw herself on the screen. She dropped the phone from her ear and turned back around.

Jillian stood with the gun in her hand, looking into the river. She was soaking wet. Her mind felt as though it were stuck in the mud of the river bottom. She couldn't imagine how cold Daniella and Kara must be.

There was no time to call Listun.

There was no time to do anything. Forcing her mind to calm itself, she kept her gaze on the two people she cared the most about.

One bullet.

One choice.

Behind her, from the tiny screen with the built-in speaker, the modulated voice said, "Tick tock, tick tock."

Jillian bolted.

Sprinting back up to her car, she yanked the passenger door open, reached inside, then half ran, half fell down the soggy grass embankment, coming to a halt at the bottom. She felt her legs shake from cold and fear as she stumbled back under the bridge to the water's edge.

Through blurry eyes, she raised the gun. Her arm shaking.

Willing it to steady, she blinked the rain and tears out of her eyes and pulled the trigger.

Though at the water's edge, she hadn't faced the river, but toward the camera. Just before she fired the gun, she said, "You don't get to watch."

Dropping the gun and her jacket, she turned and plunged fully into the river, surfacing just in front of Kara. The water was icy, though thankfully the current wasn't too strong.

She stood up and fought for her footing, as she too was now neck deep in water. Her feet kicked something hard and large. Somewhere in her mind, the word *cement* registered, but there was so little time.

Taking the straw from the chocolate shake and a hair clip she had grabbed from her car, she spoke gently. "Kara, it's Jillian."

Kara immediately tried to speak through the tape over her mouth, her head tilted back as far as it could go as she desperately tried to breathe through her nose. Jillian cut her off. "There's no time, listen to me. I have to rip this tape off . . ."

Kara tried to shake her head from side to side .

"*Listen*," Jillian said more forcefully. "As soon as I do, I'm going to put a straw in your mouth. Then I'm going to clamp your nose. I want you to breathe through the straw. Do you understand?"

Unable to speak, Kara mumbled "Mmm hmm" through the tape.

Shooting a quick glance at Daniella, Jillian feared she might already be too late. Both women were roughly the same height, and the water was now at the base of their noses.

Jillian grabbed a corner of the tape and yanked it hard. She saw air bubbles escape Kara's mouth from the scream, but she quickly shoved the straw in and then clamped the hair clip on her nose.

"Breathe slowly. I promise you I will be right back. I will *not* leave you. Keep your head back and the straw up."

Without waiting to see if Kara understood, without time to take off the blindfold, Jillian plunged back into the water, swimming over to Daniella against the current.

Coming up behind her just in case Daniella resisted, Jillian said in her ear, "I'm here, I'm here," then wrapped her arms around Daniella's waist. Planting her feet on the bottom of the river, which meant Jillian's head was now mostly underwater, she lifted.

At first, Daniella didn't move. Then, with the help of buoyancy, Jillian was able to lift her up five or six inches, but that was all. The weight was unbelievable.

After holding her as long as she could, Jillian finally let her drop back down. Daniella's feet were each encased in cement in large containers of some type, likely buckets.

There was no way she could lift Daniella out of the water; she just wasn't strong enough. Her mind was reeling, knowing she'd only bought Daniella a few seconds by lifting her to let her breathe, Jillian came up for air herself.

Though it was dark, she could see Daniella's head moving from side to side. Clearly, she was holding her breath. "I'm still here. Hang on, love, I'm going to get you out," Jillian said with more conviction than she felt.

Frustration mounting, she looked around her as she half walked, half swam in front of Daniella. Her mind raced. There simply was no way she could lift Daniella, with her legs in buckets of cement, the fifteen feet or so to the shore, and even with the help of buoyancy.

That's when it hit her. She might not be strong enough to lift Daniella, but she was incredibly strong in other ways.

Taking a deep breath, she drove down to the bottom and felt around Daniella's legs. She'd been right: they were in buckets, and buckets have handles. Grabbing one handle in each hand, she planted her feet firmly into the muddy bottom, one just in front of and one to the side of the buckets, bending her knees tightly.

Keeping her hands on the handles of the buckets, which were tightly pulled against her chest, she pushed with her legs as hard as she could. The buckets resisted, but then slid helpfully across the muddy floor toward her.

It wasn't much because her feet also slipped on the muddy floor, but the buckets and Daniella within them, moved closer to the shore.

Recocking her legs with bent knees, feet planted, she did it again and again. Then she had to let go and come up for air. Thankfully, although still neck deep, Daniella had moved close enough to the shore that she could breathe through her nose again. The water was still around her mouth.

"Hang on, it's working," Jillian said, already out of breath.

Back down she went. Plant, pull, plant, pull, breathe. Plant, pull, plant, pull, breathe. It took her five long, excruciating minutes, but she finally got Daniella close enough to the shore that she could grab her by the waist and pull her until only her legs with their cement-filled buckets remained in the river. Her hands were zip-tied behind her back, but there was nothing for it. Jillian just laid her on her back, thankful at least that the underpass shielded them from the pouring rain.

Jillian, cold and shivering, left Daniella lying on the embankment and dove back in toward Kara.

The water was above Kara's eyes now; only her hair and the top of her forehead were visible beside the straw.

Down Jillian went, grasping the bucket handles and planting her strong legs. Thankful for all the miles she had put in on her bike, she slowly but surely inched Kara closer to the shore. Her legs were on fire and her arms and hands numb from the cold and exertion.

When they were close enough for her to reach around Kara's waist, Jillian dragged with all her might, not just to the shore, but closer to Daniella.

After laying Kara down beside Daniella in the same position, Jillian wearily crawled to her phone and jacket. Grabbing both, she made her way back down to the river's edge, mostly on her backside.

Both women were shivering, and Jillian, soaked to the bone in nothing but her pajamas, threw the coat over Kara, who had been in the river the longest. Kara tried to talk through chattering teeth, but Jillian was already lying half beside and half on top of Daniella, trying to rub her ice-cold arms to get warmth back into her.

With one hand, she hit 999 on her phone.

She gave her name and warrant card number to the emergency responder that answered, then said, "Officer in distress, under Northam Bridge, west side. Send ambulance *now*." She threw the phone up higher on the bank and resumed trying to keep both women warm.

Both were shivering, though Kara seemed to be calming down a bit.

Turning to Daniella, Jillian slowly peeled back the tape on her mouth, allowing her to breathe easier. Then, gently, she removed the blindfold, but Daniella's eyes remained closed. Rubbing frantically despite the pain in her own arms, she lay against Daniella's body, in between both women, hoping some of what little body warmth she had would transfer.

Eventually, she saw Daniella's eyes flutter weakly. Jillian felt tears running down her cheeks.

Moving over, she took off Kara's blindfold. Still shivering, Kara immediately began to cry. Blinking quickly to try to clear her eyes, she would not stop staring at Jillian. Despite wanting to turn back to Daniella, Jillian felt the intensity of her stare and held it, rubbing her arms over her jacket, which seemed to help, at least a little, to keep Kara warm.

Kara's mouth moved, but her teeth were chattering so loudly she couldn't speak. She didn't need to. Even in the dim light from the streetlamps up above, Jillian could see the words she was mouthing.

"Thank you."

Jillian got onto her stomach, pulling both women as close together as she could, her body covering half of each of them. With one arm draped over each woman, she rubbed and rubbed up and down their outer arms until she could no longer move her muscles.

All three women were crying as the faint whoop of an ambulance siren off in the distance got closer.

Dropping her head onto the adjoining shoulders of Daniella and Kara, Jillian closed her eyes. She was exhausted, freezing cold, and her legs felt like jelly.

As the first medical responder descended the embankment and took in the scene, Jillian almost laughed at his expression. Almost.

With his torch shining on the three women, he saw Jillian look up and straight at him. There was no doubt that he saw exhaustion and her completely disheveled state.

What Jillian was sure he also saw as his torch shone into her eyes was something else entirely. Something that was far more than the cold, the wet, the soreness, the exhaustion, or the tears streaming down her face.

Something that up to now had not been a factor in this case, but would become the dominant factor.

Jillian Scotte was enraged.

CHAPTER 11

The long night turned into a long day. The first ambulance immediately called for fire rescue, who had to chisel and saw the cement buckets off Kara's and Daniella's feet.

The paramedics wanted Jillian to go to the hospital, but she was having none of it. She wasn't leaving until they were all on their way. When the first coppers showed up from the nearby nick, she took charge, flashing her warrant card. The paramedics looked at each other, perplexed, and even the constables didn't know what to do. *Wasn't she a victim?*

A sergeant showed up, trying to take over, and it was all Jillian could do not to bite his head off. Thankfully, DS Listun arrived at that moment, explaining to the bewildered local coppers who Jillian was, who he was, and that this was now a VCU crime scene.

Listun returned to his car and brought a proper large winter anorak back from his boot, wrapping it around Jillian's two layers of warming blankets. He knew better than to try to get her to leave. He saw it in her eyes.

Jillian just stood and watched the emergency responders do their work.

She sat in the ambulance and watched on the ride to the hospital as the medical personnel worked to get IVs started, pumping warm fluids into the two women who were her world.

She sat and stared as the doctors worked on all three of them, making sure there were no permanent injuries from the cold, wet ordeal they had endured.

She sat and stared straight ahead, answering Stephen's questions as he took down her official statement. Beyond her responses, she said not a word.

Jillian was building up her strength. She was taking in everything and nothing at the same time. Once they left the hospital, once Daniella and Kara were safe, once they were starting to heal . . .she knew she wouldn't sleep until she found him.

Having nearly lost the woman she loved, and the friend who had once saved her life and to whom she still felt beholden, Jillian Scotte had never been so focused, determined, and angry in her life. How dare he do this to them?

They were all discharged from the hospital late that Saturday evening. Jillian insisted Kara come to her flat for the night, or longer, if she wished.

Kara smiled in the car. "Your couch will be far more comfortable than the toddler bed I've been sleeping in at my mate's'."

Daniella, lying her head back in the passenger seat with her eyes closed, quietly took Jillian's hand as she drove.

Listun had already set up a round-the-clock watch for them, and even now, a police car followed them home.

Sunday brought the smell of coffee and breakfast from her kitchen as Jillian padded barefooted from her bedroom.

"What are you doing?" she asked, yawning, as she saw Kara at the stove.

"Earning my keep," Kara said, looking over her shoulder and smiling.

The morning was uneventful, the trio lounging around with Jillian fussing, only to be told by Daniella that she too needed rest. Looking over at Kara, Jillian frowned. "What are you doing on that laptop? Put that down."

Kara kept typing. "Just doing some work." She paused and looked up, meeting Jillian's eyes. "You're not the only one who's livid."

By early evening they were discussing the text message that had been sent to Daniella saying that it was Jillian, that her phone had been broken and she was stranded, she had borrowed a passerby's phone to text, and could Daniella please come and get her?

Kara had received a text that was almost identical, but with an added inducement that Jillian thought she knew who the killer was. Despite the late hour of midnight, the text had spurred Kara out of her friend's home, only to be hit over the head as she was getting in her car.

"Stupid really, I should have been more careful."

While Kara had been put into her cement bucket unconscious and placed into the river blindfolded just as she was waking up, Daniella had driven herself to the bridge, only to be grabbed from behind at gunpoint and forced down to the river for her own shoe fittings.

"You know what's interesting?" Jillian said, sipping a glass of wine. "He talked to you." She nodded at Daniella. "But not to you." Now she nodded at Kara.

Kara frowned, thinking about it. "That's true. I didn't come to until I was getting dragged in the water, and by then I was bound, gagged, and blindfolded."

Jillian nodded, turning to Daniella. "But he told you what to do."

Daniella nodded, shivering visibly. Jillian wrapped her arm around her. "Sorry, didn't mean to bring that back up."

Daniella almost laughed. "No, it's not that. I was actually cold just then." Sipping her own wine, she added, "I just wanted you closer to me," and smiled.

Just as they were about to go to bed, Kara made a triumphant noise. Daniella and Jillian turned.

Kara looked up from the laptop. "I just wanted to do a search to see if there had been others like Victoria in this part of England."

Jillian nodded.

"There have been two in the past twenty months."

Jillian sat back down. "What do you mean, *two*?"

Kara chose her words carefully. "Two women, in their twenties, found dead in the Itchen, same general appearance as Victoria." She paused, and Jillian shrugged.

"That's not that unique, Kara," she said. "Honestly, I'm surprised there haven't been more that matched that description."

Kara nodded her agreement, then added, "Both were adopted," and turned the computer around so Jillian could see the files.

That made Jillian sit up straighter.

Daniella sat back down.

The three began looking at the cases for similarities with Victoria Lessings. They knew that Royce Jones had already been picked up and was being held at the VCU. No doubt DS Listun was interviewing him as they sat in Jillian's flat. Jones said he had left the interview suite at the VCU and returned to his flat, saying he watched a match on telly and fell asleep until he was unceremoniously awoken by a warrant squad, which had detained him bright and early the next morning.

Of course, he had no one to vouch for him and no viable alibi.

They also knew that Frank Billings, Victoria's biological father, had an alibi for that night. Could it really have only been thirty-six hours ago? Jillian thought. Billings had been at home with his family all night from teatime onwards.

Jillian wondered how the interview with Jones was going. She was dying to be there, but she knew Kara and Daniella weren't ready for her to leave yet. She walked to the window at least once an hour to check that their patrol watch was outside, but that still didn't make her feel comfortable. How she was ever going to go to work in the morning and leave them here in her flat, she still hadn't figured out.

Into this ramble of thoughts, Daniella interjected. "Perhaps you're both going about this all wrong."

Kara and Jillian both looked up. They had been huddled together over a yellow lined pad and the laptop, furiously comparing notes and cross-referencing anything and everything from the case files.

Kara frowned. Jillian narrowed her eyes.

"It seems to me that you've been trying to find a pattern between the killings. Looking for some connection between the victims and the killer or how and when they were killed." She said it matter-of-factly, not as a question, but both Jillian and Kara nodded, as though this were the most obvious thing.

"Maybe," Daniella said gently, "you should look at how the killer knew they were adopted?"

Jillian's eyes widened. Bed was going to have to wait a bit longer.

CHAPTER 12

Detective Inspector Jillian Scotte hated meetings, but as she learned upon returning to work after her weekend away, they were a necessary evil of being the boss.

The week had started off normal enough. She had called the entire team into the incident room.

"We are going to take a new tack on the Lessings case." Looking around the room to make sure everyone was paying attention, she went on. "We'll still follow current lines of inquiry; however, we are adding a new one." She nodded to Kara, who filled everyone in on the development of the other two adopted victims.

"So," Jillian said, taking the lead once again, "I want to know every-one and anyone who could have known about Victoria's adoption. That means coworkers, friends, everyone will need a fresh talking-to. Let's see who knew what."

After a pause, she looked at Listun. "Sergeant Listun, I'd like you to talk to the father again."

Listun nodded, then tilted his head slightly. "Guv, didn't he have an alibi for . . ." He didn't need to finish the sentence. Everyone understood he was referring to the past weekend's events.

"Yes, but we don't know how ironclad it is. Let's dot the *i*'s and cross our *t*'s."

Still addressing him, she continued, "I also want someone looking at the entire adoption process, from the agency they used, to the court where the hearings were held. Who was there? Who was part of the process? Also, check the process from the Crown Court all the way up through that agency . . ." She couldn't remember the name. "The one with the records . . ."

Kara spoke up. "The GRO?"

Snapping her fingers, Jillian added, "Yes. Thank you."

The team immediately jumped to their tasks, and the VCU was abuzz with activity. Jillian, however, had been mostly confined to her office. Since the pandemic, everyone seemed to have realized that video conference calls made it easier to check in and communicate. While that was so, it had actually led to an increase in meetings, as executives felt they could check in more often.

One call she didn't mind was with Superintendent Maryanne Sanderson from New Scotland Yard. Maryanne, who had also called on Saturday evening, was not only calling to check in on her mentee, but also to see how the case was going. Even superintendents, friend or not, had people to answer to.

Upon finishing Sanderson's call, Jillian immediately jumped on another.

The financial people wanted an account of the already skyrocketing costs the unit was generating. The tech people wanted to discuss better security after the weekend's incidents.

Jillian spent the next several days bouncing from one call, one video conference, one meeting to another.

There were only two bright spots that came during that week . The first was when Stephen came into her office, knocking on his way in. He was getting more comfortable with his boss, which pleased Jillian, though she was careful not to let him see it.

When he closed her door, however, she sat straighter in her chair.

"I found our mole," he declared, getting straight to the point.

Jillian raised her eyebrows, nodding so he would continue.

"I set up a trap of sorts, gave a few possible suspects different pieces of information. I just received a call from DCI Walford asking me about it. What he asked about told me which one of them"—He nodded back over his shoulder—"was the one who told him."

Jillian waited.

"It's Rick Genaly," Listun said grimly.

Jillian sighed loudly. She'd liked Rick, and he was a solid copper, even if only on the administrative side. "Okay, well done, Stephen. Here's what we're going to do."

And with that, she laid out her plan. Later that day, she'd asked Genaly to accompany her, as she needed someone to take notes at an official meeting. It was all rubbish of course, but it gave her an excuse to take him with her as she drove to the Southampton Constabulary.

Meanwhile, Listun had boxed up Genaly's desk, much to the concern of the rest of the team. He'd done it quickly and then gotten into his car to meet up with Jillian, following her and Rick Genaly by about three minutes and breaking traffic laws to catch up.

Jillian had walked into the detective's room unannounced, which had set off DCI Walford.

"What are *you* doing here?" he'd asked gruffly, emerging from his office.

"Oh, hello DCI Walford," Jillian responded, as though running into him had been accidental. "I thought I'd return some of your property."

Listun had walked in at that precise moment. Looking at Jillian with the box in his arms, he said, "Where should I put this, mum?"

Jillian pointed to Walford's office. "You can put it in there, DS Listun, thank you." Then, turning to face the DCI, she said, loud enough for all to hear, "The next time you want to know what's going on in my unit, DCI Walford, you can bloody well call me."

With that, she turned on her heel and walked out. Listun, following, looked at Genaly and said, "Sorry mate, you're fired."

Genaly had looked crestfallen. Stephen and Jillian had a quick chat in the parking lot. Both felt a little sorry for Genaly, who had only been doing what he'd been told and now had to face Walford's wrath. Their sorrow didn't last long, and soon they were on their way back to the Tof.

The second bright spot was a coffee Jillian had with Amelia Hamza.

"I want you to run the adopted victim story," Jillian said straightaway.

Amelia's eyebrows rose in surprise. "But you said you didn't want us running that, what, not more than a week ago?"

"Yes, but that was because you wanted to focus on the family. I still don't want you making the focus of the piece about the family. I want you to focus on the fact that we're interested in the adoption angle and are following several lines of inquiry."

Amelia, already taking notes, looked up. "Can you give me anything specific?"

Jillian handed her a piece of paper on which she had typed up some notes. It cataloged the other two murders. After Amelia read it, Jillian said, "But you already knew that, didn't you?"

Amelia hesitated, her green eyes narrowing slightly. Then, brushing her black hair behind one ear, she said, "I knew of one of them, not the other."

Jillian nodded silently. They talked for five more minutes, Jillian giving her snippets, but nothing concrete. Enough to make the piece interesting for her editor, but nothing that would jeopardize the case.

The piece had run the next day. It was well written and well edited.

The first week back had been almost entirely taken up by meetings, but by the beginning of the second week, things began happening.

The team was working tirelessly on following up with leads, finding dead ends, and simply checking off the never-ending list of things that made up cases like these the world over.

Jillian was in her car with Kara, as they had just finished interviewing witnesses relating to the ex-boyfriend, Royce Jones, who remained an active suspect. She took a call from DS Listun.

"We've just had a call in on the hotline," Listun said, referring to the line they had set up for anyone with information relating to Victoria Lessings's murder.

"Oh yes," Jillian said, concentrating on driving more than this piece of information. "Anything to do with the murder, or just another crackpot?"

"Not exactly, mum," Listun responded.

It was the tone of his voice that made Jillian focus her attention, and Kara leaned in toward the speakerphone to hear.

"It was from a family," Listun said evenly. "They don't seem to be connected to the Lessings at all."

Jillian and Kara listened, waiting for the inevitable shoe to drop.

"Their daughter hasn't been seen of or heard from in the past six days."

Jillian felt herself go cold. "Don't tell me."

"She's adopted" was Listun's reply.

CHAPTER 13

The ferry dock came into sight intermittently between buildings as the car raced toward it. Detective Inspector Jillian Scotte drove like a woman possessed. DC Kara Devanor had her right arm fully extended against the dash and her left holding on to the "oh shit" handle above the door as the car careened around a corner, narrowly missing an oncoming lorry. The driver blared his horn angrily.

As the dock finally came into view, it was clear that they weren't going to make it in time.

***

TEN DAYS EARLIER

The desk of Detective Inspector Jillian Scotte looked like the Tasmanian Devil just had a go at organizing it. That is to say, it was a complete mess.

The meetings and endless paperwork that were the bane of her existence as the VCU leader were just going to have to wait. Having just arrived back at the Tof with DC Kara Devanor, Jillian threw her coat onto the rack by her door and walked up to the front of her desk, then turned around and leaned up against it.

DS Stephen Listun, needing no prompting, came in, notepad in hand. Kara walked in right behind him, having shed her own coat and purse across the top of her desk.

Listun began right away. "The family are Margarette and Gerald Blistoke. Their daughter's name is Alison Blistoke, adopted at six months, now aged twenty-one. She's at Southampton Uni. Normally checks in with her mum at minimum once a week, sometimes more. Mrs. Blistoke says they're quite close."

At this point, Listun looked up, and at a nod from Jillian he continued. "Six days ago, she and Margarette were texting back and forth. She, the mum, says she sensed something was going on just by the tone of the texts."

Jillian interrupted, "Does she still have them?"

Listun made a face like he'd been drinking sour milk. "No, she deleted them, silly cow." Then realizing what he's just said, added quickly, "Sorry mum."

"S'all right Stephen," Jillian said with a half smile. "I was thinking the same thing. Go on."

"She says she was supposed to meet up with her daughter the next morning for coffee and she was going to ask her about it, but her daughter never showed. Haven't heard from her since."

"So . . ." Jillian said, frowning. "What, they waited five more days to report her missing?"

"Mr. Blistoke says she's always running off unannounced for days on end," Listun responded. "It was when his wife saw the piece by the Daily Coast that they wondered . . . and then . . ." At that point, he looked up, making sure both women were paying attention.

Jillian, intrigued, turned her head a little sideways and raised her eyebrows. Kara was leaning forward in her seat.

"Yesterday, Gerald Blistoke got a call from his bank. They had set up a trust for Alison for university. Alison cleared out the account late yesterday afternoon. The banker has a personal relationship with Mr. Blistoke and thought he ought to know."

"How much?" Kara asked.

Listun looked from her to Jillian. "One hundred and fifty thousand pounds."

Kara whistled. Jillian said, "I didn't think SU was *that* expensive?"

"It can run between ten and twenty per year depending on study, but they were also expecting their daughter to go straight into postgraduate school. Apparently, she's quite bright."

Jillian turned and looked out her window, more to give herself time to think than for the view. After a time, she turned around. "Right, Stephen, check the finances of all our suspects. Anyone who didn't have an alibi. Maybe we've been thinking about the motive having to do with adoption all wrong. Maybe it's about money."

It took days to first get the approvals, and then to pull the information, and finally to go through it all. With multiple cases going on, they couldn't detail the entire team, and it was Stephen and Kara who did most of the work.

Two weeks after the attack on Daniella and Kara, the team were at it bright and early when DS Listun kicked himself back from his desk, his chair rolling back into the middle of the aisle behind him.

Kara looked up. "What's up?"

Listun looked at her, his face draining of color. Turning back to his screen, he looked for a second or two, then back at Kara. "Shit." He stood up, motioning for her to follow him, and made straight for his boss's office.

He knocked but didn't wait for an answer, even though he could see DI Scotte was on the phone.

Startled that her team would barge in when she was on the phone, Jillian turned, surprised, and just as she was about to say something, she saw the look on Stephen's face. "I'm going to have to call you back," she said, and without waiting for an answer, she hung up the phone.

"He was right in front of us the whole time."

Jillian's face hardened. "Who?"

"Nicolas Fendby."

Kara glanced at Jillian and then back to Listun, "The clerk at the Crown Court?"

"I wasn't sure at first. His standard of living didn't seem to fit much with a clerk, but it wasn't extravagant. A nicer flat than you'd expect, a newer car, but nothing ostentatious."

Jillian motioned him to hurry, waving her hand in a circle.

"I checked his records against the other victims' timelines. Each time, he had infusions of cash into his bank account."

"So," Jillian said, "he somehow gets the victims to give him money and when he's done, he kills them?"

"The thing is, boss," Listun said, "there are other infusions that don't match anything with the victims we know about."

Kara caught his meaning. "So, there may be others."

Jillian added, "Presumably still alive, or they would have fit into your search, Kara."

"One more thing," Listun said. "I left a message for the Crown Court. They just called. Fendby took a week off, rather last minute. He was due back at work yesterday. He didn't show."

The trio stood pondering for a moment. Jillian was chewing her bottom lip. Listun was shifting from foot to foot nervously. Kara was tapping the end of her pen on her lips.

Jillian, staring down at the carpet, was more thinking out loud than talking to her team. "He's running."

Kara started nodding.

Listun sighed loudly.

Looking up, Jillian said, "Check his passport, and Alison's. See if they've left the country."

Five minutes later, Kara called out, "Alison Blistoke just cleared customs pre-check at the dock in Poole. She's booked on Brittany Ferries; it departs in fifty-five minutes."

DS Listun took a police car, lights and siren blazing, and still he had to try to keep up with Scotte, who was driving like she was in the Grand Prix. To the average Englishman watching, it might have looked like a car chase.

The ferry dock came into sight intermittently between buildings as the car raced toward it. Detective Inspector Jillian Scotte drove like a woman possessed. DC Kara Devanor had her right arm fully extended against the dash and her left holding on to the "oh shit" handle above the door as the car careened around a corner, narrowly missing the oncoming lorry. The driver blared his horn angrily.

As the dock finally came into view, it was clear that they weren't going to make it in time.

CHAPTER 14

The parking lot, though full earlier, was now mostly empty, as everyone had already boarded the ferry. This didn't help the anxiety DC Kara Devanor felt as DI Scotte drove down the main row of cars, going faster than she had entered, which was saying something.

Kara bit her tongue, afraid that anything she said would disturb Jillian's concentration as they sped ever faster toward the ferry that lay ahead. Somewhere behind her, DS Listun was either following like a madman or had slowed down to a more reasonable speed.

Somehow, they got through the lot without hitting anyone, and just when Kara thought Jillian might attempt crashing through the wire barrier that closed off car access to the boat, which was already churning water from its powerful engines, she slammed on the brakes, snaking the car at an angle.

With barely time to grab the keys from the ignition, Jillian erupted out of the car. Kara, who was barely a half step behind her, suddenly realized that Listun's car had also skidded to a halt, and he too was running for the boat.

The dock attendant, in his Brittany Ferries uniform and a bright orange vest, tried to tell them they couldn't cross the barrier, but it was ignored.

With the boat just pulling away from the dock and without a word spoken between them, the trio of VCU detectives jumped.

They landed hard, each rolling on the metal loading ramp for the vehicles crossing the Channel. Another uniformed man approached; the lower deck attendant. He was looking cross and opening his mouth to begin a blistering tirade when Jillian showed him her warrant card.

Standing up and brushing off dirt and grease as best she could, she turned to Listun, ignoring the protestations of the crew member. "Get up to the bridge or whatever it's called. Get the damn captain to turn this bloody boat around. If he declines, tell him we'll arrest him for obstruction of the police under section 89 of the Police Act of 1996."

DI Scotte was definitely not in a good mood. On the Grand Prix drive over, Kara had called the ferry company, instructing them not to let the boat leave the dock, only to be told that without a warrant they would do no such thing. When she'd explained the situation, they had met her with even more resistance. They claimed that just because she said she was a police officer, they couldn't take her word for it.

The frustration from the call had made Jillian angrier and pushed her to drive faster. Now, on the boat, she was looking for anyone to get in her way as an excuse to vent her frustration.

The crew member, sensing this, wisely stepped aside as she and Kara walked toward the rows of parked cars in the bottom of the ferry. Listun made for the nearest stairwell, heading upward.

Jillian and Kara split up, walking down the rows of cars looking for Nicolas Fendby. Very few of the cars had occupants, with most opting to ride in the relative comfort of the boat with its bar and café service.

Satisfied that he wasn't in a car, they headed up to the main deck.

The boat, at full capacity, could hold nearly nine hundred passengers, and while it didn't appear to be a sold-out voyage, there were still plenty of people about. Catching a crew member, Kara flashed her warrant card and asked for a list of the reserved berths or lounge seats.

Jillian raised an eyebrow, to which Kara responded, "Had an ex who took me to Paris one weekend on one of these."

The crew member led them to a small purser's office, where they scanned the offered screen for either Blistoke or Fendby, but neither name appeared.

"Let's check the bars and café," Jillian said.

The aft bar was crowded, but there was no sign of either Fendby or Blistoke. As they were making their way toward the café, Jillian stopped. Kara, turning back, saw that Jillian was staring out one of the windows at the deck. There stood Fendby with a young woman, both leaning on the railing, looking out as the boat made its way around Brownsea Island and toward the Channel.

Making eye contact, Jillian indicated for Kara to approach from one end while she took the other.

They looked at each other as they approached. It was windy on deck, so there was little use in being quiet. Kara was approaching from Alison Blistoke's side and Jillian from Nicolas Fendby's side.

When they were within fifteen feet of him, Fendby turned his head casually, just looking around. Sensing someone walking on the deck, he half turned his upper body and made eye contact with Jillian.

His eyes grew large, and he immediately turned, grabbing Alison's shoulder to move in the opposite direction, only to see Kara approaching.

"Dad," Alison said, looking alarmed at Kara's approach. "What's wrong? Who is she?"

Jillian held up her warrant card and said, loud enough for both to hear, "Alison, my name is DI Scotte, with the Metropolitan Police."

Alison Blistoke turned and looked at her, a frown appearing on her face. Fendby looked like he was watching a ping-pong match, turning from one copper to the other, his eyes wild.

"His name is Nicolas Fendby, and he is not your dad," Jillian said, stopping ten feet from the pair. Kara did the same, effectively blocking them.

Fendby suddenly grabbed Alison and made her a shield; his arm was wrapped around her throat, lifting her smaller body up and back toward him. "Don't come any closer, or I'll break her neck."

Kara, taking her extendable baton from her purse, snapped it hard and fast so that it extended. Her eyes told Fendby all he needed to know about her intentions.

"Don't come near me!" he cried, "or I swear I'll kill her."

"Like you tried to kill me?" Kara answered coldly, taking a step toward him.

His back against the railing now, he started inching toward Jillian, who had no weapon.

"Back!" he shouted. Jillian, her hands raised, palms facing out, slowly backed up. She wasn't too worried about moving with him; he had nowhere to go. Her biggest concern was getting the girl away from him.

"What are you going to do, Nicolas?" she asked as casually as she could.

Alison tried to speak, but he was already half choking her, and all she could do was claw at his forearms, which pressed against her airway as he dragged her along.

Jillian had no intention of letting him into the main compartment, where the presence of many more passengers would complicate things further.

As she backed up, she came to stand in front of the door into the main cabin area, forcing him to continue further down the deck. Now, Kara and Jillian were together, forcing him to walk backward, pulling Alison with him.

If he let her go, he could run, but to where? They could see him processing his options as he constantly looked around.

As he passed the overhang on the back of the boat, which held the upper deck observation point, another crew member appeared and asked what was going on. Jillian told him to step back, which he dutifully did when he saw her warrant card.

Suddenly, a shadow flashed. DS Listun, at a full run, crashed into Fendby, sending him, Alison, and himself across the deck with a crash.

The force of the tackle caused Fendby to let go of Alison. As Listun tried to grapple with Fendby, Alison began crab-crawling away from the two fighting men. Kara grabbed her and pulled her to a safe distance.

Jillian watched as Listun and Fendby wrestled. Listun, trained and in shape, was getting the better of him, but Fendby wasn't giving up without a fight.

Jillian turned and motioned for Kara to throw her the baton. Swinging her arm, Kara tossed the extended police-issue black baton to Jillian, who caught it and turned, now armed, back to the fight.

Fendby, gaining a moment's advantage, shoved Listun hard against the railing. Now standing between Listun and Scotte, Fendby turned and their eyes locked. Jillian saw her opening and raised her arm. With the baton fully extended, even across the feet that separated them, she knew she could cause some damage to his legs and immobilize him.

Just as she was about to swing, Fendby turned.

He didn't try to run away; instead, he charged Listun, who was coming off the rail. Powered by fear, he careened into DS Listun and the two of them toppled over the rail, falling headfirst, into the water far below.

Jillian ran to the railing screaming, but the boat was moving too fast, and she knew they were already several feet past them now.

The crew member who had stepped back earlier saw them go over and immediately ran to an emergency box, yanking it open and pulling down the handle. A siren began wailing as Kara and Jillian stood helplessly looking over the railing into the dark churning water below.

CHAPTER 15
(EPILOGUE)

Breakfast in bed. It felt like such a luxury. The room had the requisite view of Regents Park, London, and Daniella had gotten up from the warm confines of the king-sized hotel bed, a dark brown four poster with an overstuffed white down comforter, to let the hotel attendant in.

Now Jillian and Daniella, swathed in their warm, fluffy white robes bearing the hotel emblem, were seated at the large window with a view, eating a beautifully prepared English breakfast and toasting with orange juice in champagne flutes.

They had spent the weekend house hunting in the south of England and had made an offer on a cottage that was both inviting, cozy, and modern all at the same time. In other words, perfect.

Jillian had a meeting in London, so Daniella had called in sick to her course; they were covering a section on rural mortality statistics, something she knew more about than most, so she could easily miss a day.

After they finished nibbling on breakfast, they sat back and looked out over the park.

"When is your meeting?" Daniella asked.

"Half-past twelve. Why?"

"No reason, just wondered what the morning might look like."

Jillian stood up, pushing her chair back. As Daniella looked over at her, Jillian let her robe drop to the floor and began walking back to the bed. "I thought it might look something like this," she said, looking back over her shoulder.

A few hours later, both robes were on the floor, and both women were dressed and freshly showered, strolling arm in arm out of the hotel lobby. After walking around London just looking at random shops, giggling, and enjoying some downtime, Jillian finally steered them to the small restaurant where she was to have her meeting.

After she and Daniella agreed to meet up later at a museum, Jillian entered the restaurant, coming full circle to where this had all started.

As before, Superintendent Maryanne Sanderson arrived late. "I'm so sorry I'm late again, it's been quite the busy morning."

Jillian had no qualms with the fact that, in her current role at New Scotland Yard, Superintendent Sanderson had very little time to get out of the office on any given day. That she would take what little time she had to have lunch with Jillian was not lost on her.

They ordered their food, and Sanderson wasted no time. "Fill me in on the Lessings case."

Jillian sat back, tented her fingers under her chin, and thought about where to begin.

After a few moments' pause, she said, "DC Devanor and I never expected him to charge DS Listun the way he did." Jillian was looking a little off into the distance, remembering that moment.

"When they went over the railing, I thought I'd never forgive myself." A thin smile flitted across her face. "Who knew Stephen Listun liked to scuba dive on his holidays?

"Still," she said, "it was quite a long drop into the water and the temperature wasn't too much above freezing. I have to credit Brittany Ferries though; they did a marvelous job. Whatever they do to practice for someone going overboard, it works. I don't think Listun was in the water for more than three or four minutes before they had him out."

Sanderson, who had been nodding this whole time, said, "There wasn't a single sighting of Fendby?"

"No," Jillian said wistfully. "Half the damn boat was looking over the railing by the end of it and no one saw anything. Stephen reckons that when Fendby hit the water, it must have knocked him unconscious. He said the impact of the fall and the cold were quite jarring to him, and had it not been for his proficiency at swimming and diving, he's not sure he could have made it back to the surface the way he did."

"When did they find the body?" Sanderson asked.

"Two days later," Jillian answered. "Well, almost three, really. He washed up on the Sandbank," she said, referring to the small peninsula at the mouth of Poole Harbour in Dorset.

Sanderson nodded for Jillian to continue.

"From what we've been able to piece together from Alison Blistoke, as well as another girl we got a hold of . . ."

"That's what that article in the Daily Coast was about?" Sanderson asked, interrupting.

"Yes. We asked them to help us in our search for other victims, and they agreed."

"Mmm," Sanderson said wearily. "Be careful there. The press can turn on you in a minute."

Jillian nodded solemnly. "Anyway, it seems that for Fendby it was all about the money. He used his position to target vulnerable adoptees who were just coming of age, pretending to be their biological father. He even managed to fake DNA matches. Apparently, he was quite handy with computer graphics design and mocked up a rather official-looking set of documents based on a match an actual bio parent had gotten with an adopted son. He just kept changing the names and would send them as though they were the actual results."

Jillian took a sip of water before continuing, "He mostly targeted those he thought could get money from their adoption parents under the guise that he had spent all his money looking for them for the last fifteen years, and wouldn't it be lovely if they could go away together and make up for lost time?"

"So, what happened with Victoria Lessings and the other two girls?" Sanderson asked.

"No way to know, really," Jillian answered, then holding up a finger to mark each point, she said, "More than likely they either couldn't or wouldn't get him the money he wanted, got to the end of the amount of money they could or were willing to get, or,"—she held up her third finger—"they found out about his not being their biological father."

Sanderson took in all the information, asked more questions as they ate their meals, and eventually, after paying the bill, said, "There's something I want to talk to you about, but not here."

As the two women got up and began gathering their things, Sanderson said, "Oh, so what was it with Fendby and his penchant for victims drowning in water?"

"Another mystery of sorts," Jillian said.

"Of sorts?"

"Yes, well, Kara did some digging. As it happens, Fendby's parents died when their car crashed into a river, and they drowned."

Sanderson frowned.

"The newspaper clipping from the following morning talks about the son surviving the accident." Jillian left the statement hanging.

Sanderson stopped walking, turned sideways, and looked at Jillian. "You think he killed his parents?"

Jillian raised her eyebrows but said nothing.

As they walked down the stairs to the entrance of the restaurant, there was a small sitting room off to the side.

Maryanne turned to Jillian and, opening the door, said, "Let's just step in here."

The room was small, with just a few benches along the edge, and a coffee table with some magazines laid out tastefully. A man in a dark gray suit was sitting just to the right by the door.

"Ah, good, you're here," Sanderson said.

The man got up. "Superintendent," he said, shaking her hand.

"Chief Inspector Dobson, meet Detective Inspector Scotte," Sanderson said.

Jillian shook the man's hand, wondering who he was, and why they were all here.

Maryanne waved for everyone to sit down. "Jillian," she began, "Inspector Dobson is with SCD9. They've been working on something that has moved into your neck of the woods."

Jillian's interest was piqued.

Maryanne continued. "Alan is going to be working part time in the VCU for two reasons." At this, she leaned forward, her elbows resting on her knees as she looked Jillian directly in the eye. "I know you've been reticent to tell me about how DCI Walford's been treating you and your team."

Jillian bristled a little. How did Sanderson know about Walford?

"What you don't know," Sanderson said, "is that Walford was an old school chum of Paul Davies. They went back a long time."

Jillian was taken aback by the news, but recovered quickly. "Surely he can't blame *me* for what Davies did?"

Sanderson just shook her head. "Alan will keep Walford in line, that's number one. Number two has to do with a video I'm going to show you. I want SCD9 and the VCU to team up on this, but I'm going to warn you, this is not pleasant to watch. It's actually the very antithesis of pleasant. I'll let Alan explain the rest after you see it."

With that, she took out her smartphone, and readying the video, handed it to Jillian.

Jillian hit play and began to watch.

LIGHTS,
CAMERA,
MURDER

CHAPTER 1

Detective Inspector Jillian Scotte wrapped the quilt around her like a second skin. It was late, or early, depending on your perspective. She was sitting by the window in her flat, admiring the patchwork quilt—imperfect in its handmade style but perfect for keeping her warm.

As she looked out at the rare cloudless night, she hugged herself tight with the soft, worn fabric. She remembered when she'd been given the quilt by a young twenty-something woman living in a shelter.

Jillian had possibly saved the woman's life and gotten her into a place that gave her a chance to live life on her terms. In gratitude, and as part of the "crafting" the shelter required of its occupants, the young woman had made the imperfect quilt for Jillian. It wasn't much to look at, but the colors were vibrant, and the batting had been overly done, making it warmer than it ought to be.

Jillian had spent many a night curled up in her quilt, and tonight looked to be another one.

Daniella had gone back to the University of Surrey to finish her final few weeks, and Jillian felt alone already, even though she knew soon they would be moving into their small cottage together.

If she was honest with herself, she knew she was a little anxious about this step. At the same time, it felt right. For the first time in a long time, something in her life seemed right, and she was damned if she was going to let it pass her by because she feared what might or might not be.

That anxiety, however, wasn't what had her wrapped up in her favorite quilt blanket, sipping a glass of wine in the early hours just past midnight.

The video.

She just couldn't get it out of her head.

She'd only watched the first few minutes in that vestibule with Superintendent Sanderson and Chief Inspector Dobson. Those first few minutes had been enough.

The video began with a woman sitting in a straight-back chair. She was firmly restrained; her legs bound tightly with large plastic zip ties just below the knees and again at the ankles. Her arms, held behind her out of camera view, were likely bound similarly because she clearly couldn't move despite the look of terror on her face.

There was no mistaking that look. Her eyes were wide with a fear, so primal that *terror* was the only word for it. She was gagged, so there were only muffled cries, but that wasn't what shocked Jillian. It was the contraption on her head. Some type of metal, double-ringed brace that clearly kept her head from moving.

The room was dark save for a light source out of view that illuminated the woman.

Jillian couldn't help but notice that she was pleasing to look at.

That was when the black-clad figure moved into view—dressed in nondescript black pants, a black long-sleeved jumper, and a black balaclava.

There was no warning. No preamble. He wielded a hammer, and kneeling by her feet, he began smashing her toes. One after the other, neither rushing nor waiting, just one toe, then the next, and the next. Once he finished one foot, he moved to the other with the same result.

The scream that issued from her mouth, despite the gag, was haunting.

The man—for the build, despite the black clothes, suggested a man—moved off camera.

The woman, tears streaming down her face, was gasping for air, and just as she recovered some semblance of normal breathing, her eyes went wide again as the man reappeared, this time with a sledgehammer.

Again without warning, he heaved the hammer out, then, with a sickening crack, he swung it round until it connected with her ankle. The bone shattered visibly, leaving her foot at an odd angle. He repeated it with the other side.

The woman was clearly in great distress.

He gave her no respite.

Looking back at the camera, he changed positions, so he was now perpendicular to her. Swinging the sledgehammer back toward the camera, he took a step toward her, leveraging his body as the hammer connected with her kneecap, almost knocking her entire body over.

The scream she emitted was long, sustained, and primal, in both volume and anguish. Before the man in black could connect with the other knee, the woman had already passed out from pain.

Sanderson had stopped the video at that point. Looking up at Jillian with disgust, Maryanne said, "He keeps going."

As Jillian tried to absorb what that might mean, Maryanne said something that made her blood run cold. "It gets worse."

Jillian had told Daniella about it, and they had done their best to shut it out for the rest of the day and night until Daniella left to drive back to her class.

That was when Jillian watched the rest.

The video would cut to the woman waking up in pain, and as soon as she did, the men in black would continue. And it was men, not man. There were two of them. Dressed similarly, but different in build.

The things they did would give Jillian nightmares later that night. The cutting off of each finger, not at the base, but just the first knuckle, one by one. They had turned the chair around so the camera could capture it. The burns, cuts, and mutilations they inflicted were things Jillian had never imagined.

It had all been done from the bottom up. When the woman would once again become unconscious from pain, the video would stop. In between, there would be just enough first aid to keep her alive. They always left her face intact for the next "session," when she would awake to the hell she was being subjected to.

The purpose of the contraption on her head was finally made clear when they drilled into her teeth. Not to extract them, simply to cause pain.

What they did at the end with the sledgehammer to her nearly lifeless head had been almost too much to bear, and yet Jillian watched to the very end. She forced herself, despite repeated trips to the loo to wretch. She watched because somehow, some way, she would avenge this poor woman's brutalization. Whatever the reason or justification, no human being deserved what she had endured.

For two days, Jillian felt in a fog, with the images of the video replaying in her mind. Tonight, that was changing. Her mind was shifting from being repulsed at the horror she had witnessed to what she was exceptionally good at—detecting.

The conversation between the three of them in the vestibule, brief though it had been, had centered on what they thought was the purpose of the video. It had been posted on a dark web server and then taken down within hours, but not before it had been watched hundreds of times.

As Jillian sat in her quilt sipping wine, she evaluated the "why." Two things were obvious to her. The first was that this was a message being sent by someone (or multiple someones). The second was that the two men in black had not simply done what they'd done to send the message, whether or not they were its originators. They had enjoyed what they had done. It was simply too over the top for just a message.

The next morning, Jillian woke to a text message from Amelia Hamza—journalist for the Daily Coast. Amelia wanted to meet for coffee before Jillian went in to work.

Jillian walked into the café and saw Amelia already sitting with a cup of tea at a table by the window. Amelia, with her jet-black hair straight down to her shoulders, looked up and half smiled as she saw Jillian approach.

There was something odd about the greeting that Jillian couldn't put her finger on.

After getting her mocha order in, Jillian walked over and sat down. "What's up?"

Amelia looked up with her green eyes and stared directly into Jillian's. "Do you know who Greg Slater is?"

Jillian shook her head. "Why? Should I?"

Amelia laughed a humorless laugh. Looking down briefly at her coffee, then back up, she added, "He runs all the gambling south of London."

Jillian raised an eyebrow. "Mob?"

Amelia nodded.

"What about him?"

Amelia took a deep breath. "He wants to talk to you."

That set Jillian back in her chair. She was saved from having to answer immediately by the arrival of her coffee, which she took a small sip from. Looking over the rim of her cup, she said, "Did you give him my number?"

Amelia shook her head. "He wants a tête-à-tête."

Jillian didn't know what to say, so she said nothing, looking into Amelia's eyes.

Amelia now looked a little annoyed. "He said I should tell you something that he was sure would make you want to meet with him."

That made Jillian smile. "Really? And what was that?"

Amelia's answer wiped the smile off Jillian's face. "He said to tell you it was about the video."

CHAPTER 2

"The rooftop."

Jillian sat with her mouth visibly open, looking across the table at Amelia Hamza. If the shock of what this Greg Slater had instructed Amelia to tell her wasn't enough, the follow-up had been just as much of a surprise.

"What. Here? Now?" Jillian said. She hadn't even been aware that the café had a rooftop.

"Yes."

Jillian looked at her watch. There was nothing on her schedule that couldn't be moved. She was just stalling for time, knowing that Amelia was studying her reaction.

"Want to share what this *video* is all about?" Amelia asked, using air quotes around the word.

Thank God she doesn't know, thought Jillian. She just smiled and stood up. Instead of a direct answer, she simply said, "I'll let you know." Walking to the back of the small café, she saw a door that said simply "UP." Upon opening it, she found herself in a narrow staircase built wide enough for just one person. She briefly wondered as she climbed how on earth the café servers carried trays of food up this tiny flight of stairs?

Another door greeted her at the top, and when she opened it, she found herself outside on the roof.

In contrast to the traditional café tables and chairs downstairs, the rooftop had a very modern look. Large slabs of cement had been laid, and upon them sat some of the modern outdoor furniture typically found in hotels.

Across the roof from the door she had just come through sat a man on a small sofa, looking out over the city.

Standing before her, however, was a man roughly her age, his feet shoulder-width apart, with well-shined black loafers. His gray suit was immaculately pressed, with a sharp crease in the trousers. He wore a green shirt with a maroon tie. His dark brown hair was perfectly cut and his face cleanly shaved. His blue eyes shone with a disarming brilliance as he smiled at her.

"Hello. DI Scotte, I presume?" He was English, his accent not quite discernible, though if Jillian had to bet on it, she would have placed him from Manchester. She nodded slightly.

With his hands folded respectfully in front of him, he said, "My name is Sebastian. Mr. Slater asks that I check you before your meeting."

Jillian cocked her head slightly. "Seeing as I had no idea I'd be meeting with Mr. Slater until a minute ago, I'm hardly likely to have a wire on now, am I?"

Sebastian just stood in front of her, unmoving. His smile still comfortably in place, he continued staring straight at her. As far as Jillian could discern, his expression hadn't changed, but somehow, it had. There was something resolute in his eyes.

Sighing loudly, she put her purse on the ground and raised her arms out from her sides.

She could smell a slight hint of cologne as Sebastian slowly approached her. His movements were very precise and very respectful. He didn't touch her anywhere he didn't have to. He opened each side of her suit jacket. After checking both arms, he gently pushed them down, then stepped to her side and lightly placed a hand on the small of her back and her abdomen.

When he was finished, he stepped back in front of her. "Thank you," he said. Somehow there was both a kindness and hardness in his tone. Jillian had never encountered someone so full of contradictions and yet so self-contained.

"If you would please open your purse for me and place your cell phone on that table there," he said, indicating a tall two-seat table in front of a small bar.

She opened her purse and he glanced inside, but touched nothing.

She locked her phone and placed it face down on the corner of the table. Sebastian then motioned for her to follow him and walked to the man seated on the sofa.

Greg Slater stood up as they approache. He turned and extended his hand to Jillian. "Inspector Scotte," he said with a hard Irish accent. "It's a pleasure to meet you."

Greg Slater was a big man. Not a tall man; he was thick. More solid than fat, it seemed to Jillian. His large hand had an extremely strong grip, and it took a bit of effort for Jillian not to wince.

"Thank you, Sebastian," he said, turning to his associate. "Please thank Ms. Hamza for me and wait downstairs."

Sebastian nodded, then turning to Jillian, he dipped his head. "Inspector," he said as he passed her.

"Please, sit," Slater said. "Can I get you another coffee? Something stronger?"

"No, thank you." Taking a seat on one of the chairs perpendicular to the sofa, she added, "Ms. Hamza certainly knew how to get my attention to take this meeting."

Slater was dressed in a dark blue suit with an open-necked white shirt, and though not disheveled in any sense, somehow he didn't pull off the same smart look that Sebastian had. He leaned back into the sofa cushions. "Yes," he said, smiling slightly. It was not a good look. His head seemed to sit directly on his shoulders, or perhaps because his neck was as thick as his head, it just seemed that way. "The video. Not quite cinema material, is it?"

Jillian was tiring of waiting. "Would you like to tell me what you know about it? And perhaps how you know that I've seen it?"

Slater laughed again, without humor. "Where would be the fun in that, Inspector?" Crossing one leg over the other, he reached down and adjusted his trouser leg. "Let's just say I like to stay apprised of what goes on around here."

Before Jillian could say anything, Slater continued, "I can, however, help you with one facet of the video."

It was Jillian's turn to sit back and cross her legs, noticing that Slater looked down at them as she did so before looking back up at her. He did not try to hide it; he took his time. It made the hair on the back of Jillian's neck stand up, but she tried to remain impassive. "And what is that, exactly?"

Slater gazed at her, his eyes boring into hers as if searching for something. Then he said, "I can tell you who the girl was."

Jillian now stared back at him. Trying to keep her eyes from showing any surprise. Blinking only once, then forcing herself to keep them open, despite the sun rising over the city and reflecting off some of the neighboring buildings at her.

She waited a full minute as Slater slightly cocked his head, clearly having expected some kind of response. Finally, Jillian said, "Tell me, Mr. Slater, why I shouldn't have you arrested or at the very least brought in for questioning on this matter?"

He held up his hands, palms facing up. "On what grounds, Inspector?"

Again, Jillian paused, though only slightly. "How is it you know this woman, Mr. Slater, and why would you be willing to tell me about her if you are not somehow involved?"

Slater sighed loudly, dropping his hands onto his lap. "Inspector Scotte," he said, as though he were a teacher talking to a student, "I am in the financial business . . ."

"You mean gambling," Jillian corrected.

Skipping half a beat, Slater went on. "I run a rather large organization that deals in personal and professional loans, as well as the legal, time-honored British tradition of laying wagers on all manner of activities , from sports to games and now to online video games, if you can believe it."

Jillian simply looked at him with one eyebrow raised.

"I have been in business for quite some time," he continued, "and in all that time, I have never ventured into the . . . shall we say . . . oldest profession as a means of income." He paused to ensure that Jillian was following him, which she was. "I have a modest but reasonable income, Ms. Scotte, and I see no need to fall afoul of the law by risking it on such activities."

Jillian nodded, more to keep him talking than for any specific agreement with what he was saying.

"In my line of work, however, one must keep oneself apprised of other enterprises that may or may not cross my business, whether geographically or otherwise. In any event," he said, reaching into the inner pocket of his suit jacket and pulling out a folded sheet of paper, "this is the name of the unfortunate lady in the video." He slid the paper over to her on the glass coffee table between them.

Picking up the paper, Jillian unfolded it. It was typed with only a first and last name. Petra Solanshtok. "Why tell me?" she asked again.

Slater held up his hands again. "I'm just doing my duty as a British citizen." Somehow, with his thick Irish accent, although he pronounced the words correctly, it sounded wrong.

"The thing is, Inspector," he said. His face, no longer jovial, had turned serious. "I do not meddle in the business of others. What they choose to do for income and how they do it is of no concern to me. Tarts have always been a part of life and always will be."

His eyes had become cold, and there was something behind them that Jillian couldn't quite place, but she suspected there was not a lot of truth in these words and that he very much made the business of others his business.

"I'm sure you're aware of the various gangs and organizations who dabble in the prostitution and drug trades in this area."

Jillian made no movement or sound one way or the other.

"Drugs are a nasty business and again, not something I involve myself in. As long as they leave my business alone, I have no need to . . . shall we say . . . take an interest in . . . theirs."

The way he said it and the tone of his voice made Jillian shiver.

"However," he said, looking down at his feet for a moment before looking back up at Jillian. "There has been a new . . ." He searched for the right word for a moment. "Player, on the scene. He is a man, I believe, from Poland or some such place."

Slater rubbed his hands together as though he were cold. "His name is Parav. Lomax Parav."

Jillian waited for him to continue, but he didn't. "How is this Mr. Parav connected to the girl? Is he moving in on the prostitution trade in Southern England?"

His accent thicker than ever, Slater said, "I couldn't tell ya." Then his face got that look again, hard and cold. "What I can tell ya is that he specializes in human trafficking, and this Petra was one of his."

***

Jillian grabbed her phone without breaking stride and headed down the narrow stairs. She had been polite with Slater, saying she was late for a meeting. He hadn't objected and said he hoped they could meet again sometime.

Jillian wouldn't mind never meeting him again unless he was behind bars or she had armed protection with her. Which was the thought she had in her head as she passed through the door at the bottom of the stairs and once again found Sebastian standing there. He was at the corner of the café counter, sipping coffee.

He nodded and raised his cup slightly at her. Despite herself, Jillian felt a hint of a smile cross her lips. Cursing herself, she walked past him but then stopped and turned around abruptly.

Thinking about how she wanted to say it, she said, "Do I just call you Sebastian, like Madonna or Seal, or do you have a full name?"

He was holding the coffee cup just in front of his lips, so she could only see his eyes. Though deep blue, there was something behind them that could have been a smile, though whether one of amusement or that of a shark, she couldn't tell . Without lowering the cup, he said, "Sebastian Hughes."

Jillian got into her car, hit speed dial on her phone, and, as she pulled away from the curb, said, "Kara, it's me. I want you to find out everything you can about Greg Slater and a Lomax Parav."

She had to spell the name as best as she could guess for Kara, then added, "And while you're at it, add Sebastian Hughes to the list as well."

CHAPTER 3

Homemade bread greeted Jillian as she stepped into the kitchen of the team's headquarters. The Tof occupied an old, abandoned factory that had been refurbished for them.

It was some kind of walnut banana bread with raisins by the look of it, and given the state of her nerves, Jillian cut herself a slice and ate it on the way to her desk. She greeted a few members of the team and, with her mouth full, asked DS Listun to assemble everyone in the incident room in five minutes.

Walking up to the whiteboard, Jillian wrote three names, one at the top and two below it: The first was "Petra Solanshtok," then below she wrote "Lomax Parav—Human Trafficking" and "Greg Slater—Gambling."

"Right," she said, turning to her team. "Here's where we start." Pointing her marker at Parav's name, she continued, "We have reason to believe that our victim was tied to this Parav." Nodding to Stacey Alston, one of the unit's admins, she said, "Stacey, I want you to do a full workup on Parav, whatever we can find."

Alston nodded and began making notes on her iPad.

Next, Jillian spoke to PC Stella Dawson. "Stella, I want you to see what we can find out about . . ." At that point, Jillian noticed Chief Inspector Alan Dobson walking into the unit. While not a complete surprise, it was the person tagging along with him that caused Jillian to pause.

It was a roguish gent in faded jeans, a sweater, and a windbreaker, with dark curly hair and a swagger that followed him wherever he went: Detective Sergeant Rob Milston.

The pair approached the incident room. Dobson, in a suit rather than in uniform, walked in and looked around. Milston just leaned against the doorframe.

"Ladies and gentlemen," Jillian said, "meet Chief Inspector Dobson of SCD9. We'll be working closely with his team on this case."

Dobson looked around, nodding his head slightly.

"And that refuse he dragged in here with him," Jillian said, nodding at the man leaning in the doorway, "is Detective Sergeant Milston, also of SCD9, though he'll have to do something about his god-awful Cockney accent if he wants to blend in down here."

Milston didn't move, just grinned as he looked straight at Jillian.

Dobson looked from Jillian to Milston and back. "You two know each other?"

"I taught her everything she knows," Milston said in a low, deep voice, still grinning from ear to ear.

"Mostly how to lose at chess," Jillian quipped without missing a beat. That prompted a genuine laugh from Milston.

DCI Dobson said, "Please continue, don't let us stop you."

"Yes sir," Jillian said, then, pausing to remember where she'd been, she turned back to Stella. "As I was saying, PC Dawson, look into our victim, see what you can find out on the street."

Dobson looked up at the board. "Is that the name of the victim? Christ, that didn't take you long." He seemed genuinely surprised.

Jillian wasn't about to tell him where she got the information. Milston just looked over at his boss and in a conspiratorial tone said, "Told ya."

The rest of the meeting was perfunctory, and soon Dobson, Milston, and Jillian were headed into her office.

Kara caught up to them and punched Milston on the arm. "I see they've let you out of London then, or did you do something to deserve it?"

Milston turned and smiled. "Hey you." Then, flashing his boyish grin, he said, "Either way, would have been worth it just to come down here and see you two again."

As Kara returned to her desk, Listun said, "You know them as well? Who else knows those two?"

Kara smiled to herself, sitting down. "I only know the sergeant, never met the DCI before."

After a few minutes, Jillian called both Stephen and Kara into her office.

Following the introductions, she filled everyone in on what they knew so far, which wasn't much. Jillian asked, "What does SCD9 know about this Lomax Parav?" She was mostly talking to DS Milston.

Milston took a seat in one of the chairs across from her desk and said, "We know of him, but very little. We don't even have a photo."

Dobson chimed in. "He came on the scene just about two years ago. He took over the human trafficking scene here, consolidating warring factions, but no one seems to know much about him. We're not even sure it's his real name."

"How can he be that big of a presence and not be seen?" Jillian asked.

"Part of 'is charm, love," Milston said, his accent sneaking back, "'E's somewhat of an enigma. Makes 'im sort of folklore, don' it?"

"Told you you'd better watch that accent if you're going to work cover down here, Rob," Jillian said seriously, and Dobson looked over at his sergeant with a look that suggested he'd said the same thing before.

"What?" Miston said, throwing up his hands, palms facing up. "She brings it outta me." Putting his hands back down, he said, "Besides, he doesn't need ta be seen. 'E's got a gorilla who does all 'is work for 'im. Goes by the name of Gorski."

Dobson and Milston eventually left. Kara and Listun were discussing next steps when Stacey Alston knocked on the door. "Mum, we have a possible address on Lomax Parav."

Now it was Jillian's turn to be impressed. "That was fast, Stacey."

"We got lucky, mum," she replied. "He made a donation to an MP's race last month."

Jillian wouldn't have thought to check there. A mental note she now filed away. "Well done," she said, meaning it.

"Kara. Work with the team and dig into those names. I want to know whatever we can about them," Jillian said. Then, nodding at her sergeant, she said, "Grab your coat. Let's pay this Lomax a visit."

As the pair were leaving her office, Jillian said, "Oh, who made the bread in the kitchen?"

Kara looked at Listun. Jillian stopped with her coat over her arm, eyeing him with skepticism. "Wife made it then?" she said with a deadpan face.

Listun managed to look hurt. "What? A bloke can't bake a loaf of bread?"

It was Kara's turn to appear skeptical, which she did exaggeratedly, cocking her head heavily to one side and putting an arm on her hip, looking right at him.

Listun looked from her to his boss. "All right, yeah, it was her."

The three managed a quick laugh, and then Kara said, "Well, if she wants to make any more now that she's home, tell her we'll gladly let her experiment on us."

"Hang on," Jillian said. "What do you mean *now that she's home?*" Looking at her sergeant, she asked worriedly, "What's happened?"

"Shit," Kara said. Ducking out quickly, she added to Listun, "Sorry."

DS Listun didn't look all that upset; if anything, he looked a little relieved. "Uhm . . ." he said, suddenly awkward, "We're uh . . . well she's . . . expecting like . . ."

Jillian, unable to control herself, threw her coat down on the chair and ran up to him, wrapping him in a hug. "Oh Stephen, that's wonderful news."

Listun didn't know quite what to do. He was half returning the hug when Jillian realized he probably didn't know her well enough or her him to have done it, but she wasn't going to apologize. "That really is great news. Congratulations. When is she due?"

"'Bout six months," he said sheepishly. "She's going to work part-time from home now, so that's why the bread-baking happened."

"Well, Kara's right. It's delicious." And with that, she and DS Listun headed out to the address of one Mr. Lomax Parav.

The address was a Russian tea shop, of all things, close to the docks in Hythe. As they walked in, there was an aroma of spice and a jingling of bells on the door. The shop was nearly deserted and had only two occupants. A man was sitting in a booth along one side reading a newspaper, and a woman stood behind a counter smoking a cigarette and looking at them through dark-lidded eyes.

Listun and Jillian flashed their warrant cards and asked if Mr. Parav was available. The woman simply stared at them, unblinking. Finally, she shook her head slowly, pursed her lips, and said, "No one here by dat name." Her accent was thickly Slavic.

Jillian looked around the room, then back at the woman. "This is the address Mr. Parav gave. Do you know when he'll be back?" The woman just shook her head and blew cigarette smoke from her mouth.

Listun said, "Maybe we can ask some of your customers if they know him? We can come back when there are . . ." He paused, then added, "More of them."

Suddenly, from a door at the back, there was a flush of a toilet, and a man walked out. He could barely fit through the doorway. He said something in Russian to the woman, who replied in kind. He walked up to Listun and got very close to his face. He was easily several inches taller and quite a bit bigger and stronger than Listun. "Marda tell you, there no one here by dat name. You go now."

His voice was not exactly threatening, but there was a finality to it, a command.

To his credit, Jillian thought, Listun didn't move. He didn't even flinch.

Jillian had her phone out and was working the screen with the thumb of the same hand, while with the other, she pulled her warrant card out of her purse and showed it to the enormous man. She said, "Does he come here often?" After a pause, she added, "Lomax Parav?"

The man turned around with his arms outstretched. "Lady. You see much peoples in dis place ?" Then, dropping his hands, he turned back around slowly. The look on his face was menacing.

Listun was looking hard at Jillian, but not because of the menacing look the man was giving her. It was before that. When the man had turned around and his back was toward them, he'd felt Jillian shiver.

As they climbed back into their car, Listun looked over at her before starting the ignition. "You okay, guv?"

Jillian just kept staring straight ahead through the windshield at the door to the tea house. Finally, without turning or looking at him, she said, "When he turned around, he was in shadow for a second."

Listun waited, saying nothing.

Then Jillian said, "He had the same silhouette as one of the men in black in the video."

CHAPTER 4

Horses—actually, they were ponies—were standing in the middle of the road. They were in the New Forest, where roughly five thousand or more ponies had the run of the place.

Jillian and Daniella sat in their car, smiling.

"They're lovely," Daniella said. Jillian agreed.

They needed a break from their crazy life. What with Daniella now in her final three weeks at "school," their move into their new cottage coming up at about the same time, and Jillian's workload, a trip to the New Forest was just what the doctor ordered.

Daniella had bought one of the guidebooks and was reading some of the history. "Did you know that the New Forest was formally designated by William the Conqueror in 1079? So that's what . . ." She half closed her eyes, trying to do the math. "It's almost nine hundred and fifty years old. Not so bloody new, is it?" Both women laughed.

As they watched a small group of ponies, eight of them, slowly moving off the road into the field beyond, Jillian was still marveling at something Daniella had said to her earlier.

"It's got one hundred and forty miles of cycle tracks in it." She'd looked over at Jillian with shock on her face. "If you set loose in here on your bike, I'll never see you again."

Jillian had assured her that wouldn't happen, but she couldn't help but feel the pull to get on her bike and come for a ride. Maybe next weekend she'd give it a go.

They drove for a while and then stopped at the Café Parisien for a cuppa and a quick bite to eat.

They spent a blissful day wandering around, shopping in the quaint villages, strolling hand in hand through the trails. The fresh air and silence, coupled with each other's company, was soothing to both of their souls.

They often walked without saying a word, just happy in each other's company. Other times they couldn't stop talking or giggling, even occasionally having to stop, bent over in laughter from something or other one of them said.

It wasn't until they were back in Jillian's apartment, having eaten, cleaned away the dishes, and started getting ready for bed, that work came up. Jillian was checking her emails, Daniella brushing her teeth.

From the bathroom, Daniella said, "So, you really think this bloke . . . the big one . . . the Russian. You think he's one of the men in the video?"

"Don't you?" Jillian asked, typing away on her laptop.

"Well, love," Daniella said, coming out of the bathroom in her terry robe with her hair still wet from a shower. She tried to dry it with a towel. "I didn't see him. I'll admit, the men in black did not look small, and certainly your description would fit, but . . ."

Jillian stopped typing and looked over at her. "I wish I could describe it, Dani," Jillian said, a far-off look in her eye as the memory came back. "It was something about the way he moved when he turned his back, or maybe the light . . . I don't know. But I swear to you, that was one of the men in that video."

Focusing her eyes back on the present, she looked straight at Daniella, who was standing next to her own side of the bed. "I just need to prove it." Then she shuddered again.

Daniella looked at her and said, "I'm sorry he made you feel that way."

Jillian smiled and reached out for a hand.

Daniella smiled back, but before she took the offered hand, she let her robe drop to the floor, quickly jumping into bed with nothing on. "I know how to warm you back up."

Jillian, never having lost her smile, replied, "Why do I suddenly feel overdressed?"

***

The next morning as the two readied to part for the week, Daniella stopped by the front door. "You know, I've been thinking about what you said about the video." Jillian stopped and looked at her. "About how you think they wore all black because they would just get rid of everything so there wouldn't be any evidence."

Jillian nodded.

"What about the shoes?"

Jillian frowned. "They were just trainers."

"They weren't black," Daniella pressed.

That made Jillian's head tilt slightly. "Meaning?"

"Meaning they weren't black, and they weren't cheap. They probably had other clothes on under the black, but they might not have had an extra pair of shoes."

"Yes . . ." Jillian said thoughtfully, trying to remember what shoes they were wearing, "But that is a popular type of shoe. They could just say anyone with the same size shoe could have been there."

Daniella had a look in her eyes that Jillian had seen before. A look that said there was more to it than what she'd said. Finally, giving her a quick kiss before heading out the door, Daniella said, "Yes, but with what they did to that poor woman, I'll bet my first paycheck from the job I don't have yet that some of her DNA made it onto those trainers, inside the back, down the laces, somewhere."

Jillian's first question when she made it in to the Tof was to Detective Sergeant Listun. "Stephen, what shoes was that rhinoceros wearing?"

That garnered a few looks from other members of the team, but Listun knew exactly who she meant. He thought for a minute, then said, "Trainers, I think—why, guv?"

Jillian just proceeded to her office. "I'll tell you later."

Later that morning, Jillian left for a small café a few blocks away that was beginning to become "their" meeting place, as it was the third time she had been there to meet the same person.

That person was Amelia Hamza, journalist. Jillian had a courteous, if not quite friendly, relationship with Amelia. One of cautious mutual respect.

She knew how to dig up and research stories, could write exceptionally well, and was good in front of her own camera, creating YouTube videos that she used to present her stories through the digital site.

Amelia had been texting ever since she'd introduced Jillian to the gambling mob boss, Greg Slater. *What video?* had been how most of her texts started. It was time to pay the piper, and Jillian had agreed to meet at the café where she'd met Greg Slater.

After the drinks were ordered, Amelia got straight to work. "So, a man like Slater wants to meet with you, and all it takes is mentioning that his request has something to do with a video and you didn't give it a second thought."

Jillian just looked back at the beautiful journalist with her straight black hair and bright green eyes.

After a moment of silence, Amelia said, "Are you going to tell me about this video or not?"

"Yes," Jillian said, wanting to make sure she had Amelia's attention. "But first, I want to know how you know Greg Slater."

Amelia half smiled and sat back in her chair as the server brought over their coffees. Stirring in some sugar, she looked over the cup at Jillian. "In my job, I sometimes have to make deals with people I'd rather not make deals with so that I can get the information I need to do my job."

Jillian knew there was an allusion to the deal she had with Amelia there, but she didn't think Amelia was actually hesitant about their relationship. Jillian was pretty sure that part of her comment was reserved solely for Slater.

"Do you have earphones on you?" Jillian asked.

Reaching into her purse, Amelia pulled out a pair of black, corded earphones.

"This is off the record. It has to be. You'll understand why."

Amelia nodded; their unspoken pact was part of what kept each of them tied to the other. Jillian plugged the earphones into her phone and cued up the video. It was only the first two minutes of it; she had expected this and wasn't about to show her all of it. Two minutes was more than enough.

Jillian watched the journalist's face. What began as her trademark hard stare turned curious, then at once repulsed. By the time the two minutes were up, she raised her gaze to Jillian, and the DI could see that she was fighting back the tears that were welling up in her eyes.

Taking her phone back and handing back the earphone plug, Jillian said nothing, giving Amelia a few minutes to compose herself.

When Amelia was ready, Jillian said, "We believe she was part of the recently resurrected human trafficking trade down here."

"Do you think Slater's involved?"

"I don't know," Jillian answered truthfully. "Doesn't seem his gambit, does it?"

"So why the meeting, then?"

That was the question, wasn't it? Jillian thought. "He wants to help?"

Amelia snorted, which made Jillian raise her eyebrows.

"Slater doesn't do anything that doesn't benefit Slater," Amelia said by way of an answer. She followed it up with, "Is there a body?"

Jillian shook her head. "What do you know about his bodyguard, Sebastian Hughes?"

Amelia got a strange look on her face, as though an icy shiver had just gone through her. "I know he's dangerous," she said with a stern look.

Jillian nodded in understanding.

"What else can you tell me about this? I assume the girl doesn't live . . ."

"How do you know that wasn't the end of the video?" Jillian asked.

Amelia just shook her head. "That was a warning for someone, maybe more than one someone. You don't record something like that and not finish making your point."

Jillian was quiet for a moment, then said, "No, she doesn't live."

"You're certain?"

"One hundred percent."

Amelia let out a long sigh, as though she'd been holding her breath.

"There's no story here," Jillian said, "yet."

Amelia simply pursed her lips, not wanting to acquiesce on that point just yet.

"But," Jillian said, setting the hook, "I can tell you the girl's name."

CHAPTER 5

Lights in the rain often look like a kaleidoscope, thought Detective Constable Kara Devanor as she shivered from the cold.

Not that it was a particularly cold night temperature-wise. It was that Kara wasn't wearing much. Her frizzy black hair had extra hair spray on it, making it the only part of her body that was decently covered. Her makeup was so overdone she almost looked like a drag queen.

She was wearing a tight leather miniskirt, emphasis on the mini, with a hot-pink, short-cut top that was one size too small. Her black skin gleamed in the reflection of neon lights that made up the part of Millbrook near the Western Docks. Her high-heeled shoes clicked loudly despite the falling rain.

She'd grabbed one of those cheap purse-sized umbrellas at a local Boots and purposefully broken one of the metal braces to give it a disheveled look, a decision she was now regretting as the rain came in at a slant and her legs below the skirt were getting soaked.

It was her fifth night out "on the street" and she was tired.

It was easy to put on a bored expression and walk drearily up and down the streets like a lost junkie or expectant prostitute. When the occasional punter would pull up and roll down a window, she just named a price no one would accept, and they drove off.

She wasn't here for them.

She was trying, desperately trying, to get information on their victim, not that anyone was talking.

She couldn't show Petra's photo around; they hadn't got one, and taking a still from the video was not a good idea. Besides, Jillian had said, it would make her look too much like a copper.

Instead, Kara, going by the name Cassie, was working a story about Petra owing her some money.

PC Dawson was her "chaperone" for this evening's stroll through scum town. Parked halfway down a side street in the middle of the grid Kara was working, Stella Dawson was in a disheveled old van, probably with a warm blanket pulled over her and a thermos full of coffee, listening to the rain hitting Kara's umbrella through a hidden microphone disguised as bling at the crux of her exposed bra.

***

Back at the Tof, Detective Inspector Jillian Scotte was working late. She didn't want to go back to her empty flat, and she was more than a little apprehensive about having Kara out on the street. Kara was a good copper, that much Jillian knew. She was also a young, attractive black woman walking in one of the most dangerous parts of Southampton.

Jillian tried to shake the nagging thoughts from her mind and concentrate on the pile of work on her desk. The truth was, she had far too much on her mind at present, and it wasn't just Kara walking the streets at night dressed up like a tart.

Reaching into her desk drawer, she grabbed two paracetamol tablets to help with the headache that was coming on. Jillian leaned back in her chair and turned around, facing out her window, her mind returning to earlier in the day.

***

Everyone was working in shifts now. Kara doing her nightwalking and requiring someone on scene for backup meant the team was half-staffed in the morning, with the other half working in the afternoon. Jillian was splitting the difference, coming in at late morning, knowing she would stay until Kara was on her way back.

Just after lunch, Kara had walked in, checked in with DS Listun, who was working the morning shift, and then knocked on Jillian's door.

"Mum?" she said, looking down at some papers. "Something odd about the financials."

"What financials?"

"Sorry," Kara said absentmindedly. "Look at Parav, for instance." Kara spread out what looked like HMRC (Her Majesty's Revenue and Customs) statements for various business ventures. Kara explained, "The morning crew have been compiling all the various businesses that Parav funnels money through. It's quite a web, and when you focus on one of them, there's not much to see. One year it's doing well, the next it's flailing. Anyway, I started looking at it from the whole and not the individual pieces. Parav seems to be doing quite well over the last two years from where he started."

Looking at the charts Kara was showing her, Jillian nodded.

"I checked with SCD9, and that made sense to them given the uptick in his . . . uhm . . . primary business since he took over." Kara paused and then pulled some other sheets to the front. "The thing is, Milston also said the gambling has finally made the lucrative jump from on-site to online, meaning that Slater should also show considerable growth, but when you take his various businesses and look at them collectively, this past year was rather flat."

Jillian looked up. "That doesn't make sense."

Kara just stared back.

"Perhaps we need to have another chat with Mr. Slater."

The two detectives pulled up in front of the Bantry Club . As it was the middle of the afternoon, the place was just setting up for the evening's club scene and the only people inside were employees.

Jillian and Kara held up their warrant cards to the bouncer, who looked like he'd boxed one too many times, with a nose that was decidedly out of joint in the middle.

"We'd like to speak to Mr. Slater," Jillian said.

The bouncer looked hard at the warrant cards as though trying to determine whether they were real. More likely because he couldn't read, Kara thought, but kept it to herself. The bouncer lifted his eyes and said, "Sorry, no one 'ere by that name."

"That's funny," Kara said, not able to keep the sarcasm out of her voice, "'cause he's listed as the owner."

"Don't know oo owns the place, love, but there's no Mr. Slater works 'ere." The bouncer was dressed in black jeans and a black shirt a size too small that emphasized his formidable biceps. The shirt had the club's name printed in white with a spotlight on it.

Jillian, tiring of the game, took a step closer to the bouncer, but instead of looking up at him, she turned her head sideways and peered deeper into the main room. After a moment, she looked up slightly at the bouncer and said, "Tell Mr. Slater that DI Scotte wishes to speak to him."

"Look, I tole ya . . ."

Jillian put a finger to the bouncer's lips, saying, "Shhh . . . just tell him."

The bouncer wasn't sure what to do. It wouldn't look good trying to usher police out the door, especially because they were female.

Throwing his hands up, he sighed loudly and said, "Wait 'ere." He lumbered off, climbing some steps to the right of the main dance floor and disappearing from view.

After a few minutes, Sebastian Hughes descended the steps. He wore a light gray suit and a purple shirt, open at the neck, with a matching handkerchief in the suit pocket. His black shoes were highly polished and made no sound as he descended the steps.

His eyes sparkled a little as he walked up. "Detective Inspector Scotte, how nice to see you." He then turned to Kara.

"This is Detective Constable Devanor," Jillian said. Hughes nodded, his hands casually in his pockets. "We'd like to speak to Mr. Slater."

Hughes's expression didn't change. "I'm afraid he's not here." Looking around him, he added, "He doesn't spend much time visiting his . . . uhm . . . businesses."

"That's what he has you for?" Jillian said.

Hughes made a slight nod with his head. Not quite agreeing, but more an acknowledgment.

"Is there something I can help you with?"

"Perhaps," Jillian said, after a pause.

"Please," Hughes said, motioning for them to come in and then turning to go back up the stairs. Pausing with his hand on the railing, he said, "Can I get you something? Coffee, Tea?" Then, raising an eyebrow mischievously, he added, "Something stronger?"

"Tea would be lovely," Jillian said. Hughes looked over at Kara, who said, "Yes, please."

As he began climbing the stairs, Hughes called out to an employee walking past. "Linda, can you have a pot of tea for three sent up to my office please?"

The woman nodded and smiled. "Right away, Mr. Hughes."

From the top of the stairs, they made their way across a walkway over the middle of the dance floor to a gleaming oak door marked "Private" with a centered gold plate.

Inside was a simple room where a man sat behind a desk. He stood up as they entered.

"Pat, I've had some tea sent up. When it arrives, bring it in, will you?" It was said not as a question but rather as a statement. The man, dressed in a three-piece, dark blue suit with a silver tie, cuff links on his shirt, and dark black hair combed to one side, simply said, "Of course, sir."

With that, Sebastian Hughes ushered the detectives into his office.

Unlike the outer room, which had a desk, two chairs, and little else, Hughes's office was twice, if not three times its size. A large, dark brown leather sofa sat against one wall, potted plants on either side. A Persian-looking rug filled the middle of the room with a circular glass table and four comfortable padded chairs.

Beyond the table, in front of a large window, was a large oak desk, meticulously kept, with a blotter, a small artisan lamp, and a penholder. In front of the desk were two overstuffed chairs that matched the sofa. Two of the walls were decorated with art of varying types—mostly colorful contemporary pieces. The last wall was a bank of video screens, each with a different view of part of the club.

Hughes walked over to the glass table and pulled out two of the chairs. He waited until Jillian and Kara were seated before sitting down in a third chair.

"Now, how can I help, Inspector?" he asked.

"Would you say business is going well?" Jillian asked.

After a slight pause, he said, "I assume you're not asking about the club."

"No, Mr. Hughes, I'm not asking about the club."

"Please," he answered, tilting his head forward and slightly sideways, "call me Sebastian."

Jillian nodded. "All right, Sebastian. How is the gambling business?"

He paused again, putting his elbows on the side of the chair and his fingertips together against his lips. Finally, he said, "I'd say business is better than ever, Inspector. Why do you ask?"

Ignoring his question, Jillian said, "So, no recent financial problems?"

Sebastian paused. There was still a glint of something behind his eyes. He smiled faintly, then said, "Not recently, no. It took a while for us to figure out how to ah . . . adjust . . . to the online competition." He spread his hands apart and shrugged. "Of course, as soon as we did that, the pandemic hit and we were affected the same as everyone else."

He clasped his hands in front of his chest, fingers intertwined. "But I'd say the last eighteen months have seen some of our best yet." Now his eyes narrowed a bit. "And again, I have to ask, Inspector. Why?"

Jillian turned and looked at Kara. Kara reached into her bag and pulled out a sheet of paper. Sliding it across the table, she said, "According to what we were able to learn about Mr. Slater's business dealings, and his reporting to HMRC, it would seem as though business has been rather lax of late."

Hughes studied the form for a minute.

There was a knock at the door, and the blue-suited gentleman came in with a tray and set down the tea. He poured three cups, asking the ladies if they wanted milk and sugar: just sugar for Jillian, milk and sugar for Kara. He then made a cup for Sebastian with one sugar, no milk, before leaving quietly.

Sebastian took a sip of his tea. "Mr. Slater has some rather, shall we say, creative accountants, Inspector. Surely you can understand that what gets reported to HMRC isn't . . .well . . . let's just say it's not complete."

Jillian smiled at his choice of words, which garnered an equal smile from Sebastian in return.

Having taken a drink of her own tea, which was excellent, she leaned forward and pointed to the chart on the paper in front of him. "No Sebastian, I don't imagine that HMRC has a full accounting of Mr. Slater's affairs, nor do I imagine these numbers represent even half of the income his businesses take in."

Sebastian kept his gaze steadily on her as she talked.

"However," she continued as she pointed to another chart on the paper, "when we look back historically, and again assuming that this is . . . how did you put it . . . incomplete? We can at least assume that it is consistent."

At this, she saw a slight frown cross Sebastian's features, but he recovered quickly, and it vanished just as abruptly as it had appeared.

"I just find it odd that after a few years of less-than-stellar performance," she continued, her finger tracing along the line in the graph, "followed by two years ago when there was a significant improvement"—again her finger traced the line on the graph—"that this past year was flat when, as you say, these have been some of your best months yet."

Sebastian looked at the graph, then up at Jillian, his face completely unreadable. He glanced at Kara, then back at Jillian. Taking a deep breath, he said, "Well, detectives, I wish I could help, but I'm afraid accounting is not my area of expertise."

He reached down, held up the page, and looked at Kara. "May I keep this? I can certainly ask the accountant to explain it and make sure Mr. Slater is aware of the filing with the HMRC."

Kara nodded.

When they were back in the car heading to the Tof so Kara could begin getting into costume, she looked over at Jillian and said, "He's quite charming, isn't he?"

Jillian gave her a quick look. "Hughes? Yes, he can be."

Kara then added, "He's also lying."

Jillian smiled. "Yes." Then, shooting another glance at Kara, she said, "But about which bits?"

***

PC Stella Dawson was doing her best to stay awake. She'd dressed warmer tonight than she had two nights ago when she'd been first assigned inside the van. God, that had been a cold five hours. Tonight, she had a hot thermos of hot chocolate, two layers of pants and jumpers under her warmest coat, and a woolen hat and gloves sitting beside her just in case it came to that.

She had the sound on the wireless receiver on low so any passersby wouldn't be able to hear it. She was getting DC Devanor's signal loud and clear, though. She heard Kara swear about how cold and wet she was after leaving yet another dead-end conversation with a cross-dressed prostitute named, unoriginally, Lola.

Suddenly, a large lorry pulled up and blocked the intersection in front of the street where Dawson had parked the van. While she wasn't worried about having to drive anywhere quickly, since the intersection behind her was wide open, she could no longer see Kara.

Grabbing her hat, she jumped out of the van and jogged down half the length of the lorry, her heart pounding. *Nothing to be worried about,* she told herself before quickly making her way around the back of the lorry. She looked across the street and sighed in relief as she saw Kara standing on the corner, her pitiful umbrella still doing its best to keep her somewhat dry. Continuing around the other side of the lorry, Stella approached the cab, which suddenly opened. A burly man jumped down, his boots splashing in the water on the street.

"Oy," she shouted. "You can't park this here. You'll have to shift it."

"Says who?" the man said, turning toward her and squinting in the rain. As Stella approached him, reaching into her jacket pocket for her warrant card, the man took a step toward her, then shoved her so hard she fell on the pavement. "Piss off, you stupid tart." Then he turned and walked away around the front of the lorry.

Water soaking through her pants, Stella started getting up, anger rising inside of her, but as she put one of her hands down on the ground, twisting herself to get back to her feet, ice flooded through her veins.

As she slowly stood, she glanced up at the corner where Kara had been.

Looking quickly left and right, she jogged over to see down the side street. She looked left and right again, then turned all the way around.

DC Devanor was nowhere to be seen.

CHAPTER 6

The tall building by the river came into view through the intermittent windshield wipers. Sitting on a still ancient-looking road with cobblestones wet from the rain that had all but stopped. The cobblestones weren't ancient, of course. They had been "restored" with new ones before the turn of the century.

Detective Constable Kara Devanor, dressed decidedly un-police-like, sat in the back of the sedan with the large-framed man who had approached her nearly twenty minutes ago. She had been standing on the corner, wondering which of the ladies of the night she hadn't yet talked to, when the dark-colored sedan had pulled up and the man had extricated himself mightily from the back seat.

He was easily close to six and a half feet tall and probably close to two hundred and fifty pounds. He was hard. The extra weight carried as muscle, not fat, and no neck that she could see. His face was round. Hair cut very short, more stubble than actual hair. Eyes a dark color she couldn't make out in the dim light and falling rain.

He walked up to her, his voice low and raspy. "My boss wants a word."

It wasn't spoken harshly. He hadn't touched her. He merely stood before her. Somehow, though his voice was calm, she understood she had little choice in the matter. There was noise across the street. A commotion that somehow sounded familiar, but she was concentrating too much on trying not to shake as the man gestured to the open car door and she complied. Besides, Kara knew Stella would be listening and would soon follow.

It was only as the door closed behind her that she understood that amid the commotion across the street; it had been Stella's voice she'd heard . There would be no cavalry to the rescue this time. Stella would likely not even know which direction she was headed in.

She'd asked the bull of a man who'd climbed into the backseat beside her, taking up most of the remaining space in the car, who his boss was.

He simply stared ahead silently.

Kara had tried to talk occasionally. Questioning. "Where are we going? Why are we headed down Pilemont Street? We're leaving the docks, where are you taking me?"

She had to be careful not to be too obvious. To appear nervous and scared, which was easy at this point, but not inquisitive, which was the more challenging aspect. Besides, Kara thought, there was no way her hidden microphone would travel this far without Stella following, but she had to try.

Now they pulled to a stop in front of the tall building. Gray stone, with a polished red door neatly flanked with potted trees on either side, just up a few steps from the street. There was no visible address on the door, and the bull simply got out of the car and waited for her to follow. Then he led her up the steps and opened the door for her.

She walked inside.

***

Detective Inspector Jillian Scotte felt herself go cold from head to toe. The call had come straight to her phone; she gave Stella credit for that. "What do you mean you've lost her?" Jillian said, trying to keep the anger out of her voice and remain calm.

PC Dawson explained about the lorry, about seeing Kara on the corner, about the distraction with the lorry driver, and then . . .

Jillian put her head in her hands, thinking. Whatever happened or didn't happen, whatever purpose they had had for being there, none of that mattered now. She told Stella to walk every road from that corner for two blocks in either direction and ask if anyone saw anything, then hung up the phone.

Grabbing her coat and purse, she slammed open her office door, garnering the attention of the limited evening staff, which had been her aim. "Right!" she yelled, not slowing down as she pivoted and headed toward the exit. "We've lost DC Devanor. Everyone. Cars. Now!"

There was a scraping of chairs and a rustling of coats. Soon everyone was running to cars in the parking lot, and a convoy of lights and sirens accompanied them as they headed toward Millbrook.

They came into the docks with sirens and lights blazing, tires screeching to a halt and blocking both sides of the main road. PC Dawson came running up in her layered clothes. She and Jillian conferred for a moment, and then Jillian dispatched the team with orders to interview and detain anyone who might have seen anything. It was going to be a slow-profit night for the tarts, and the punters would have to look elsewhere.

She had called Southampton Constabulary on the way to ask for additional resources, but she didn't hold out much hope that she'd get any. She then called Chief Inspector Dobson, interrupting his supper. He said he knew the night sergeant at a police nick nearby and would see what he could do.

Meanwhile, Jillian turned around in the middle of the street. The flashing lights of her team's cars bounced off the disheveled and abandoned buildings that littered this part of Southampton. The damp post-rain air was not fresh, but stale and all too humid, mixing with the seawater nearby. It was neither a pleasant feeling nor smell.

She could be anywhere by now, Jillian thought, and she felt the bile building in her stomach.

***

Kara could not see much of the outside of the building, from her brief exit of the sedan to the front door. It had seemed to her unassuming. Not plain, but not indicative of anything. It didn't have the air of a block of flats or an industrial building, nor did it seem like some posh hotel or abandoned old factory.

The simple yet bright door was solid and thick. She noticed her bull-like companion's muscles bunch as he pulled it open for her. This was meant to be a fortress, not somewhere one came in and out without being asked.

Inside was not what she expected. It was like walking into a home. The black-and-white marble flooring of a narrow hallway ended in an interior door, half frosted glass, which was opened from the other side before she reached it by an unseen hand.

While walking through, she saw a butler, black tails and all, bow slightly as she passed, which she found absurd, dressed as she was. The bull, who had been walking behind her, now came forward and indicated a doorway to her left, and she followed him into a beautifully appointed library with a crackling fireplace and floor-to-ceiling shelves lined with books.

The bull offered her the choice of one of the many comfortable-looking armchairs or the worn leather couch. She chose the couch, not wanting to be confined by the arms of the chairs. The butler, who had followed them, said, "Would miss care for anything? Tea, coffee, wine?"

Still unsure of what this was all about, she managed to say without her voice shaking, "Tea," and then added, "please." She instantly regretted it, as it wasn't exactly in character for her to say.

The bull simply stood to one side of the doorway, looking at her silently.

After a few moments, a woman walked in. She was tall, slender, in her fifties, if Kara had to guess, and quite striking in a classic sort of way. Her dress, a tight-fitting blue number with a slim black belt across her hips, showcased her well-maintained figure. Her jewelry was sparkling and looked expensively real. She had light brown hair cascaded in waves down to her shoulders. Her eyes, a deep brown, studied Kara for a moment. Then she walked over to the fireplace and stood staring down at it.

The butler returned with a tray, a teapot, two cups, milk, sugar, and spoons on what looked to be silk napkins.

The woman turned around. "Please, help yourself," she said, her accent British, local. "You must be cold after all that rain."

Kara tried not to let her hands shake as she poured, but the pot was full and heavier than she'd imagined, and the spout rattled as it tapped against her cup.

After her cup was filled, she decided a tart wouldn't offer to pour the woman's tea. She simply picked up the cup without the saucer and held it in her hands, blowing softly over the surface to cool it.

The woman turned and smiled, though there was little warmth in it. "Why don't we get to know each other a little bit, shall we?" she asked, walking over and taking a seat across from Kara. "Who exactly are you?" Before Kara could answer, she said, "Vice? Or some poor low-on-the-totem-pole constable they forced to play dress up out in the rain?"

Kara opened her mouth to protest, or at least redirect the woman's line of thought, but one look at her face and Kara knew it was pointless. She closed her mouth and took a sip of tea, trying to buy herself time.

"Those shoes, love," the woman said. "They're far too uncomfortable to be walking all night in. Dead giveaway. Coppers always think they have to look the part, but never think of the details of the person who would wear them. No tart on the street would be found wearing that brand, far too expensive, and much too uncomfortable.

"So," she added matter-of-factly, "why don't we start with your name?"

Kara thought it over, then said, "Jaine." Which was her middle name, so not exactly a lie.

The woman paused, as if considering whether to believe her, then said, "And where do you work, Jaine?"

Kara couldn't think of a reason to keep up any pretenses, so she said, "Violent Crime."

This caused the woman to raise her eyebrows in surprise. "You're part of that new unit that was set up? You work for Inspector Scotte?"

Kara ignored the question and just took another sip of her tea.

"Why are you looking for Petra Solanshtok?" the woman asked.

Kara decided to go on the offensive. "Why do you want to know? Do you know where she is?"

For the second time, the woman seemed slightly taken aback by Kara's answer. She leaned forward, her elbows on her knees and her clasped hands just under her chin, studying Kara intently. "I'm afraid not," she said. "I rather fear something has happened to her."

"Why do you say that?" Kara asked.

The woman let a thin smile flit across her face. "First, tell me why you're looking for her."

Kara wasn't sure where this dance was headed, but she knew she needed to play for time. "Actually, we're looking for people who know her." She almost said *knew her* but caught herself at the last second.

"And why is that?" the woman asked.

"Sorry," Kara said as though she had called this meeting and not the other way around. "Part of an ongoing investigation."

"Investigation into what exactly?" the woman asked, letting her hands fall forward, her forearms now resting on her knees.

The bull by the door hadn't moved and seemed neither bored nor interested in their conversation.

Kara took a breath. "Human trafficking," she said finally.

Again, the woman paused, sitting more upright in her chair, her hands now properly folded in her lap. She looked across at Kara, her eyes squinting slightly. Her gaze was intense, despite her unassuming appearance. This was not a woman to be trifled with.

"She's dead, isn't she?" she blurted. Her voice was calm and resolute. It was almost a statement, more than a question, though she was definitely waiting for an answer.

"Again," Kara said, still stalling and hoping to gain some advantage. "What makes you say that?"

The woman leaned forward and began pouring more tea into Kara's cup, then her own. "Because, my dear Jaine, or whatever your name is, you said you work at the VCU. Why else would a copper from Violent Crime be asking after someone who's been missing unless she was a victim of a violent crime?"

***

True to his word, Dobson had delivered with three pairs of constables from the nearest nick, and now the sidewalks were crowded with lines of tarts and a few punters as they all underwent questioning.

Despite Jillian's insistence that he stay home, DS Listun had come down. They'd talked to a fair number of people at this point. "Boss," Listun said, his tall, angular frame further emphasized by the trainers and jogging pants he'd been wearing when he heard the news. He hadn't bothered to change, which spoke to his commitment to his team, as far as Jillian was concerned.

Jillian turned to him. "Two people now corroborate the Pakistani gent from the tobacconist. Devanor was on that corner there," he said, pointing, "when a dark-colored four-door sedan came down along here." He pointed down the street they were on. "Turned the corner in front of her, a rather large bloke got out, spoke to her, she got in the car and it drove off. Less than a minute."

"Anyone get a good look at him?"

Listun shook his head.

"Registration plate?"

Again, Listun shook his head.

Jillian threw her hands up, knowing the answer even before she asked it. "Any working CCTV?"

"Sorry guv," Listun said, shaking his head.

Jillian looked up and down the street. Her voice was loud as she cried out, "Shit!"

CHAPTER 7

The Bentley caught PC Stella Dawson's eye. She was standing in DI Scotte's office with DS Listun. They'd come back from the docks two hours ago. Scotte had called most of the team in despite the late, now early, hour.

They had pored through CCTV from surrounding streets, but at ten o'clock on a Friday, traffic had been heavy. They had tried to chase down a couple of dark sedans, but without a number plate, they were looking for the proverbial needle in a haystack.

DS Listun looked as tired as Stella felt. Scotte looked both worried and angry at the same time—not a good combination. Listun had been going through options, grasping at straws about where, who, or why someone would abduct DC Devanor.

Stella, who was supposed to have been her backup and had lost her, was doing her best to blend into the wall when she noticed the lights of a car that had stopped outside the gate of their discreet parking area. The presence of a car had caught her eye, never mind the sight of an actual Bentley at this time of night.

Then her eyes went wide. "Mum," she said, trying to interrupt the conversation between DI Scotte and DS Listun, but Scotte ignored her, so she said louder, "*Mum*!"

Scotte, looking annoyed, replied, "What?"

Stella pointed outside. "It's DC Devanor."

Scotte swung her head around, and Listun joined her as the three of them took a step toward the window. There she was, trudging along in the drizzle, looking like a worn-out tart after a busy night, her shoes in hand, walking barefoot across the wet parking lot.

Scotte was out the door and halfway down the corridor before the other two managed to turn around.

When Kara walked through the unit door, Jillian stood with her hands on her hips, unsure whether to yell at her officer or hug her. Kara looked so tired.

Kara looked up and saw Jillian's face. "Sorry boss." She was shivering from the chilly rain. Jillian turned around. "Stephen, get a blanket." Then she ushered Kara into her office.

Listun returned and wrapped a blanket around Kara's shoulders while she smiled tiredly at him. Stella brought Kara's gym bag from the lockers and put it down beside her in case she wanted any of her regular clothes. She touched Kara's arm lightly. Kara put her hand on top of Stella's and squeezed gently.

"Now that we're all here," Jillian began, taking her place behind her desk, "where the *hell* have you been?"

Kara recounted her evening abduction, the drive to the building, and her conversation with a woman called Lilian Delacroix.

"After we got the preliminaries out of the way, she told me she runs a brothel to legitimize her *girls*." Kara held up air quotes as she said the last word.

"What do you mean legitimize?" Jillian asked.

"She says she helps them get their lives back on track. She even helps them take classes at uni, if you can believe it. She claims that she pays them fairly, gives them a clean and safe place to ply their trade."

Jillian could hear the tone Kara was using and suspected that she was repeating some of this word for word. She would have Listun take a full statement later. "So, she considers herself some kind of Joan-of-Arc madam?"

"I'm not sure, mum," Kara said, shaking her head, "but she did seem to care about the girls in her charge."

"How do you mean?" Jillian asked. Both Listun and Dawson kept quiet.

"She called down one of her girls. Her name was Rosa. She was maybe twenty if a day. Had an Eastern European accent, couldn't be more specific than that." Kara pulled the blanket tighter around her. "She told the girl that Petra was dead, and the girl practically collapsed right on the spot.

"Delacroix jumped up and ran to her. Even the bodyguard got down and helped the girl up. Turns out this Rosa and Petra were friends. She, Rosa, had brought Petra to the house a few weeks ago, I think to try and get Delacroix to take her in."

Jillian nodded for her to go on.

"Anyway, apparently Petra had seen or heard a conversation. I'm not sure, Rosa's accent is quite thick. Anyway, according to Delacroix, she was quite scared. They had agreed to have her come and stay at the house.

Petra said she was just going to go and get her things and would come back that night. They never saw her again."

"Did you find out more about what it was she saw or heard?"

"Not exactly," Kara said, taking a sip of a cup of tea that Listun had made for her. "It was apparently a meeting that someone wanted kept quiet, but she didn't know who the people at the meeting were or exactly what they had said, as she had been hiding in a back room, having gone there to uhm . . ."

"Yes," Jillian said, "we get the gist. What about her punter? Was he still there with her?"

"She said he had just left, and she was getting herself together when the men came in to have their meeting. According to Rosa, there had been three men, and guv," she said, looking up at Jillian, "the only thing Rosa remembers Petra saying to her was a name."

Jillian waited.

"Parav," Kara said.

***

Jillian sent everyone home and decided she didn't want to go back to her empty flat, so she drove up to the university, arriving just after sunrise.

Daniella opened the door bleary eyed, still in her pajamas. "Jillian!" she said, "What are you doing here?" She gave her a hug and pulled her inside.

After Daniella made some coffee, they sat on the small couch in her single dormitory room while Jillian recounted the events of the past few days, culminating in the evening's excitement.

"Have you asked SDC9 about this Delacroix woman?" Daniella asked.

"Not yet," Jillian replied. "I will on Monday. Sorry to show up like this. I just didn't want to be alone this weekend."

"Well," Daniella replied, "I have labs this afternoon and tomorrow, but I'll be free tonight for dinner."

"What about this morning?" Jillian asked.

Daniella smiled warmly. "Nothing." Then she pulled Jillian to her and grabbed her head, resting it against her shoulder and saying, "I'm not going anywhere." She kissed the top of her head and settled back into the couch with her arm holding Jillian tightly.

Later that day, after Daniella went to her lab, Jillian dialed the phone number of the Bantry Club. When the call was picked up, she said, "This is Detective Inspector Jillian Scotte. I'd like to speak to Mr. Hughes, please."

There was a pause, and then she was put on hold to some awful hold music.

After a moment, the line clicked and Hughes said, "Ms. Scotte, what can I do for you?"

"I'd like to know if you know a woman named Lilian Delacroix?"

There was a pause; she imagined Sebastian Hughes weighing the request's pros and cons. "I know of her," was all he finally said.

"Do you know if there would be any connection between her and Parav?"

"I doubt it," Hughes said.

"Why?"

"As I understand it, she has a rather minor operation. She used to be a . . ." Hughes paused, catching himself. "She used to work the streets herself when she was younger. Now she tries to save some of those like her."

Before Jillian could ask another question, Hughes continued, "But she has a dozen girls at best at any given time. She's not exactly competition for those in that trade."

Jillian considered what he'd told her.

"What's this got to do with Parav? Was the girl one of Delacroix's?" Hughes asked.

"What girl?" Jillian asked, her eyes narrowing.

"I saw the piece on the Daily Coast," Hughes replied, saying nothing more.

Jillian paused again. Finally, she said, "Not that I'm aware of." There was silence on the line, neither of them saying anything for a moment. "Sebastian?" Jillian asked, "Did you talk to your accountant yet?"

Again, Hughes was silent on the end of the line. Jillian waited without saying anything. Finally, Hughes said, "Is there anything else I can help you with, Detective Inspector?"

"No," Jillian answered. "Thank you for your help."

"Anytime," Hughes said, and hung up the phone.

CHAPTER 8

To call it a bike path was being generous.

Detective Inspector Jillian Scotte, looking anything but the part of a DI, pedaled furiously on her Cannondale SuperX Force 1 bicycle. Its Tec-Carbon frame and Vittoria Terreno Mix tires took curves at speed and accelerated through straightaways like a bullet.

Jillian was "exercising" her demons on this early Sunday trek through the New Forest, just after the sun had crested the horizon.

The so-called bike path was more of a pedestrian walkway. Later in the day, it would be littered with tourists and walkers who would just get in the way.

It was much too early for that, and despite the chill in the air, Jillian was already sweating through her riding gear.

This case, Petra Solanshtok, was gnawing at her. After a lovely day and supper with Daniella, Jillian had decided to drive back to her flat after all. She needed to work through some things, and Daniella had to work Sunday anyway, hence the early-morning ride through the woods.

She shifted gears and stood in the saddle, pedaling up a slight incline until she reached the speed she wanted. Then she settled back in the saddle and inched up another gear, cruising as the trees flashed by at a rapid clip.

Parav and his Neanderthal Gorski were clearly involved. Something was going on with Slater and his business, at least on the financial side of things.

Then there was Hughes. And now this woman Delacroix.

Somehow all connected, but there were more questions than answers.

Jillian took a turn at a frightful angle, but her tires held their grip, and she slingshotted out of the turn, rocketing down the straightaway that would take her back to her car in the layby where she'd started.

Questions like, What was Slater playing at by getting her involved? Why was he hiding money, and if Hughes ran his day-to-day business operations, or at least some of them, didn't it stand to reason that he would know?

The only thing she was fairly certain of was that Gorski had been one of the people in that awful video.

Pulling up to her car, she dismounted and put the bicycle on the rack attached to the boot.

As she got in and turned on the car, there was one more thing she was certain of.

She was tired of not having answers.

***

"Boss," Listun said, entering Jillian's office with a knock on her open doorframe. She looked up.

"We've been trying to look deeper into the financial aspect of this case." Listun had a bundle of papers in his hand, and he was flipping through them, looking for something.

He stopped as he sat down in one of her "client" chairs in front of her desk and looked at her. "With everything going on, it sort of took a back seat, but we've been back on it the past few days. Anyway, we finally pulled the thread and figured out where Parav reports his income through."

Jillian gave him a look that said *Get to the point*, so he did. "Turns out he owns a few buildings through a holding company, and that appears to be where he funnels his money through."

"What sort of buildings?" Jillian asked.

"That's the thing," DS Listun responded. "They're buildings that used to be small-scale homes for old pensioners. One was a care home for the elderly."

Jillian frowned. "He's running elder care facilities?"

"Not quite. They used to be but went out of business or needed too many repairs, et cetera, so he buys them cheap."

"What does he do with them?"

Listun, rifling through the pages again, said, "So far he hasn't done anything with them."

Jillian sat back in her chair, one hand twirling a pen.

"Anyway, that's not all," Listun said, pulling a stack of papers out and placing them on top of his file. "The purchase of the buildings, or at least some of them, and the repair costs, came at the same time as the holding company saw an increase in revenue."

"Go on."

"The amounts fluctuate over the course of about twelve months."

She could almost sense where he was going, but she let him say it.

He paused as if thinking out loud. "The thing is . . . those twelve months are the same period of time where Slater's business seemed to dry up, at least according to his tax reports."

Jillian stopped spinning her pen.

Just then, her phone rang. She picked up the handset. "DI Scotte." Then, after a pause, she said, "Hang on, I'm putting you on speaker. DS Listun is with me."

She mouthed "Milston" as she hit the speaker button and hung up the handset. "Go on, Rob."

DS Milston's voice came through wearily in mid-yawn. "Sorry, been a long night."

"Enough about your sex life, Rob, what have you got."

"Hey," Milston said, sounding hurt, "I was working all night, thank you very much."

"Is that what the kids are calling it these days," Jillian said teasingly.

"Look, Inspector," he responded, "I don't have to take this abuse from you, that's why you have DS Listun on your team or that cute DC what's-'er-name."

Jillian smiled, looking up at Listun, who rolled his eyes. "You know perfectly well what her name is, Rob. Now, what's up?"

"As I was saying, word on the street is that the gorilla Gorski has a chum in town. Someone almost as ugly but just as big. A Chechen named Kerim. No one knows his last name."

After a pause Milston went on. "The two apparently are thick as thieves when they're together, which isn't often. The last time was about the same time the girl in the video went missing."

Jillian felt herself go cold all over. Milston wasn't finished.

"Anyway," he said, yawning again. "He might be the second man in black on the video."

That didn't do anything to warm Jillian up, and she reached across herself to rub both her arms. What DS Milston said next, however, made her stop, her arms frozen in mid-motion.

"Anyway, they're apparently looking for one of their stable that's gone missing. A girl named Rosa."

CHAPTER 9

The diary came as quite a shock.

DI Scotte, DS Listun, and DC Devanor all turned to look at each other.

Jillian's head was muddled as she thought about the steps that had gotten them here.

***

Halfway through the week, with the team picking away at finances and cold tips from various informants, Milston had called about the strongman Gorski, who apparently had another giant of a friend named Kerim in town.

Interesting as that might be, it was the fact that the pair were looking for a prostitute named Rosa that had scrambled everything. Rosa was the woman Kara had seen at Madame Delacroix's "home for wayward tarts" (a term Listun had said out loud, which prompted a reproachful look from Jillian).

Rosa and Petra had obviously been close, given Rosa's reaction to the news of Petra's death.

Jillian had hung up from her call with DS Milston, grabbed Listun by the elbow and told him to get his jacket, then shouted to Kara across the main room of the Violent Crime Unit to grab her coat and "come on." They all piled into one car, with Listun driving.

Kara had paid attention on her previous ride back from Delacroix's house, which seemed so long ago, and directed them more or less straight there. The car pulled up just as the late afternoon sun began to cast shadows.

Jillian, sensing Kara's discomfort, turned in her seat to face the back. "You don't have to come in if you don't want to."

Of course, Kara's response of "no problem" was what Jillian expected, but it never hurt to ask. The trio walked up to the gray stone building with its polished red door and potted trees on either side.

Listun grabbed the brass lion head knocker and clapped it three times.

Presently, the man who had served Kara tea opened the door. On seeing Kara, his eyebrows rose imperceptibly, but otherwise, he kept his composure. "Good afternoon," he said in his clipped voice. "May I help you?"

Jillian held up her warrant card. "I'm Detective Inspector Scotte. This is DS Listun, DC Devanor," she said, nodding to each in turn. "We'd like to speak to Ms. Delacroix."

With the briefest of hesitations, the man nodded and opened the door wider. After showing them into the library room, he said he would see if Ms. Delacroix was available.

Kara was explaining that this was the very room where her conversation had taken place when the door opened and none other than Lilian Delacroix herself walked in, followed by the bull-like bodyguard.

Delacroix was wearing a beige business suit and pants with a deep burgundy silk blouse; her shoes matched her suit. The bull seemed to wear the same thing he'd worn not quite a week ago.

"Detective Inspector Scotte," she said, crossing the room and walking straight up to Jillian, arm extended. "What a pleasant surprise."

Jillian shook the woman's hand, aware that she was being appraised and not caring much. "Madame Delacroix," she said politely. Nodding to either side of her, she said, "This is DS Listun, and I believe you've already met Detective Constable Devanor when you abducted her last week?"

Delacroix smiled, made a clicking sound, and said, "Come now, I would hardly call it an abduction. I simply invited her to have a chat. No harm came to her." Then, turning, she added, "Did it, Kara?"

Kara was surprised Delacroix knew her first name, but said nothing, letting Jillian do the talking.

Delacroix, crossing over to a small couch for two, added, "And please, call me Lilian."

Everyone sat down except for the bull, who walked over to the fireplace and stood next to it.

"What can I do for you, Inspector?"

"I'd like to talk to one of your girls. Rosa," Jillian said, getting straight to the point.

"I'm afraid that's impossible."

"Why is that?"

"Because she's not here," Lilian said, her face impassive.

Before Jillian could ask another question, there was a commotion in the hallway. The door burst open, and a giant of a man filled the frame. Jillian and Kara recognized him immediately.

Viktor Gorski.

He entered the room and stood to the side. Listun stood up, and the bull had already moved over to stand beside Lilian Delacroix, his arms hanging loose at his sides.

Following Gorski was an older gentleman in a light brown raincoat, wearing a brimmed hat, which he removed. Behind the old man, another giant came in and took up the position on the opposite side of the door from Gorski.

The butler, looking somewhat disheveled, said, "I'm sorry, madam, they barged straight in."

"That's quite all right, Baldwin." Then, turning to the old man, she said, "Hello Lomax. You could have called on the telephone. I'm sure there's no need for all this . . . drama."

Jillian looked at the old man. So, this was Lomax Parav. His eyes were black, like small lumps of coal with no soul behind them . His skin was gaunt and tight on his face, his lips so devoid of color they looked almost gray.

The old man's lip curled up at the corner. His voice when he spoke was raspy, like that of a smoker. "What I require cannot be retrieved by phone."

Looking away from Lilian Delacroix and her bodyguard, who was staring intently at the two giants by the door, Parav turned his gaze to Jillian, ignoring both Listun and Devanor.

Slowly, he walked over so he was closer to the group of chairs and sofas where everyone except Listun and the bodyguard sat.

If it were possible, the disgust on his face and in his voice deepened. "Detective Inspector Scotte, VCU. What brings you out here on this fine day?"

As he moved closer, the two giants moved with him, one circling the group to stand to the right of Kara; Jillian was on Kara's left, with Listun beyond her. Their positioning made it so that neither Listun nor the body-guard could look simultaneously at Gorski or his friend.

Jillian looked up unblinkingly at Parav. "Same as you, Mr. Parav. I just came here for a chat with Madame Delacroix."

Parav sneered unpleasantly. "Let us . . . how do you English say this . . ." he began, his Slavic accent heavy. "Cut the bullshit. We are both here for the same person."

Turning to Delacroix, he opened his mouth to speak when suddenly two more men walked through the door.

Jillian wanted to roll her eyes. What the hell was going on here?

Sebastian Hughes, looking dapper in a dark blue pinstriped suit, wing-tipped shoes, and a black shirt and tie, entered, followed by someone she didn't know. The stranger was big. Not as big as the giants and perhaps not as big as the bull, but there was no denying he was solidly built. The arms of his suit were bursting at the seams. Neither Hughes nor his associate said anything, both standing with their suit coats open, no raincoats, and their arms at their sides. Hughes looked around the room, and Jillian thought she caught a hint of amusement in his eyes, but his face remained stoic.

"What the hell are you doing here?" Parav rasped sharply, looking over at Sebastian.

Turning his head slowly until he was looking directly at Parav, Hughes said, "We were just in the neighborhood. Looked like there was a party going on, so we thought we'd join the fun."

The tension in the air was palatable. Parav was not happy. "Get the hell out of here. This doesn't concern you or your employer."

Hughes didn't move. His associate stood still, staring directly at Kerim without blinking.

Parav turned back to Delacroix and nearly shouted, "You will bring the girl Rosa, or I will kill you and get her myself!"

Delacroix, full of poise, responded gently, "I don't think that would be wise in front of the police, Lomax."

A vein in Parav's head throbbed, and blood rushed to his ears. As he took a step closer to Delacroix, the bull straightened up slightly and stood taller. Parav spat as he spoke. "I do not care about this bitch police. I will kill you all."

He then turned and nodded to Gorski, who looked at his friend Kerim, and both men reached inside their coats for their weapons.

"Uh uhhh." The voice was loud and crisp. It had come from Sebastian Hughes.

If Jillian hadn't been facing in that direction, she wouldn't have believed what she saw. One moment, Sebastian was standing still, the next there was a gun in his hand. Fast didn't even begin to describe how quickly he was able to pull it.

His associate, though not as fast, now had his gun out as well, pointed directly at Kerim's head.

Hughes did not have his gun pointed at Gorski; his was pointing directly at Parav.

If Parav had been angry before, he was close to apoplectic now. "What the hell are you doing? How dare you point your gun at me, Lomax Parav."

"Killing three police officers will bring far too much unwanted attention here." Hughes's voice was even; his arm, sticking straight out, did not waver or tremble. "Whatever your business is here, it can wait. The party's over for tonight."

Parav, Gorski, and Kerim didn't like it, but since the two giants had not been able to fully pull their weapons before Hughes and his associate, they were at a disadvantage.

Without a word, Parav put on his hat and walked out the door. As he passed, he leered at Sebastian Hughes. "You are a dead man."

The giants also tried to look tough, which is difficult to do when there are guns pointed at you.

Sebastian holstered his weapon and nodded to his accomplice, who walked into the hallway.

Jillian met Sebastian's eyes, but as usual, she couldn't read them. She opened her mouth to speak, but Hughes said, "Sorry to have interrupted the party." Then, with a nod of his head, he said, "Madam," looking at Delacroix, then "Detectives" with a nod to Jillian and her team, and he turned and left the room.

The bull left Delacroix's side and went into the hall. He came back after a few minutes and, looking at Delacroix, said, "They're gone."

Lilian Delacroix still appeared composed, but Jillian noticed that some color had drained from her face. She stood up and addressed her bodyguard. "Fetch my bag from the study, please." He nodded and left.

"After our little chat," she said, indicating Kara, "I sent Rosa away. Too much attention is never a good sign, and I feared something like this might happen."

"Where is she?" Jillian asked.

"Somewhere safe" was all Delacroix said.

The bodyguard returned with a polished leather bag that looked more like a briefcase but had the strap of a handbag. He handed it to Delacroix and moved closer to the door, where he kept an eye on the entryway.

Reaching inside the bag, Delacroix pulled out a small book with a strap wrapped around it.

"Before she left, Rosa handed me this." She looked down at it for a moment, then handed it to DS Listun, who handed it to Jillian.

Before opening it, Jillian asked, "What is it?"

"It's Petra's diary."

Jillian, DS Listun, and DC Devanor all turned to look at one another.

CHAPTER 10

Detective Inspector Jillian Scotte was having dinner with Amelia Hamza, journalist for the online newspaper Daily Coast. Although the two were not quite allies, Jillian knew Amelia enjoyed some of the information she could get via the tenuous relationship, though she wasn't sure who was getting the better end of the deal.

Jillian had asked Amelia to meet her for dinner. She had a lot to talk about, and a quick meeting over coffee wasn't going to do it. She'd told Amelia to pick the restaurant, and she had chosen an out-of-the-way Chinese place—an actual restaurant.

Amelia was already seated, and Jillian slid into the booth opposite her. "Thank you for making the time," she said, smiling as she set her coat and purse beside her.

Amelia said she was always glad of a free meal. She was wearing a cream blouse, with a jade pendant hanging from a silver chain around her neck.

Jillian got straight to it. "I'm not going to mess about; I need a favor." Amelia began rolling her eyes, but Jillian quickly said, "For which I'm willing to give you a lot of information."

That got Amelia's attention.

"You've been a big help to me in past investigations, Amelia, and I'd like to think I've been fair with you in exchange."

Amelia stared, choosing not to respond.

"What I want to discuss has to be off the record for a bit." Jillian could sense Amelia's hesitation. "*Just* for a bit. You'll understand why as we go, but I need your assurance up front."

Amelia was used to this from various sources, and more often than not, she could wrangle a compromise on the off-the-record gambit, but she knew better than to try with Jillian Scotte. She also knew that whatever information she would get, even if she had to sit on it for a short while, was likely to be something big. It was worth the gamble.

"Off the record," she said. Her slight Middle Eastern accent, mixed with the English one she had picked up since moving to the UK in her teens, was coming out.

The server came by, and the pair ordered some food. A pad Thai dish with tofu for Jillian; Amelia ordered vegetable chow mein. They both ordered hot tea to drink.

Once the server left, Jillian told her about the case, not going into too much detail but outlining the general situation. Amelia already knew about the dead woman, Petra. Jillian having given her that information earlier.

"We have a diary, supposedly written by Petra," Jillian announced.

The server had just dropped off tea, and Amelia was pouring. She paused with her hand over the pot lid. "What does it say?"

"We don't know yet," Jillian answered. "We're getting a translator, as it's written in Crimean, her native tongue apparently."

Jillian talked about the human trafficking and prostitution trade; she mentioned Parav, Gorski, and Slater. She even touched on Kerim but didn't mention Delacroix or Hughes.

"I'm quite certain that Parav ordered Petra Solanshtok to be killed," Jillian said. "I'm equally confident that Gorski and his friend Kerim may have been the killers."

"The men in black in the video," Amelia said.

"Yes," Jillian responded, "but I can't prove it yet."

"What about Slater?"

"I don't know." This is where Jillian paused, which was fortunate— the server had just brought their food. Once the server departed, she continued, "I'm not sure what role Slater plays, if any. Prostitution's not his thing."

Amelia shrugged, which caught Jillian's attention. "What do you know about Slater that I don't know?"

Amelia looked up. She had just put a mountain of chow mein into her mouth . After chewing for a moment, she said, "Nothing. Only that Slater didn't always run gambling."

Jillian ate some of her own food and nodded for Amelia to go on.

"Before he came down here, the word on the street was that he started up in Dublin, where he worked for the O'Malley Brothers. He was an enforcer."

Jillian looked across at Amelia. "I'm not sure I understand. What does being an enforcer for a mob outfit in Dublin have to do with this?"

Amelia paused, meeting Jillian's gaze. "The O'Malley Brothers ran all the tarts on the east side of Dublin."

Jillian sat back, her hands falling to either side of her plate.

"So," Amelia continued, "what's this favor you need?"

Jillian was thinking, working out whether this new bit of information might alter her original plan. "I need to rattle some cages. I'd like you to do a piece on organized crime here in Southampton, focused on both Slater and Parav specifically. Don't tie them together. Treat them as two separate entities within the same piece."

Jillian knew this wasn't anything exciting to write about and might not even get past Amelia's editor, so she quickly added, "You can cite unnamed sources within the VCU as saying they are taking a keen interest in both men following the death of Petra Solanshtok. Furthermore, you can mention that new evidence has been discovered that may soon lead to arrests."

That was enough to get Amelia's interest. Still, her eyes narrowed slightly as she took it all in. Finally she said, "I'd want to see the diary."

"No," Jillian said quickly.

"Jillian, come on."

"Look," Jillian responded, "I can't agree to let you see something until I know what it contains. If,"—at this Jillian held up her index finger—"If there is something relevant or that won't compromise this woman, and yes, I know that she's dead," Jillian added as Amelia opened her mouth to speak. "But she is still a victim and I have to protect her rights."

Jillian paused to make sure that got through before continuing. "If there is something that you can use, you have my word that I'll get it to you, but only after we've had it translated and I know what's in it."

Amelia knew that was the best she was going to get, and she honestly hadn't expected to get that much. She nodded.

They ate the rest of their meal companionably, talking over mundane details of life and work. By the time they were ready to leave, they paused outside on the sidewalk, neither quite knowing what to say. The meal had been almost friendly.

Finally, Amelia straightened her back and said, "I'll write the story for tomorrow."

"Thank you," Jillian said, holding out her hand, which Amelia took with a smile.

***

Back in her office the next morning, Jillian attended to the mountain of paperwork she had piling up as the team continued to track down leads.

When it was nearing lunchtime, Chief Inspector Alan Dobson walked in, accompanied by a middle-aged woman with dark hair and black-rimmed glasses. "DI Scotte, meet Marcia Palenova of His Majesty's Diplomatic Service," he said by way of introduction.

Jillian and the woman shook hands, and then Jillian called in DS Listun to escort her to the incident room so she could begin work on the translation.

"Thank you, sir," Jillian said to Dobson. "I know we're already over budget on this, but if there's something in that diary that can help us nail Parav, it will have been worth it."

Dobson was looking at the translator and Listun as they walked away. He nodded silently, then slowly turned back to Jillian.

"Look Jillian," he began, but he was clearly troubled. "SCD9 just got a call from our London branch, actually north of London, but anyway . . ."

He was still stalling; she thought.

"What is it?" she asked, bracing herself.

"They found a body," he said plainly, and she knew even before he said it, feeling herself go cold as she slowly sat down in her chair. "They sent over a photo. It's Rosa Acolpina."

Jillian was numb.

Dobson wasn't finished, "I won't give you the details, but it wasn't pretty. Whoever did this tortured her, and they weren't subtle about it."

Jillian looked through the glass window of her office that looked onto the team room and beyond it to the incident room. "They were looking for that diary."

Dobson nodded.

"How the hell did they find her so quickly?"

"We think Parav's operation here is just the intake point."

Jillian studied him. Dobson looked a little sheepish. "We didn't tell you because we didn't think it mattered, and we thought it might distract from your investigation." Dobson swallowed hard, then continued. "Parav brings girls in through multiple points on the coastline of the UK, and while many of them come through Southampton, it's only one of his entry points. His biggest operation is actually in London, which he runs remotely from here. We think it's a way of distancing himself should things go tits up."

"How long have you known this?" Jillian asked, trying to keep her anger in check.

Dobson held up his palms. "We didn't know at first. We've been following that thread while you were chasing the Petra woman's death." Straightening up a little, he added, "Parav got an influx of cash recently that fueled his expansion. His outfit has been systematically, and force-fully, I might add, taking over smaller operations all over the city and suburbs beyond."

Jillian sighed.

"That giant Kerim didn't just arrive from across the Channel," Dobson said pointedly. "He came down from London. He's Parav's mus-cle man there the same way Gorski is here."

Jillian sat, staring at the window again, trying to connect the dots. "If Kerim is the muscle, and Parav and Gorski are here, who's running the show in London?"

Dobson shrugged. "We don't know yet. We're working on it."

Jillian watched as DS Listun left the incident room, having set up the translator with a computer. He nodded to her, meeting her gaze, before heading back to his desk.

One way or another, they would get some answers later that evening.

A ping came from Jillian's computer. It was an alert. Amelia's story had just been posted.

Jillian felt like she was juggling too many balls in the air. One of them had already fallen. She closed her eyes briefly, wondering how many more would fall before this was all over.

CHAPTER 11

Mindfulness was not something Jillian Scotte was good at, but she was working at it.

Dr. Daniella Morales had suggested she try it to combat stress for those times when going on a ten-mile bike ride just wasn't possible.

Times like now.

She had called Daniella, more to just have someone to talk to than anything else, while they waited for the translator to finish the diary. Daniella could hear and sense the stress in Jillian's voice. When Jillian told her they'd found the body, Daniella knew that her stress level would go through the roof.

"Jills," Daniella said, her calming voice now assuming a little more of a doctorly tone.

"Yes," Jillian responded with a sigh—not particularly because she knew she was in for a lecture, just because she was exhausted. It had been a long day of waiting and her nerves were frayed.

"You know that woman's death wasn't your fault, don't you?"

Jillian paused. "Do I?" she answered, almost absentmindedly.

"Yes, you do!" The forcefulness of Daniella's response woke Jillian up out of her dreamlike state.

"Sorry Dani, what did you say?"

"I said." This time her voice was much lower, calmer, kinder. "You know that woman's death wasn't your fault."

This time the pause was genuine, thoughtful. "Yes," Jillian said, "but it doesn't make it easier."

It was Daniella's turn to pause. "No, I don't suppose it does." Then she added, "It's one of the reasons why I love you."

Jillian smiled. "Look, I've got to go. Listun's headed my way."

"Do you want me to come down?" Daniella added hastily.

"No, really, I'll be fine, and God knows how long we'll be here tonight anyway. Got to run, love you, bye," Jillian finished just as DS Listun knocked on her door and entered, his bright red hair looking a little worse for wear. It reminded Jillian that she wasn't the only one stressed at the moment.

"Boss," he announced, "the translator has a rough draft. She says she'll need to go through it again tomorrow to check for errors, but . . ."

Jillian was already out of her chair and moving. "I'll take a draft."

DC Kara Devanor was at the main section printer, taking sheets as fast as the printer was printing them and making piles of them. She looked up as Listun and Jillian approached. "I've started sorting by weeks, so roughly one week in each pile. Some weeks she wrote more often than others, but I figure this might be the best way to get through it, if we split it up throughout the team."

"Excellent, Kara," Listun said.

Jillian added, "Perfect. Let's the three of us take the last three weeks."

Kara coordinated, handing out stacks to the team as they came out of the printer, then she, Jillian, and Listun went into the incident room, now vacated by the translator, who had gone home to sleep.

Spreading out the sheets, they began to read their week's entries.

Listun, who had the earliest of the three weeks, spoke up. "She says something here about that night. Just a mention of almost getting caught with her punter, nothing specific about the meeting."

Time went on, and Jillian said, "Wait, here's something. She talks about being scared, about V wanting to talk to her. Says she's not sure if he knows or if it's just about work." Jillian looked up. "V has to be Viktor Gorski."

Listun nodded. "Odd how she talks about it as 'work', though, isn't it?"

Kara chimed in. "What's she supposed to call it though? I mean, it's what she does . . ." Then, as an afterthought, she said, ". . . did."

On that somber thought, they all went back to flipping pages.

Suddenly Kara exclaimed, "Found it!" Then she began reading out loud. "I shouldn't have been there. I didn't know Mr. Parav was going to have a meeting. Don't know who the other man was. Taller than Parav. Nice clothes. Not from the same country. Parav was angry at the talk. The other man also got angry. They talked about money, I didn't understand. I left quickly but didn't know if someone saw me. Girls talk." She looked up to see Listun and Jillian staring at her. "That's it. It's the last thing she wrote."

A lengthy silence filled the room.

Listun spoke first. "Taller than Parav, nice clothes. Could be Hughes."

Jillian nodded. "Or Slater. He's bigger than Parav, and maybe by taller she meant bigger, or it got lost in translation. And let's face it, it wouldn't take much to dress nicer than Parav in his old hat and worn trench coat."

Kara said, "Right, but if it was Slater, wouldn't Hughes be with him? I mean he wouldn't go to a meeting with Parav alone."

Listun, as if trying to poke holes in his own theory, said, "He might have gone to the meeting with Hughes, but had his bodyguard wait outside, not in the actual meeting. Petra doesn't say whether anyone else was there, because she had to sneak out."

Kara murmured her agreement. Jillian sat thoughtfully, nodding and chewing on the end of a pen.

"What about that bit where the other man wasn't from the same country?"

They thought about that for a moment, and Kara said, "She and Gorski and Parav are presumably all from the same country, so must mean he wasn't from there. Of course, doesn't tell us which country he was from."

Listun, tapping his own pencil on the table, said, "That last bit is odd though, don't you think? Girls talk?"

"I thought about that too," Jillian said. "It's as if she thinks another tart had seen her."

"Rosa?" Listun asked.

Jillian made a murmuring sound. "I don't know. Why confide in her and give her your diary if you think she's the one who *talked*?" She made air quotes around the last word.

"Someone else saw her there," Kara said.

"It would explain why she was scared, and how Gorski would have known she'd been privy to the meeting in the first place," Jillian agreed. Turning to Kara, she leaned over the table. "We need to find the other girl."

"Yes, mum," Kara said, a determined look on her face.

"Right," Jillian said, standing up. "Let's get everything from the rest of the team and piece together whatever we can from this diary. It won't hold up in court, but it might lead us to evidence that could nail these bastards."

CHAPTER 12

The kitchen in the Tof was the one thing DI Scotte had insisted they splurge on. Nothing fancy, just a nice area for her team to make a "cuppa," brew some coffee, or heat up some food. She didn't want the typical plastic, sterile space so many police nicks had in them.

She wanted something that felt warm and comforting and where one could actually have a proper meal if they wanted, not that coppers were known to be gourmands.

Jillian plopped down the obligatory pastries she had picked up on the way in, and some fruit salad as well. She'd be surprised later to find all the fruit salad gone and only half of the pastries.

The team had spent the better part of the last day going over the diary and looking for further clues, but they'd found little. After the morning meeting, she met with the senior team in her office.

"Kara," she said, "I want you down on the docks this afternoon talking to the girls. We need to find out who else knew about this meeting."

DC Kara Devanor nodded.

"And I want Dawson walking beside you, in uniform. We're not hiding this; we're going to be in full view."

Jillian needed Dawson to know that she hadn't lost trust in her. Putting her back out there with Kara would go a long way to help that.

Listun seemed agitated, rocking from side to side and chewing the end of his pen. "Stephen, something on your mind?"

He looked up, surprised she had noticed. "Uhm, yes mum," he said point-blank. "I think sending Kara back there, even with PC Dawson, is dangerous. I think they should have backup."

"I agree," Jillian said, "which is why I have a call in to Dobson and expect to hear back sometime this morning." She smiled at her DS, and he nodded, smiling back.

They went over some more items, and then everyone returned to their desks to work.

Just before lunchtime, Jillian's phone rang.

"Hello Jillian." It was Chief Inspector Dobson.

"Hello sir," she replied.

"Listen, we have a bit of a problem."

"What's that, sir?" She frowned.

"I need you to keep this between us, but we've had a tipoff that one of the container ships coming into port tonight has a shipment of girls and it's supposed to be rather packed."

Jillian didn't say anything, so Dobson continued. "Normally, I'd give you one of my team for backup for your DC—what's her name again?"

"DC Devanor, sir."

"Right, Devanor. Anyway, I'd give you one of mine, but it's all hands on deck tonight. However," he began before she could argue, "I've arranged for a car and two officers from the constabulary to be with her tonight, all night if necessary."

"Thank you, sir, I appreciate that."

"It's not a problem, Jillian. I'm sorry it can't be one of us, but they'll see her right."

"Yes, sir."

"How's the rest of the investigation going?" he asked.

"We're still working the money angles," she said carefully. "We're attacking it from all sides."

"Good," Dobson said. "I don't have to tell you that London is pressing for a result here."

"No, sir."

"Right, well, I've got to go coordinate this raid tonight. Call if you need anything else."

"Thank you, sir."

Hanging up the phone, she sat back in her chair. She had hoped, and had in fact asked for, DS Milston to accompany Kara and Dawson. A car with two plods would be fine, but she'd feel better with someone she knew. Part of being the boss was not always being able to control everything, and she knew it. That didn't mean she had to like it though.

In the middle of the afternoon, Kara and Dawson prepared to leave. Listun and Jillian walked outside with them. Kara looked back at them as she approached the car. "Would the two of you stop worrying? We're going to be fine. We'll have our chaperones and everything."

PC Dawson looked from Kara to Jillian and back, unsure how to react.

Jillian smiled thinly. "Check in every thirty minutes, no exceptions."

Listun added, "We're only twenty minutes away if you need us."

Their concern made Kara pause, but she was determined to get back on the horse. She nodded. "Yes boss," she said, speaking to both of them, then she climbed in the car and drove away.

Jillian, not taking her eyes off the car, said, "The constabulary car?"

Listun, without averting his gaze from the departing vehicle, said, "It's already there, waiting for them to arrive."

Jillian nodded, and once the car was out of sight, she turned to walk inside. It wasn't Madame Delacroix's abduction of Kara that had them concerned. It was the fact that Parav knew they had the diary and that they were putting two of their own into the lion's den that worried them.

As they were walking back to her office, Jillian's phone beeped. Taking it out of her pocket, she saw a text from an unknown number. Upon opening it, she stopped walking.

Listun, who was walking with her, turned back. "Everything all right, boss?"

Jillian was frowning.

She read the text again.

We need to talk. I found something I need to show you. Tonight, seven.

The rest of the message was an address and a signature—Sebastian.

"Boss?" Listun asked again.

"I just got a text from Sebastian Hughes. He wants to meet tonight." She turned her phone and showed him the text.

Listun took a deep breath. "Could be a trap."

Jillian nodded. "Yes. It could also be the break we've been waiting for."

"Wait," Listun said, reading it more closely. "That address looks familiar." He went over to his desk, with Jillian following close behind. He rifled through some papers, looking down a list. Then he reached for another pile and thumbed through a few pages until he finally pulled out a sheet and turned back to her.

Jillian showed him her phone again, and he glanced between the address and the paper in his hand. "Here it is," he said, pointing to the sheet and showing it to her. "This is one of Parav's buildings. He bought it about a year ago. It's not currently occupied that we know of. There has been some renovation going on."

Jillian considered this for a moment. "We have to be missing something. Maybe Hughes found it or found something that will fill in the gap."

Listun put the paper back on his desk, then turned back to her. "I'm coming with you."

"No," Jillian replied automatically, "I need you here in case something happens with Kara."

"I'll have the calls sent to the desk sergeant," he replied, and before she could begin to argue with him again, he added, "Guv. We just sent

Kara with PC Dawson and a backup car. You're not going to meet Hughes by yourself. This case is getting too close."

Jillian wanted to tell him she'd be fine and that he needed to stay here, but she knew he was right. Besides, the address was actually closer to the docks, so if Kara needed help, they'd be even closer than if they stayed at the Tof all night.

"Okay," she said, and returned to her office.

Kara started calling in. Nothing much to report: they were making the rounds, talking to the girls, but were met with suspicion and more than their share of distaste. Coppers and tarts weren't on the best of terms on the best of days.

"Everyone seems on edge," Kara said, talking to Listun, who relayed the conversation to Jillian later in her office.

"Did she say why?" Jillian asked.

"No," Listun responded. "I asked her. She said it was just something she felt. Said Dawson mentioned the same thing."

At half-past six, Jillian and Listun got into a car, the DS driving, and began heading toward their meeting with Sebastian Hughes.

As they got closer, Listun said, "Do you think we should have notified Dobson about this meeting?"

Jillian looked over at her DC. "Why?"

He shrugged. "I dunno, in case it's a trap?"

Jillian looked out the window. "I don't think Hughes would send me a text to trap me. He knows where to find me, and the text would implicate him. Besides," she added, "Dobson's busy tonight."

Listun looked over at her inquiringly.

Glancing back at him, she said, "They're doing a raid tonight, all hands on deck."

Jillian was eager to talk to Sebastian. If he had something, she needed to hear about it. And if it wasn't something that could help them, she was going to push him until he gave her something. This whole affair was off from the start, and she was tired of being in the dark.

They pulled up to the address, parking next to a single car in front of the main entrance. Although it was clear there was renovation going on from the large skip next to the main entrance and various pieces of construction equipment strewn about, it appeared that most of the work was being done on the interior.

There was a notice on the door that hard hats needed to be worn at all times inside the construction area. Listun pulled the door open, and Jillian stepped through into a small vestibule with a set of double doors. Light shone through a small porthole-like window in each door.

Jillian pulled a door open and stepped into the large open room.

The moment she walked in, she knew she'd made a mistake.

It was a trap.

CHAPTER 13

Light bulbs hung from extension cords in the largely empty space. Walls in half-states of construction. Cement floor covered with dust. Eerily quiet, without the usual noises associated with construction sites. The closing outer door echoed in the space.

None of this, however, registered beyond the periphery in Jillian Scotte's brain.

Two things registered simultaneously. The first was the form of a man standing next to some plastic chairs. The thin, raincoated form of Lomax Parav.

The second was the cold steel barrel of a gun against her temple the moment she walked through the interiror door.

She felt Listun stop suddenly beside her. He had walked in after her, and he too had a gun similarly placed from the other side of the door.

Through her peripheral vision, she could see the two giants holding the guns: Gorski and Kerim.

Parav's raspy voice filled the room. "Welcome, Inspector. I am happy to see you arrive with punctuality." His accent filled the empty room.

The brutes shoved both Jillian and Listun toward their boss. Listun exchanged a nervous glance with Jillian.

As they approached, Jillian noticed that Parav's right arm had been hanging down out of their view, and as he turned, she saw that he, too, was holding a gun. It seemed to her a lot of firepower for police who are normally unarmed.

Waving the gun nonchalantly, Parav indicated two of the plastic chairs. "Please," he said almost politely. "Take a seat."

Listun was forcibly shoved into one chair. Jillian took the other one a few feet away from him.

The larger brute, Kerim, walked away as another man appeared—a tall, heavyset man also brandishing a gun. He spoke into Parav's ear.

226 | Trouble Comes In Threes

Parav nodded, and the man retreated, leaving Parav and Gorski standing before the two detectives.

Jillian could feel cool sweat running down the back of her neck. This did not bode well. Parav was a dangerous man and his henchmen were completely unpredictable. She stole a quick glance at Gorski and instantly regretted it.

The man had a nasty smile plastered across his face and he was staring directly at her. It sent a shiver down her spine, and try as she might, she couldn't prevent herself from outwardly showing it. She glanced back at Parav, who was glancing back and forth between Jillian and Listun.

Parav lifted his gun hand and held the weapon in front of him, not pointing at either of them, just in their general direction. Gorski, putting his gun into the waistband of his pants, walked behind Listun, yanked his arms back behind the chair, and placed a set of plastic tie cuffs around his wrists, cinching them with a yank that made the DS grimace.

Parav didn't say a word as he watched, his gun making a clear point that any defiance would not be tolerated.

Gorski walked over behind Jillian's chair. Despite an urge to do otherwise, she moved her arms back before he could grab them. Still, he placed the cuffs around her wrists and yanked on the end, tightening them far more than necessary. Out of sheer willpower, she kept her eyes locked on Parav.

She could feel the plastic already cutting through her skin.

Gorski leaned forward and put his face next to her, his cheek resting against her head just behind her ear. He took a long, slow, deep breath in. Held it, then slowly exhaled with a low murmur. If she hadn't already been scared, she was now.

At that moment, the main door she and her sergeant had just come through opened. Everyone turned and looked over.

In walked Greg Slater, followed by Sebastian Hughes. Both men surveyed the room as they approached. Slater wore a fashionable black pinstriped suit with a white pocket handkerchief. Hughes was in a light gray suit, dark blue shirt, and yellow tie. Somehow, he made Slater look like his attire came from a secondhand store, which it most certainly did not.

Hughes's eyes darted around the room, returning to where Jillian and Listun were sitting.

Slater approached Parav. "Lomax, what the hell's goin' on?" Slater did not look happy. Jillian looked at Hughes, but he was locked into a stare with Gorski. It was hard to read his face. He seemed impassive, almost bored.

Parav turned slightly toward Slater. "I am taking care of our problem."

Slater opened his mouth to say something, but nothing came out.

Into the silence, Hughes's voice startled everyone. "Slater," he said, his eyes never leaving Gorski. "What are we doing here?"

Jillian frowned.

Slater waved his hand as though he were swatting away a fly. "Not now."

Hughes pressed on. "Is there something I should know?"

Slater turned his head and spoke in a stern voice, his Irish accent heavy. "I said, *not now!*"

Hughes, without turning his head, moved his eyes until he was looking at Slater. For a moment, neither spoke, but Jillian noticed that something in Slater's face had changed. What had been hard now seemed . . . almost frightened.

Hughes spoke. "You've been funneling money to him." It wasn't a question, and no one had any doubt who "him" was. Hughes's eyes were now back on Gorski, who had moved next to Parav, facing directly opposite Hughes.

Parav looked at Slater. "You need to control your dog."

Slater turned from looking at Hughes to face Parav. "Lomax, I donna work for ya. We might be in business together, but that doesna' mean you can tell me what to do." Slater was trying to project strength, but he was no match for the older man.

Parav sneered. "I do not think of you enough to tell you what to do.." He turned his body now and faced Slater directly. "But since you do not have the strength to keep this dog in line, I will do it for you."

Gorski, who had been staring directly at Hughes, didn't move. He didn't flinch. Didn't even blink. Perhaps it was meant to be an old cowboy showdown between the two, but it never came to that.

There was a loud click as Kerim, who had walked up silently out of the shadows behind Hughes, suddenly appeared. He pressed his gun to the back of Sebastian's head and cocked it. Everyone except Hughes had been focused on Parav, so it came as a surprise. Except perhaps to Hughes, who hadn't moved a muscle.

Slater turned around quickly. Seeing Kerim with a gun to Sebastian's head, he whirled back around. "What do ya think yo'r doin'?" he asked Parav aggressively.

Parav looked briefly at Slater, then turned back to face Jillian. "I already told you. I'm taking care of problem."

Slater opened his mouth to speak, but Parav held up his left hand, palm facing toward him. Slater closed his mouth.

"Now," Parav said, directing the full weight of his soulless eyes on Jillian, "you will tell me what is in diary."

Jillian had spent the few minutes of this exchange wracking her brain for a way out of the situation she and her DS were in. She hadn't come up with much.

Again, Hughes's voice broke in. "Killing police will only bring more attention. This is not a smart play."

Jillian saw something in Parav's eyes. It was a flicker behind the emptiness of his coal-black pupils. She wasn't exactly sure what it was, but it was not pleasant.

Slowly, the old man turned and took a step toward Hughes. "I am tired of you interfering in matters that do not concern you." He then spoke in some Slavic language Jillian didn't understand.

Kerim, his gun still pressed firmly against the back of Hughes's head, said, "Two fingers. Slowly."

Hughes didn't move at first. Then, slowly, reaching with his thumb and forefinger, he removed a gun from a shoulder holster under his coat.

Parav stepped back and raised his gun, now pointing it directly at Hughes's chest.

Sebastian held the gun out to his side. Kerim took a tentative step forward and took it from him. He then grabbed Hughes by his neck and shoved him toward a small door at the back of the room. As Sebastian opened it, Jillian could see it led out behind the building into what was likely an alley.

Parav turned once again and faced Jillian. Slater was standing a little behind him and to his left.

"I will not ask you again," Parav said, his voice menacing. "What is in diary of the whore girl?"

Jillian swallowed hard. "We . . ." she didn't have much saliva in her mouth. "We . . . haven't finished translating it yet," she said, hoping to stall. She had to find some way to gain an advantage, some way to figure out how to get out of all this.

Parav stared at her, his dark eyes boring into hers. She tried not to blink but couldn't help herself.

She saw the flicker in his eyes again. This time, he didn't turn. He kept his eyes locked straight into her, and without blinking, without so much as breathing, he raised the gun, pointed it at Listun, and fired.

The shot echoed loudly in the empty room. The shot hit Listun in the chest, knocking him back so that his chair fell over and to the side. He cried out when the shot hit him, and now he lay on his side with his back to Jillian, his arms still bound behind the chair.

There had been a scream, and Jillian realized it was her own. She stared down at the back of Stephen's body, trying to see if he was breathing, but the chair obscured much of her view. He certainly wasn't moving.

"Jesus, Lomax!" Slater cried. "What the fek are ya doin'?"

Parav turned his head partially toward Slater. He didn't even look at him. Jillian could see the blood drain from the Irishman's face.

Her mind was recoiling as though she couldn't quite believe what had just happened. This couldn't be happening. Listun was going to be a father. Her breathing was coming in brief gasps, and she was in danger of hyperventilating.

Parav, turning his attention back, now leaned down a little, placing his head just above Jillian's.

"I do not like waiting."

"Please," Jillian said, her voice cracking. "Please let me help him."

Without warning, Parav brought his gun hand up and backhanded her across the face. The gun caught her lip and cut it, making it instantly swell and bleed.

She turned her head back, the metallic taste of blood on her tongue. She met Parav's stare, and despite her own inclination for self-preservation, she stared back defiantly.

Perhaps he saw her determination. Perhaps he simply was tired of waiting. Whatever the reason, he took a step back until he was standing next to Slater. Then, looking over at Gorski, he simply said, "Viktor."

It had the same effect as letting go of a dog's leash when it had been salivating in front of a bowl of fresh meat.

Viktor stood in front of Jillian. The look on his face held nothing short of bloodlust. His eyes were gleaming. After placing his gun in the small of his back beneath his trouser waistband, he cracked the knuckles of one large, menacing hand with the other.

Jillian's mind instantly went back to the video. This was definitely one of the men in black. In a flash, she remembered what they had done to Petra, and her heart stopped beating. Her mind was flashing black-and-white images in front of her. Her pulse was quickening, her heart now hammering in her chest. What she saw in front of her, as she stared into his eyes, was pure evil.

Viktor Gorski turned his torso halfway to the left as though stretching, only this wasn't a stretch. He cocked his arm back, and using the momentum of his torso as it twisted, he brought his arm toward her face at lightning speed, his large hand now balled into a fist.

She tried to brace for it, but you can't brace for something like that.

His fist connected with the right side of her face, hitting the side of her eye and cheek.

The force of it was tremendous. Her head snapped to her shoulder. The blow launched her body sideways, still connected to the chair.

Her whole body almost lifted the chair off the ground for a fleeting moment before landing all at once on the cold, hard cement. She couldn't breathe. Couldn't get her lungs to start. She was in shock and trying to understand . . .

That's when the pain hit. Her eyes, closed from the blackout of the impact, now saw shards of light, which stabbed at her senses. The entire right side of her face was swelling and every nerve in her head was screaming.

With the left side of her head against the floor, she half opened one eye. Even the act of taking in images from one eye was enough to send another flood of pain through her.

What happened next was so fast she wasn't sure she actually saw it.

The back door of the room burst open. Hughes entered and quickly fired two shots. The first hit Gorski, who had turned toward the sound, square in the middle of his forehead, almost certainly killing him instantly.

The second shot was fired into the shadows behind Parav and Slater, presumably where the taller guard had been standing. Jillian couldn't see, but she heard a loud thud as a body fell to the floor.

Jillian tried to swallow, but her throat protested from the pain. She watched as Hughes, who hadn't broken stride after coming through the door, advanced with his gun pointed straight at Parav.

Parav, with no time to even raise his gun, simply stared.

Hughes, whose nose was bleeding, also had blood smeared across the front of his shirt. Far more blood than his nose could account for.

Jillian blinked slowly. She was going to lose consciousness soon; she could feel it.

Hughes walked over to the group. He stole a glance at Listun and then at Jillian. Their eyes met for a brief second. Then Hughes turned and shot Parav in the head. Slater recoiled as blood splattered on his face.

"Christ!" Slater yelled as Parav fell to the ground, his gun still in his hand.

Hughes bent down next to Listun.

Jillian couldn't see what he was doing. Her vision was blurring. She willed herself to stay awake despite the pain in her head.

Hughes stood up and walked over to Gorski. Reaching down, he grabbed the gun from behind the man's back. Standing up, his hands by his side, a gun in each hand, he looked up at Slater.

"You knew about the girl," he said plainly.

"What?" Slater asked, confusion on his face. "What are you talking about?" Before Sebastian could answer, he said quickly, "Sebastian. We need to get out. What's happened here . . . we can use it . . . we can take over . . . we can . . ."

Hughes interrupted him. "The video. You knew."

Slater stopped talking. He still looked confused, but then realized what Hughes was saying. "Yes," he said, almost defiantly. "Yes. I knew. Look Sebastian, she was only a . . ."

He never finished. Sebastian raised Gorski's gun and fired three times directly into the center of his boss's chest.

Slater looked shocked for a moment, then simply crumpled to the ground where he'd been standing.

Jillian sensed more than saw Hughes walk over to her and crouch down. She could feel his hand on her neck. Things were getting darker now. She heard him move over to Listun. She could hear sirens in the distance.

More movement.

Then quiet.

Except for the sirens. The sirens were getting louder.

Then everything went black.

CHAPTER 14

Flash.

Another flash.

Why the hell was the press here?

The thoughts ran through Detective Inspector Jillian Scotte's mind as the flashbulbs went off and the nerves from her eyes signaled her brain.

Just as quickly, however, her brain caught up to reality, and she realized they weren't flash bulbs from paparazzi cameras. It was an emergency medical technician, shining a light into her eyes.

She groaned from the pain. Tried to speak, but there was a mask over her face. Oxygen.

She felt the world move, and suddenly she could see the ceiling rushing by above her as they transferred her to an ambulance. She closed her eyes and tried to fight back the pain.

She woke up again with a dulled sense of reality.

She was lying on a bed. Tubes. Blinking machines. A nurse was talking to someone who turned toward her, and Jillian's heart rate increased. Kara.

Kara Devanor moved quickly to the side of the bed and spoke clearly and purposefully, without rushing. "You're in the emergency room. You've been here just under an hour. Stephen is in surgery. We don't know anything yet. He was alive when he went into the surgical theater."

Jillian took a deep breath. Her head still hurt, but the pain was dull, not sharp like before.

A doctor in scrubs walked in. "Hello Ms. Scotte," he said. "My name is Doctor Branson. Your right cheek has several minor fractures which will heal in time. Your eye will, I'm afraid, take quite a while to heal, but there appears to be no permanent damage there, either. You have had a nasty concussion and I'd like to keep you for a few hours' observation, possibly overnight." He didn't wait for her to answer. "I don't think there's anything to worry about, but we'd like to make sure just the same."

Jillian raised her hand and took off the mask. Her voice was weak and slow. "Thank you . . . can't stay . . . I've had enough . . . of hospital beds . . . lately."

Despite strong protestations from the doctor and the nurse, Jillian Scotte slowly but resolutely disentangled herself from the various machines.

Kara, seeing the determination in her boss's face, said nothing and merely helped with clothes and belongings. After a time, the pair headed toward the surgical theater waiting area.

Jillian's gait was slow, and Kara offered an arm, which she readily took to steady herself. Her voice was as weak as she felt. "Did someone . . . call Deborah?" she asked, referring to DS Listun's pregnant wife.

"Yes, mum," Kara said. "A car went to fetch her thirty minutes ago. She should be here any minute now."

In the empty waiting room, Jillian sat down gratefully, only to get back up again as Deborah Listun walked in, looking worried and scared. A nurse was telling her they would be in shortly to update her on her husband's surgery as soon as they knew something. It was then that she turned and saw Jillian.

Deborah Listun almost fainted on the spot. Thankfully, Kara was there in an instant and helped her to a seat. Jillian forgot that her appearance must look as bad, or worse, than she felt. Half of her face was black and blue; her mouth was swollen, affecting her ability to speak.

Jillian wanted to say something, to comfort the poor woman. To tell her that her husband would be all right, but she honestly had no idea of the extent of his injuries or what his chances were. She remembered he'd been shot, but she couldn't even be sure where he'd been shot; it had all happened so fast.

She just sat across from Deborah and tried to think of something to say when nothing could be said.

That's when Daniella arrived in a flurry, her raincoat flying as she passed the waiting room, then doubled back and stepped inside. One look at Jillian and she cried out, "Oh my God!" She quickly rushed forward and knelt in front of her. "Jills . . ." she said, reaching up but stopping short of touching her face. "You need to get back into a bed, you shouldn't be up and about."

Slowly, Jillian grabbed her hand. "I'm okay," she said. Seeing the disbelief in Daniella's eyes, she gently lowered her head until her good eye met those of her lover. "Really . . . I'm okay . . . Or . . ." With a twisted smile, she added, "I will be."

Jillian looked across the room. "Daniella," she said, struggling to speak clearly around her swollen lips. "This is Stephen Listun's wife, Deborah."

Daniella turned her head and noticed the tear-streaked face and swollen eyes. She said hello, though she doubted the woman, lost in her own private thoughts, heard her. Turning back to Jillian, she lowered her voice. "What happened?"

Jillian looked at Daniella, and in that instant, Daniella saw all the pain and hurt in her gaze. She knew the agony she saw was not from Jillian's own wounds. "Shot . . . In theater now" was all Jillian said as her eye brimmed with tears that swelled out and cascaded down her cheek.

Daniella reached up and brushed the tears away, then leaned up and kissed Jillian's cheek gently where they had been. Turning to Kara, she asked, "What are they saying?"

Kara shook her head. "We don't know anything yet."

Daniella switched immediately into doctor mode and stood up. "We'll see about that." And she strode out of the waiting room.

After a few minutes, two more people came in.

Chief Inspector Alan Dobson and Detective Sergeant Rob Milston. Both took one look at Jillian and stopped dead in their tracks. After a pause, as if on some silent cue, Dobson turned and sat next to Deborah to offer comfort and support as Milston moved beside Jillian.

"Look Scotte," he said. "We've got to stop meeting like this. People are going to talk, and I'm not sure your coroner friend is going to be happy about it."

Jillian tried to smile, but it hurt too much. "Shut up," was all she said.

Turning to Kara and back to Jillian, he said, "I know this isn't good timing, but I really need to talk to you."

Kara went out and returned, saying there was an exam room down the hall they could use, and the three of them went inside and closed the door.

"I've just come back from the scene," DS Milston said. "Quite the cock-up. Lots of blood." He paused, taking out his notebook. "Looks like Dobson and I were deliberately sent off on a wild goose chase while they lured you into the trap."

Jillian listened impassively.

"Can you tell me what happened?" he said, his pen hovering above his pad of paper.

Jillian told him everything. Almost everything. Up to the point when Sebastian came back in. At that point in the story, she said, "I was losing consciousness. I remember the back door opening. Large man. Couldn't see clearly." She rubbed her head, not for effect, but because it did really hurt.

Milston interrupted her. "Could it have been Kerim?"

Jillian tilted her head. "Possibly, but I don't know. Couldn't see."

"What about Hughes? Could it have been him?"

Jillian paused. Everyone was silent, and finally Milston said, "Detective?"

Jillian looked over at him. "No, I don't think so . . . I couldn't see clearly . . . but the man in the door . . . was bigger . . . not slender."

"But you're sure it was a man?" Milston asked.

Jillian waved her hand dismissively. "I suppose it could . . . have been a large woman . . . I really don't know . . . blacked out."

"Do you know what happened when this person opened the door?"

"Shots," Jillian said, "I heard more shots." Then, sighing loudly, she said, "That's all . . . I remember . . . sorry."

Milston wrote something in his book, then closed it. "Most of what you said adds up with what we found, though it's a mess. SOCO will tell us more in the morning, but none of it makes sense. Why would Kerim shoot his own people?"

Jillian shrugged, instantly regretting it as her head began to spin.

Milston headed to the door and then turned with his hand on the handle. "You know the strangest bit?"

Jillian just looked at him. Kara actually spoke up. "What's that?"

Milston looked down for a moment at the floor, then looked back up and gazed straight into Jillian's beat-up face. "Someone took the time to apply a makeshift pressure bandage to DS Listun. Looks like it might have been handkerchiefs from some of the other victims' suits, held in place with a belt tied round Listun's torso."

Jillian tried to show no emotion. Kara looked from Jillian to DS Milston and said, "Who would do that?"

"Exactly," Milston replied as he opened the door, and they headed back to the waiting room.

Soon after they got back to their seats in the waiting room, Daniella returned. She looked at Jillian, the worry on her face no doubt caused by the pallor of Jillian's skin from shock and exhaustion. Still, she turned and knelt in front of Deborah Listun.

"I've spoken to the head of surgery and the lead nurse who stepped out to talk to me briefly," she said, keeping her voice steady. "Stephen was shot in the upper-left part of his chest."

Deborah's hand shot up to her mouth and she gasped.

Daniella raised her hand slightly and quickly added, "It didn't hit his heart, which is a good thing."

Deborah Listun nodded, but kept her hand over her mouth. Daniella continued, now looking around the room at everyone as she spoke. "The surgeon is one of the best in Southampton, and the team working on him is top-notch. He lost a lot of blood, but so far, everything is going well."

Turning back to Deborah, she said, "He's not out of the woods yet. I'm not going to lie to you, but there is cause for hope. We won't know for another few hours, but he's doing very well so far."

Deborah Listun thanked Daniella profusely, and eventually everyone settled in for a long night.

***

The hospital was overrun with police over the course of the next few hours. Everyone from the VCU and SCD9 turned up. The surgeon emerged around two in the morning to say that the surgery had gone very well, but the next eight to twelve hours would be key. Once Listun came out of anesthesia, they would know more. All they could do now was wait.

Kara took over organizing shifts to guard Listun's room once he was out of surgery. No one was taking any chances. He would be in the intensive care unit for at least a few days.

Everyone tried to get Jillian to go home, to bed, to rest.

It was like talking to a brick wall. She wasn't leaving until she knew he was okay. Eventually Deborah moved over and sat next to her, and the two talked. They talked about the baby, about what Stephen was like at home, at work, and even at one point about what had happened.

Coffee was drunk by the gallon. Time ticked excruciatingly slowly by.

Around midmorning, a head nurse took Deborah to see her husband. He wouldn't likely be awake until tomorrow at the earliest, but she could sit with him. He was still critical; the nurse told the group of detectives and other police hanging about, but his vital signs were stabilizing, which was a good sign.

For the umpteenth time, she urged everyone to go home. Word would be sent to them once they knew more.

No one listened.

Jillian dozed on and off on one of the uncomfortable sofas in the waiting lounge, resting her head on Daniella's lap. Daniella gently stroked her hair. Kara made sure everyone was eating and drinking something besides coffee, taking charge in the absence of her sergeant and while her boss was asleep.

As the sun was setting, a doctor came in. "Detective Scotte?" he inquired.

Jillian sat up stiffly. "Yes?"

He stepped into the crowded room as people parted to make way for him. "I'm Doctor Inslay. I'm on rotation tonight in the intensive care unit. I wanted to give you an update on Sergeant Listun."

"Yes?" Jillian asked carefully.

"He's improving," the doctor said quickly, attempting to allay everyone's fears as he picked up the intensity of the stares. "He is showing no signs of infection. His blood pressure and vital signs are moving in the correct direction."

Jillian closed her one good eye as tears once again leaked down her face. Daniella put an arm around her shoulder and squeezed. Jillian didn't care that everyone could see her cry. To hell with being the strong boss and all that rubbish. This was real life.

The doctor continued, "We'll keep him in the unit at least until tomorrow. We've got him on a rather high sedative at present, so he won't wake until then, if not the day after. The bullet did quite a bit of damage and he lost a great deal of blood. His body needs to heal."

The doctor looked around as everyone nodded their understanding. "At this point, I'm confident in saying that we are going to upgrade his status to still critical, but stable."

There was applause at that point as the room erupted with relief.

The doctor gave one last update before he left. "While we all appreciate the need for you to be here for your fellow officer, I would like to remind you that this is a hospital which sees a great deal of other patients. As such, we would really like to have our waiting room back, so . . ." He chose his words carefully. "I think it's safe for you all to go home now."

Jillian thanked the doctor and told Kara to get everyone moving.

"Come on, you lot!" Kara shouted. "Shift it."

Everyone grinned, and there were a few giggles and some grumbles of "Yes, mum," but they did, in fact, begin to disperse.

CHAPTER 15
(EPILOGUE)

It was dark as Jillian, with a great deal of support from Daniella, made her way to the door of their still somewhat new-to-them cottage. It was a tiny home that sat on a hill in the middle of a small suburb of Southampton, but if you looked down the road as it swept away and turned a curve, you could just see the river Itchen. It was perfect for them.

Daniella opened the door and helped Jillian in, along with carrying some food they had stopped to grab for a quick takeaway.

Jillian turned around slowly once inside, closing the door.

That's when Daniella screamed.

Jillian turned far faster than she should have. Her head immediately pounded in protest, causing her to lean heavily into the wall.

Daniella was standing rigid, having dropped the bags of food. She had turned on the hall light, and there, in the half-lit small sitting room, was a man sitting in their armchair, looking straight at them, mostly hidden in half shadow.

"It's all right," Jillian croaked. Then, trying a little louder, she said, "Dani, it's okay."

Daniella turned, a look of terror still on her face.

"It's okay," Jillian assured her, pushing herself off the wall slowly. "Daniella Morales, meet Sebastian Hughes."

Hughes stood up slowly, his hands out to his side. "I'm very sorry to have frightened you, Dr. Morales."

Daniella squinted with distrust. Jillian moved up beside her. Touching her arm, she said, "Could you get me a glass of water?"

Sebastian took a step forward. "Please, let me help you with . . ."

But Daniella was already bending down to pick up the dropped items. "No," she said sternly. He stopped and stepped back slowly.

Jillian looked at him, trying to keep herself as steady as possible. He looked back.

"Shouldn't you sit down?" he said gently. He waited until she took a place on the sofa and then carefully sat back down in the chair.

Daniella came back with three glasses of water, handing one to Jillian and one to Hughes, who, eyebrow raised, said thank you. She then sat down on the arm of the sofa as if protecting Jillian, who simply stared at Hughes.

"What are you doing here?" Jillian asked finally.

Hughes took a sip of water. He was wearing a different suit from the one she'd last seen him in, but there was something off about him. His clothes were still impeccably tailored, his shirt crisp, his shoes polished, his hair neatly combed. It took a few seconds, but she finally found it. His nose was somewhat swollen and he looked exhausted, as though he had not slept.

Setting the water glass down gently on the low coffee table, he said, "I wanted to see if you were okay. And to see about . . ." He waved a hand in a gesture that indicated something else.

Jillian spoke slowly, her swollen lip still making speech difficult. "DS Listun is in critical care, but stable."

Hughes nodded.

Daniella stood up abruptly. She had been up all night and all day, so she too was exhausted, and it wasn't until that moment that she'd connected the dots. She looked at Hughes, then at Jillian and back at Hughes. "*You* were *there!*" she said, pointing an accusing finger at him.

"Dani," Jillian said softly, but Daniella didn't move.

"Yes," Sebastian said.

Pointing at Jillian, Daniella said, "She could have been *killed.*"

"Dani," Jillian said again.

Still Daniella didn't move, her breathing coming in larger and larger gasps, her chest rising and falling. "You left her there to *die!*"

"Dani!" Jillian said as loudly as she could, which wasn't very, but got Daniella's attention.

"What?" Daniella said, whirling her head around to look at Jillian.

Jillian held up her hand, palm forward, trying to calm Daniella down. "He saved my life."

Daniella glanced at Hughes, then back again at Jillian, then back at Hughes again. Finally, she turned back to Jillian. "But, I thought you said . . ."

Jillian nodded slightly, careful not to move her head too much or too fast. "I'll explain later." Then turning to Hughes, she said, "I think you might have saved Listun's life too. Thank you for that."

Sebastian's expression didn't change. He waited a few moments, then said, "The other reason I came was to ask . . ." He stopped, seeming at a loss for words, then said, "Why aren't the police for me?"

Jillian stared at him for a long while. No one spoke. Daniella kept shifting her gaze from one to the other. Sebastian's gaze held Jillian's.

Finally, Jillian spoke up and told him what she'd told DS Milston. "I'm sure at some point they're going to want to talk to you. They'll also be looking for Kerim."

Something in Hughes's expression changed, or rather, Jillian thought, something in his eyes flickered. "They won't find Kerim."

The way he said it made Daniella shiver.

Jillian said nothing.

Hughes stood up. "I'd better be going."

Jillian got slowly to her feet. They walked to the door, which Daniella opened.

"I hope I didn't ruin your supper," he said as he walked past. As he turned back and looked at Jillian, he studied her face. "Will you be all right?" he asked.

Holding his gaze with her one open eye, she said, "Eventually."

Hughes nodded once and turned to leave.

"Sebastian," Jillian called out, and he turned back around. She paused, her one good eye welling up a bit, and then she said softly into the cool night air, "Thank you."

He looked back at her, his eyes glinting in the light from the hallway. "For what?" he asked, then smiled, turned, and walked away.

Acknowledgements

Writing is often a lonely endeavour. I am fortunate to have been assisted on my journey with this book by a number of people who made it all possible.

First, to the members of the *Journey Institute Press Writing Prompt Group* who not only encouraged (and some times good naturedly harrassed) me to continue with these stories, but also went on to cheer on their publication.

Second, to the members of my *advanced readers team* who gave of their time and talents and were not afraid to provide honest and well directed feedback to make these stories much better than they originally were. To, Brittany, Claudia, Kelly, Peggy, Robert, Sara, Shannon, and Shawna, my heartfelt thanks and appreciation for your support, your encouragement, and your time.

To my editor Jessica Medberry at InkWhale Editorial, your editing skill and talent in catching details continues to astound me. Everything you did made the book better and any remaining errors are mine alone.

To my wife Dafna, for her unwavering belief in me and my stories. None of this would be possible, or worth it, without you.

Finally, to you, dear reader. I write these stories because I need to, and I write them for you. I hope they bring you a moment of escape from the trials and tribulations of our world. I hope you enjoy reading them as much as I enjoyed writing them.

MJ

ABOUT THE AUTHOR

Michael Jenet was born in Belgium and moved to the United States when he was seven years old. He is an eight-year veteran of the U.S. Air Force. A self-described "recovering corporate CEO", he now devotes himself full time as the publisher for Journey Institute Press.

An international best-selling and award-winning author, his first two books were in the self-improvement genre: *ASK: The Questions to Empower Your Life*, and *A Better Life*. He lives in Colorado with his wife and family.

Journey Institute Press

Journey Institute Press is a non-profit publishing house created by authors to flip the publishing model for new authors. Created with intention and purpose to provide the highest quality publishing resources available to authors whose stories might otherwise not be told.

JI Press focusses on women, BIPOC, and LGBTQ+ authors without regard to the genre of their work.

As a Publishing House, our goal is to create a supportive, nurturing, and encouraging environment that puts the author above the publisher in the publishing model.

Wordbinders Publishing is an Imprint of Journey Institute Press, a Division of 50 in 52 Journey, Inc.